The Trail

Visit www.booksurge.com to order additional copies.

NATALIA PRENTICE

THE TRAIL

2007

The Trail

PROLOGUE

Sharon Thomas had one concern upon waking. *Can I move?*

She slowly wriggled her toes and tensed her quads. *My legs work*, she thought with surprise, recalling how they'd smashed onto the pavement. *Good sign.* She lifted her head an inch from the hospital pillow, inhaling a lungful of sterile air, and grimaced mid-breath at the pain. Her fingertips traveled over the heavy gauze bandages that wrapped her left side. Her milk-chocolate eyes darted around the ICU at Columbia Presbyterian Hospital. They settled on the IV bag hovering over her bed, and the yellow food drip oozing down into the rubber tube stuck in her wrist.

Then, another fear hit her. Hard as the bullet had. Clearing the post-coma fog.

Oh my God, what have I missed?

Sharon had no idea how long she'd been lying in this bed, but she knew it was too long. Her eyes fluttered weakly. The phone beside her rang, calling her whole body to attention. Reaching through the metal bed rails, she lifted the receiver. "Hello," she said, her voice scratchy and unused, as she gulped against her dry throat.

"Sharon, we all wish you the best for a speedy recovery," said a deep male voice.

"Who is...?" She struggled for recognition, frustrated. She wondered how many times this phone had rung to no answer. *How many?* Her obsession. Numbers. *Numbers told everything.*

"Sam Peterson," the voice said, matter-of-factly.

"Sam," her breath shortened as she recognized her boss, the CEO of the most powerful investment bank in the world, Silverman & Sons. The green lines monitoring her heart rate staggered. *Former boss*, she reminded herself. She had quit her banking job a week before the street mugger left her for dead.

"Uh, thanks," she replied hesitantly. She knew that Sam didn't offer warm and fuzzy support.

"You know, we'll always think of you as family. Be well, Sharon." He ended his call as abruptly as he began it.

Sharon shivered, amazed at how even a few words from this mogul conjured her deepest pangs of anxiety. Guilt and fear. Part of the reason she quit.

Then a doctor wandered in and looked her over, seemingly unimpressed that she was awake and talking. A gaggle of nurses checked her and fussed over her, and the enormous pull of Sam and Silverman receded from her mind. The women left an hour later, and as she was dozing off, pumped with pain-killers, her phone chimed again.

"Sharon here," she answered, sharpening her professional voice, swallowing saliva.

"Hey, patient," said a pleasant voice, coated with relief. "You know, there are better ways to get out of your first writing assignment."

She smiled through the agony. It was her new and highly attractive boss, Damon Matthews, editor of *Riche$*, the most powerful business magazine in the world.

"So, you mean, I didn't have to get shot?" she joked nervously, smoothing her long dark hair off her forehead. Blinking away the memory of her attacker's eyes.

"Nah," he said, "a simple 'need more time' would have worked."

"I'll keep that in mind," she replied, sinking back into her pillow, losing grasp of the phone.

She sighed. *Career transitions weren't supposed to lead to extended hospital stays.* Her intent was to slide from banking to reporting. Like she escaped her marriage. *Move on. Don't look back.*

"Well, take all the time you need," said Damon. "I'll be here waiting for you."

Close one door and open the next, she thought, as the phone receiver was suddenly too heavy and fell out of her hand. Her ribs throbbed. That's how it was supposed to be. She caught a spasm of pain jutting up her left side. But nothing was ever that easy. Doors swing both ways.

CHAPTER 1
(Two Years Later)

WORLD WELL BANK BUSTED!

EXCLUSIVE BY DAMON MATTHEWS

RICHE$ MAGAZINE

The story blazed across the glossy black cover of the mid-August issue. It was the first thing to bring a genuine smile to Damon's face in a long time. He inhaled a breath of pride, puffing his chest out like a lion king. A sigh of sadness followed, as he thought of Marsha. *A very long time.*

Shrugging his grief momentarily aside, he refocused on his achievement. WorldWell Bank Bust. The scoop of a lifetime. The envy of all his fellow journalists. Even his star reporter, Sharon Thomas, had eyed him with a brand new respect. "Way to go, boss!" she thumbs-upped him the morning it came out.

Hell, didn't he deserve this attention after all he'd been through? He reclined in his chair, hands behind his head, shoes off, the heels of his argyle socks resting on his desk. "Like I've said before," his voice boomed into the speakerphone, "when you know you've got a scoop, you gotta go for the jugular, take it down, get it out first...Yeah, thanks, Stan...Drinks after Labor Day? Sure, let me check my calendar."

While Damon pretend-paused, his publisher appeared in the office doorway. Catching Ralph Stetson's wrinkled grey eyes with his own piercing cobalt ones, Damon pointed to the phone and mouthed, "Stan Johnson." Stan worked for the *Wall Street Tribune*. He had won three Pulitzers. He was journalism royalty.

"Got it," Ralph mouthed back, unimpressed. He spun his index finger in a tight circle, motioning for his editor to wrap up.

"Stan, I'll call you early September, we'll do dinner." Damon clicked off and smoothed his polo shirt. "Ralph," he said, planting his Clarks Wallabees on the floor beneath his desk. "Come in. Take a seat."

"Thanks," said Ralph, still standing. "I'm good."

"What's up?" Damon ran a hand through his sandy-brown hair. *Managing editor, here I come.*

Ralph drew a deep breath, the knobby outline of his thin shoulders visible through his light-blue button down shirt. "Let me get right into this. You've been a bit, well, tense lately."

"Sorry?" Damon's jaw dropped. *Did I hear that wrong?*

"I need you to take it down a notch—you know, lighten up." His words hit the air like a bad headline.

Lighten up? Damon was unable to hide the exasperation in his voice. "We just unleashed the biggest bomb Wall Street has ever seen."

"I know. Great story. The best. It's just that, maybe you need some time off, now," said Ralph.

"Time off? Look, if you're afraid of a lawsuit, we're clear. I fact-checked every word."

"It's not the story, it's not the lawsuit. It's you." Ralph leaned in, "Elsa left in tears yesterday."

Damon's explanation sounded absurd, even to him. "She used the wrong color for the stock chart."

"The wrong color?" Ralph's voice was tinged with impatience, his hands stuck to his khakis.

"We were going to print," Damon spat back. "I needed red. WorldWell Bank was in the *red*. That was the whole point." He shoved up his shirt sleeves in two abrupt motions.

"John in graphics says you drop-kicked a wastebasket because your locals were on the wrong size paper."

"I didn't *kick* it. I moved it to hand over the proper..." Damon demonstrated as he spoke, thinking his publisher hadn't a clue what really mattered.

Ralph sighed and took a seat. "It was a fabulous piece. Wall Street's on pins and needles. So maybe it's time for you to get away. Look, I know the Marsha thing is still..."

"Okay. I'll start my weekend early." He couldn't talk about Marsha.

"Actually," said Ralph, "I was thinking more like a week." He rose to leave.

"What? I can't take a week off now, there's follow-up and..." Damon's face reddened.

"Good, then. It's settled," said Ralph, walking out the door. "See you in a week."

As Ralph's back went out of view, Damon turned to his computer and shook his head. He emailed all of his WorldWell files and notes to his personal hotmail account. After they transferred, he deleted them from the *Riche$* database. And then again from the recycle bin on his PC. He might have to be out of the office, but no one was muscling in on his turf. No one was going to stop him now. Not on this story.

CHAPTER 2

Every night Sharon Thomas died again. Once, if she was lucky. More often than not, she died multiple times. Two years of hell. Nothing natural helped. She'd tried therapy, hypnosis, hours of grueling workouts at the gym. Even the psychic she had consulted in desperation to bring peace couldn't make the nightmares disappear.

The only reason she got any sleep at all was by the miracle of Ambien. She never considered herself someone who relied on drugs. Not her nature to be dependent. On anything. But that was before. Now, even when she slept, death penetrated every dream.

Deep in the throes of REM slumber, the side of Sharon's head buried into the creases of her pillow. The auburn highlights of her dark brown hair draped languidly across the peach lines of the soft linen. Her breathing slowed as her body relaxed into the medicinal lull of her downers.

And, just like that, she was back. Back to that stifling summer. That Sunday evening on the Upper East Side. The sun had set, but the air was still oppressively humid, peppered with the stench of uncollected garbage. She was walking home along the quaint tree-lined block of Seventy-fifth Street, past ornate nineteenth-century brownstones, all pastel shutters and steep steps. She was returning from a movie. Lost in thought. Fantasizing about what Colin Farrell would be like in bed.

By the time she noticed the gunman, it was too late. In one swift motion, he grabbed hold of her arm, spun her around, and pointed a Glock at her heart. Her eyes darted toward the black weapon, then upward to the face of her attacker. They locked with his charcoal ones, pupils as dark as his irises. They widened as he pressed the trigger. The single shot that followed was silent.

She felt the warm sensation of fresh blood pouring down her chest. Snaking its way down the punctured skin covering her rib cage. Her white cotton T-shirt soiled to crimson. Everything unfolded in slow motion until she crashed to the ground. The faint scrunch of the shooter's canvas sneakers against the pavement, cushioning his getaway. Losing consciousness at the shrill sound of screeching tires. Of approaching sirens. *Resounding louder and louder.* Then, Sharon heard the sharp pop of an exploding bullet.

CHAPTER 3

Only a few days into his forced break, and Damon was already stir-crazy. He checked his watch for the millionth time. 1:30 a.m. He paced the wooden floor of his study. He and his wife, Marsha, had bought the 1887 house in a state of decaying shambles. Together, they transformed it into a romantic weekend getaway. Easton, Pennsylvania, was everything they needed, he had believed. An hour and a half drive from Manhattan. A world away from the scum his stories centered on. A world away from Park Avenue penthouses and Sutton Place mistresses.

And now he was surrounded by nothing but kayaking, hiking, and all the reading he wanted to catch up on. He tried to convince himself that he needed this. The recent pace had certainly added lines to his thirty-seven-year-old face. He had busted his balls to get his writers to step up to the plate. Not to mention his own contribution to the mix. The result was some of the best stories *Riche$ Magazine* had ever published.

The timing couldn't be better. Competing magazines were struggling for cash. The post-millennium recession was eating into advertising budgets. Promised pages were being yanked at the last minute. But not at *Riche$*. There, ad sales were setting new records. Because of him.

It wasn't easy to pull off. Exhaustion seeped through his veins. He hadn't slept more than three consecutive hours in weeks, maybe months. But who cared? It was August. The time when new stories slowed to a trickle.

Company CEOs were lounging at their Hampton estates. Performing their annual familial duty, logging face-time with their wives and kids before they could return to Manhattan and be important. Corporations were on half-staff. Washington, too, was essentially shut down. The stock market was barely conscious. Junior traders were scared to make a move—afraid their bosses would return and blame them for some screw-up that a magazine like *Riche$* could turn into a scandal. Everyone and everything was taking a breather before fall. Good a time as any to get away. At least, that's what he kept telling himself.

He looked at his watch again. 1:35 a.m. He flipped open the planner by his bedside, hoping to find something more than a series of blank pages. Then it hit him like a ton of wet cement. It was the anniversary. A year ago, on this day, his wife had left him. *A whole year.*

He closed his eyes and concentrated. The scent of her cherry perfume arose immediately. Pictures of her still adorned the fireplace mantel. Marsha horseback riding along the Pacific Ocean in San Diego, smiling at him. Marsha setting up her scuba gear on a Cayman Islands dive-boat, waving at him. Marsha blowing him a kiss from a beach-front hut in Belize. The Kodak moments that frame a marriage. The promise of eternal love and a hopeful future. The pictures that outlast the sentiment. The pictures that mask reality. *The pictures that lie.*

Damon, she had texted him (text being the only mode of communication he responded to readily), *I can't do this anymore. Goodbye.*

He hadn't seen it coming. She had never been one for expanded explanation. In fact, she rarely talked much at all. She was more into conveying than articulating. Sometimes, she would emphasize a thought with a flip of her shoulder-length auburn hair. "Come *on*, Damon," she'd say with a flip to the right, indicating something he'd done was ridiculous, or merely stupid.

Or she'd pin him with the glare of her jet-black eyes that said, "Damon, enough." *Enough*, come home before midnight tonight. *Enough,* come to bed. *Enough, love me.*

He hadn't had time to tell her how important she was to him. How he loved her even though he was barely ever around to show her. How his journalistic ambitions were a part of who he was. How they were the only thing that made him feel alive. How hours passed into nothing while he dug for stories, creating buzz out of hunches. Building up and destroying companies and careers. It made him feel he could make a difference.

It was like *playing God.*

He hadn't had time to try and get her back because Marsha was found dead in a Pierre Hotel suite two days after she had texted him. At the time he was notified, he had no idea what a woman with zero tolerance for opulence was doing at the Pierre on Fifth Avenue. It was a pretentious place where the ancient clientele wore their finest tuxedos and biggest diamonds to afternoon tea. A place stuck in some macabre time warp of charity events and watch fobs.

He discovered that her reason for being there made a mockery of all he had taken for granted. He thought her fidelity was a given. It was not. He was wrong. Deeply wrong. The shock of this knowledge transcended that of her murder. Marsha. *His* Marsha.

His Marsha was discovered lying at the foot of a cream-iron radiator. Her lifeless body was clad in scarlet lace lingerie. She was wearing a diamond toe-ring Damon had never seen before. She had been choked to death by the heavy gold and maroon curtain tassels. The police who searched the room found no fingerprints, no errant hair strands, no footprints, and no trace of the killer. The coroner found no signs of a struggle. There was a brief murder investigation, but the case was shelved three months after it opened. Another sordid murder following an affair gone wrong.

Damon hadn't aided the investigation. First, because he was the prime suspect. Second, because he couldn't bring himself to think about it. He wanted to, but just couldn't. All of a sudden, his experience, his objective reporting instincts, his ability to track down information about everything, didn't amount to anything. Marsha was gone. He couldn't bring her back. He couldn't ask her why she'd cheated on him. He couldn't do a goddamn thing.

He hated himself for not putting in more effort. For letting the trauma of her transgressions numb his brain. So, he did the only thing he knew how to do. The only thing that made sense. He threw himself into his work the day after the funeral.

He hated himself for that, too. Damon shuffled listlessly into the tiny kitchen at the back of the house. It had been Marsha's favorite room. Sorrow, guilt, and the heavy stillness of the summer night weighed on his every movement. He leaned forward over the kitchen sink, staring through the window above it. The garden she had been so proud of was now fully overgrown. He hadn't had the heart to touch it.

Marsha loved waking up early Saturday mornings. She'd spend long moments nuzzling her coffee mug, looking out the same window at the tangle of fauna she had tamed. Occasionally, a deer pranced into the yard from the forest to say good morning. Birds flocked in to breakfast on her homemade granola feeders. He would come up from behind her, slip his arms around her waist, and hold her close.

The kitchen was a hodge-podge of appliances from different decades; 1940s cupboards with butter-yellow peeling paint, a cook's stainless-steel 1950s oven, a rust-colored Frigidaire from the 1970s, before sub-zeros existed. The only updated appliance was the microwave he'd bought recently, to reheat stale cups of black coffee more quickly, to stave off sleep for longer.

Damon extracted a ceramic mug from one of the cabinets. He poured himself some of yesterday's cold coffee and nuked it. Sitting at the antique oak table in the dining room, he remembered them buying the mugs at a shack that called itself a country art gallery. "All items designed by owner," the sign outside said. Marsha, a real art dealer, bought a dozen. Her contribution to the local economy, she said, laughing. The memory evoked a faint smile. He still loved her. Always would.

His eyes glassed over as he shifted his gaze through the bay window, onto the dark hill that cut up the side of the forest to the main street above. There was only a faint glimmer from the crescent moon. Most of his neighbors were New Yorkers. They only showed up on weekends, even in August. Broadway producers, photographers, interior designers, novelists.

But it was Monday. His was the only house with lights on. The silence thickened. He moved to the high-backed Amish chair in the corner of the room, oblivious to its hard angles. His watch read 2:35 a.m. He had managed to waste an hour. He had been avoiding this for a year. Now, to commemorate the occasion, he turned on the lamp and opened the drawer of the side-table. Self-torture. Extracting a manila folder, he carefully removed the yellowing newspaper clippings. He willed the stale words to provide meaning. To offer closure.

The headline of the top article pierced his gut:
"Woman Found Slain at the Pierre."
He buried his forehead in the heels of his hands. His depression engulfed him like a tsunami. His mind instinctively returned to the safer focus—the next step in the WorldWell

Bank crackdown, and the harder one, his personal loss. He slowly flipped to the second clipping:

"Riche\$ Editor: Chief \$uspect."

Trust editors to pick headlines that add insult to pain, he thought to himself. He was about to flip to a third clipping when he heard the screen porch door slamming against its frame. Once. Twice. Damon shoved his chair back. His ears pricked up to the sound. He walked through the kitchen to the porch to check it out. In the mud room, he stepped around a pile of old paint cans, a rusty hoe, stacks of chopped logs for winter fires. He reached for the handle of the porch door and tried to move it. It was locked. He jiggled it again to make sure. The latch was fastened, too. He didn't remember having fastened it.

CHAPTER 4

The cell phone tucked beneath her pillow vibrated into a beep, thrusting Sharon mercilessly from her dream. The relentless montage of her nightmares left a residue of fear coating her body. Like a full-body Novocain shot wearing off, one tingle at a time.

Her cell phone blared again. She squinted at her clock radio: 3:07 a.m. She knew who was calling before she saw the illuminated caller ID. The man who never slept—even, apparently, while on vacation. Her editor and boss, Damon Matthews.

"Hello," she said, cradling her cell phone between her ear and shoulder, head still on the pillow.

"Sharon," he said.

The nervousness in his voice made Sharon sit upright, wiping the sweat from her brow. "Damon, what is it?"

"Sharon," he repeated, after a several second pause.

"Damon, you're breaking up," She strained to hear over the bad wireless connection.

But there was nothing more to hear. The line had gone dead. *That's weird*, she thought. She usually had great service in her apartment. *It must be something on Damon's end.*

Sharon shut her cell phone, placed it on the nightstand, and tucked a strand of hair behind her ear. She knew he'd call back. She fumbled for her contact lens case and popped in her eyes. Some story idea had probably struck him. She understood the impulse to share it.

She glanced at the man lying beside her, oblivious to the noise. A trainer from her gym. Sometimes they boxed there. Sometimes they sparred later, in her bed. He had the most amazing body she'd ever seen. Biceps the width of her thighs. Thighs thicker than her waist. They had been sleeping together casually. Randall somebody.

Since her divorce a year earlier and a string of subsequent infatuations with even bigger disasters, thirty-three-year-old Sharon Thomas was more wary than she had ever been of trusting men. Her solution was simple: sleep around, keep them at arm's length. Her men offered good eye candy, decent company, and no conflict. She was good at scoring; she was good at playing tough, hiding the enormous hole of her own insecurities, and shielding herself against all attachments.

She nudged Randall awake, trailing her fingers down the small of his back, over his taut butt cheeks. "Randall," she whispered, "you have to go."

He rolled onto his back and smiled slyly, eyes half-closed. "You mean, you want to go again?"

"No, Randall. I don't. Not tonight. You have to get up. I have to work," she said.

"I'll sleep while you work." He propped himself on his elbow, circling her nipple with the tip of his tongue, slipping a strong arm around her waist.

"You know I can't work while you're here. It's kind of... distracting."

Sharon had established an ironclad rule after her divorce. No man was more important than her work. She didn't want a second marriage. She didn't want a relationship. She wanted a Pulitzer.

Randall had known the deal going in. He sighed and swiveled his stunningly muscular cocoa legs off the bed. He fumbled around for his underwear, T-shirt, and jeans. The bulge in his crotch revealed both his desire and disappointment.

As he dressed, she threw on a black silk robe. "Sorry, Randy, it's just that, you know..."

"Yeah, yeah, I know," he grumbled, walking to the door.

"I'll call you." She pecked his cheek and squeezed his hand. Maybe one day there'd be a man she would open herself to, but that was a matter for her and her therapist. Her cell chimed again as she shut the door behind Randall, still feeling the moist heat between her legs.

"Damon. What's up?" she answered cheerfully, like it was perfectly normal to be discussing anything at this hour. Journalists were consummate night owls. You interviewed people in the daytime; you figured it all out at night.

"Do you remember that ITA story?" he asked abruptly.

"Which one?" She detected breathlessness in his tone.

"The one that matters," he answered.

"Yeah, I do. Not clearly at three a.m., but yeah, what about it?" She knew which one he was talking about. The ITA investigation scoop that past spring, the piece she thought would catapult her career.

"Do you remember their SEC filings from March?"

"Uh," she hesitated, raking her fingers through her hair. "Well, there was a massive debt issue at the end of March. And a board member change just before that bond deal."

"When? Around the fifteenth?" he prompted.

Sharon's heart rate quickened, but she composed herself. "No, it would have been after that."

"What happened on the fifteenth?" he asked. His voice sounded stilted to her.

That's something I still haven't figured out. "I don't know. They didn't file anything with the SEC then."

"Sharon, what happened on the fifteenth?" he repeated.

Why is he repeating himself? she thought. *Is he drunk?* "I just told you, nothing was filed then."

"Are you sure?" His voice cracked.

"They had no March 15 filing," she said. *Technically, that was true.*

There was a long pause over the wireless network. Then he asked, "Are you alone?"

"Damon, what's going on?" Sharon demanded, now pacing. The uneven wood floors creaked beneath her.

"Do you have the notes on ITA at your place?" asked Damon, ignoring her question.

"Yes," she answered, glancing through her dark living room through the bedroom door frame at her desk against the far wall.

"Dig out everything you have," said Damon. "I'll be there in about two hours."

"Okay, but what about your vac—?" she started.

But the phone had gone dead. Again.

CHAPTER 5

Sharon tied the belt of her robe in a loose knot, clicked on the light in the living room, and approached her desk. She had just powered on her PC when the building buzzer sounded. With a small huff, she reluctantly buzzed him back in. Randall was less sexy when he got too needy. Everyone was.

She spent her life shunning need. Need compromised you, caught you off balance, got you into trouble. She had just as little patience for other people's dependence. It was reflexive thinking, since every time she became dependant, she got burned.

Randall's return was flattering, but distracting. Still, she thought, reflecting on their earlier escapades, he had his positive qualities. She smiled to herself and opened the door with her tough face: "Hey, I said I had to work." But the hulking man before her was definitely not Randall.

A brute sporting a frayed jean jacket and a scraggly face stood in her doorway. His sullen slits for eyes peeked at her from beneath his Mets cap. "Surprise," said his raspy voice as he extended his arms toward her throat. "Remember me?"

Sharon leapt back. She tried crushing his encroaching hand between the door and frame. He was too overpowering. He shoved himself into her apartment, quietly so as not to wake the neighbors, clicking the door shut behind him.

Then he lunged at her, covering her mouth with one hand and landing a sharp right hook to her cheekbone with the other. The crushing pain spread through her brain instantly, like tributaries rushing to an ocean. The feeling of explosion in her left eye came next.

She stumbled backward under the force of his blow. He belted her a second time, in the ribs, winding her. Knocking her to the ground. As he extended his leg to kick her fallen body, she rolled away onto her good side. Wincing, she glared up at the man out of her working eye, trying to rub away the excruciating ache with the back of her hand.

"Yeah, it's all coming back to me," she panted, clutching her side.

Everything swirled through her throbbing head. The brute. The story. The call from Damon. The recurring nightmare. Five minutes ago, she had been sleeping. Five months ago, she had come home to the same guy, rummaging through papers in her desk. She had been ferocious—and lucky; she had managed to surprise him bent over her desk. He was not expecting her. Her Aikido training from after her Upper East Side attack came flooding back to her, and a few moments and an expertly applied joint lock later, stunned, he had run off.

Now, she tried to maintain clarity, despite the fact that her head was spinning. She didn't know what he was doing back. But things didn't end well the last time, for him especially. She realized this time was only going to get worse. Much worse. Now he wanted revenge.

He clenched his fist and lunged to strike again. This time she was prepared. Her training allowed her to keep her sanity and reduce the constant paranoia after she was shot and left for dead.

She jumped away from the incoming punch. Simultaneously, she pivoted 180 degrees, deflecting his fist with the palm of her nearest hand. With the other, she reached over his arm, grabbed his hand, and snapped his wrist sideways and up toward his shoulder. The unnatural position brought him to his knees.

"Urghh!" he emitted in discomfort. "You little bitch!"

He swung his free hand around, landing another body blow to her ribs. Sharon dropped back, wheezing. Her grip loosened. He quickly spun her into a half-nelson. The crook of his arm clamped like a vise against her throat. She instinctively ducked her chin into her clavicle to alleviate some of the pressure.

"Now you're really pissing me off," he said, squeezing harder.

Sharon tried to swallow and gather air. But the hold was too tight. She changed tactics. She relaxed slightly, telling him he was in command of the situation. *Keep your attackers guessing.*

It didn't seem like he was falling for it; he didn't loosen his hold. "Where's the file?"

She could barely breathe. She felt trapped. Powerless.

"Where's the fucking file?" he asked again.

"Which file?" she wheezed. She knew she was close to blacking out.

She reasoned that if he wanted to kill her, given their last encounter, he would have by now. At least that what's she told herself to keep calm. He needed her information. He might have gone away abruptly last time, but he certainly hadn't disappeared.

"You know damn well which one. Tell me where it is or I'll choke the life right outta you," he demanded, corking her neck.

Her arm fluttered in the direction of an old carved Indian cabinet in the corner of her living room. "Over there," she sputtered, trying to find the floor with her tiptoes to lessen the strain. She felt her robe belt loosening.

He slammed her to the floor. She smashed onto her good side, crushing her right shoulder against the wooden boards.

She tried to rise. He pulled a 9mm from inside his jacket and aimed it at her.

"Don't. Move," he said.

The sight of the gun made her freeze, eyes fixed on the barrel. "What do you want?" she whispered.

"The file. Bitch. You know which one."

Sharon knew which one. The one he tried to get on his last visit. She still wasn't sure what it was about that file that was so important, but she knew enough to know she had to keep it, no matter what. She steadied her breath and watched. He was clawing through her cabinet like an angry, overgrown rodent, flinging files around the room with one hand, gun pointed at Sharon with the other. He stopped at a folder marked 'SEC.'

"Here we are," he said, holding it up.

Sharon didn't react. *Never move until you've assessed the situation. Never give anything away.* She had made that mistake once.

He was about to leave with the folder when he paused and turned around. "Wait a minute," he said. "This is bullshit! You think I'm some sort of an idiot!" He leafed through it. There was nothing in it but a couple of press releases and some CEO photos.

Sharon's lips tightened, which raised his ire further. "Now, I don't think you fully understand me," he hissed. "Let me spell it out for you, I'm after the trail. If you don't get it to me in the next ten seconds, I'm blowing a hole through your head."

He hovered closer, menacing. She could smell his sour garlic breath over her. He turned the gun around, butt toward her, and smacked the side of her head with it. She crashed flat to the unyielding floor. Blood trickled from her scalp. She wiped some of it away with the back of her hand, maintaining eye contact. The room was getting blurrier. She knew she had to give him more before he'd go away.

"It's in the 'Big Bank' folder. In the desk." She tasted blood. Her vision was getting darker. But she needed to keep alert until he left. *Just stay with him.*

"You better not be fucking with me!" Pointing the gun at her again, he opened desk drawers one at a time.

Sharon's heart was ramming against her chest. She was losing blood and consciousness. She watched him retrieve the WorldWell Bank folder and page through its contents. She decided there was no way he could know what he was looking at, but hoped the official-looking financial documents would reassure him.

"That's more like it," he said, plodding toward the door. "Good seeing you again, Thomas. Hope it's not so long next time."

She stared at him, her lungs heaving. The room spun faster. Her head felt like it was being assailed by an avalanche of migraines. She could barely keep her working eye open as she watched him stomp toward the door. She tried lifting herself up, palms pushing into the floor, but couldn't manage.

"Wait another minute," he said, turning back toward her. "I'll be taking this, too. Just to be sure." Sharon's heart sank as she watched him unplug her hard drive. He slammed the door behind him. She struggled to get up and started crawling to the cabinet, but it was too much of an effort. She slumped back to the floor in a heap.

The trail. Then everything went black.

CHAPTER 6

D amon was sitting at his dining room table, a shot glass and a spread of articles about his wife's murder before him. His palms were clammy. His throat dry. The mouth of the woman's 9mm pressed uncomfortably against his temple. Having attempted otherwise, he was left with no other option. So, he let go of the words she had instructed him to speak.

There was a long pause over the wireless network.

"Like we discussed," she whispered in his ear.

Damon's body strained as he recited his lines. The woman cocked the trigger.

As per her instructions, he asked Sharon, *"Are you alone?"*

Damon had been utterly stunned by the blonde with the revolver. He walked back from the kitchen, shot glass in hand, and there she was. Hunched over his post at the dining room table leafing through the articles about Marsha's death. She seemed to glance at them, impersonal and voyeuristic. A faint smirk across her lips. She was wearing a tight red T-shirt and jean shorts, like she was coming back from a picnic. Her cropped pixie hair and freckled face at complete odds with the calm handling of her gun.

"Do exactly as I say," she had ordered, looking up casually from her reading, stroking the gun's barrel with her long, slender fingers. "And I won't be forced to use this."

"Who the hell are you? How did you...?" He couldn't believe he was being held hostage by this waif.

"Sit down! Where you were before," she commanded, her voice transforming into a drill sergeant's. "Now!"

Damon's feet remained stuck to the floor. He processed the fact that she knew where he had been sitting. She must have been watching him. Waiting for him. He thought that maybe he had touched too raw a nerve in the WorldWell Bank boardroom. This was the first time a story of his had produced this kind of result. It was—oddly liberating.

"I said, NOW! I'm not screwing around!" She stood up deliberately and fired at him. The bullet barely missed his left ear as it sailed into the wall behind him, cracking the plaster on its way in.

"Okay, I'm sorry," said Damon, fingers extended, palms out, in a wait-right-there pose. Liberating had turned to terrifying. He'd never been so close to a gun before, or a bullet for that matter. "I'm sitting."

She kept her gun poised at him, guiding him back to the table with it. She positioned herself behind him after he sat down. Slowly, she trailed the tip of the gun over his tousled hair, before steadying it by the side of this head. Following her next command, he speed-dialed Sharon Thomas.

"Do you have the notes on ITA at your place?" he had asked, not sure what this had to do with WorldWell Bank.

She nodded approval to his back as he continued delivering the lines she had placed in front of him.

Until, without any notice, he changed the script. "I'll be there in about two hours," he had told Sharon, and snapped his cell phone shut.

Two shots rang out as the woman stepped back, firing to the right and left of his head, spraying two clean bullet holes into the wall in front of him. He dropped the cell phone, startled.

"What the hell was that?" she demanded. "I don't recall telling you to set up a date with the bitch."

He didn't think she was after an explanation. He offered none.

"Please," Damon pleaded, "no one's going to hurt her, right?"

"No comment, Mr. Matthews."

She slowly sauntered toward the front door, holding her gun cop-style on its side, still pointed at him. Giving him a better glimpse of her. She moved with the coolness of a millionaire socialite. "I'll be going now," she said.

He glanced down at his cell. She noticed.

"What—you gonna call the police, Matthews?" she goaded. "I'd strongly advise against it, what with your star reporter under threat and all. Wouldn't want her to get the same treatment Marsha got."

The use of his wife's name sickened him. He nodded, his stomach churning.

"And remember," she said, "this never happened—you *never* saw me."

* * *

After he heard the back door shut behind her, Damon tiptoed across the living room toward the study on the opposite side of the house. Through the side window, he watched the woman enter her car and drive off. He steadied his breath and dried his palms on his pant legs. He thought about calling the police, despite her warning.

But the police in that town still considered him responsible for his wife's death. Marsha had become the town martyr. No, he couldn't call them. But Sharon was in danger. Of that he was certain. He couldn't have another tragedy on his head.

Grabbing his keys, he darted to his own car, driveway pebbles crunching loudly under each step. He peeked around the driver's seat, relieved to find the back empty; no one hiding out, no one lying in wait. Then he cranked on the radio for company. And sped off.

Partly because there was no traffic in the middle of the night and partly because he had to see Sharon, Damon flew down I-78 toward Manhattan. On the way, he repeatedly called her cell phone and land line. She answered neither. *Maybe she just went back to sleep.* He floored the gas pedal.

Eyes fixed on the highway, he shifted focus away from his encounter with the gunwoman. He was caught between concern for Sharon and the desire to keep certain information from her. In his zeal to get his story to print and, if he had to admit to himself, use it to jumpstart his career, which had shifted from solid reporting to internal politics, he hadn't told anyone the real details. So, he also couldn't tell Sharon about the woman in his house. Not that he knew who she was. Or what she really wanted.

As he hit the toll bridge, he shuddered. There was an attendant at the booth he selected, a woman with short blonde hair. Spitting image of the one who'd just been in his dining room. His mind was playing tricks. He rubbed the skin of his temple, fingering the indent from the tip of her gun.

HONK! blasted the car behind him. His back stiffened. HONK! HONK!

Damon glanced at the rearview mirror with his eyes, the rest of his body paralyzed.

He saw a blonde.

CHAPTER 7

When Damon reached the East Village, the sky was striped with a few streaks of peeking light, the first preparations for the morning sun. The streets were almost empty, only the last of the night people straggling about. A few teenagers were laughing on the corner, probably just having been kicked out of some bar. A group of homeless men were smoking cigarettes by the Mexican bodega. There was a couple making out against the side of a phone booth. One of the teenagers shouted, "Hey, get a room!" Damon slowed his car to a stop.

He parked his white Chevy Impala on Fourth Street beneath an alternate side of the street parking sign. It promised a tow truck or a parking ticket at 8:30 a.m. Slamming his car door shut, he raced up the front steps of Sharon's building and buzzed her apartment. There was no answer. He buzzed a second apartment. *Come on, Sharon.* And a third. A fourth.

A corporate neighbor headed to work finally let Damon into Sharon's walk-up. He sped up the four flights of stairs, taking three steps at a time. He leaned on her doorbell while gathering his breath. "Sharon," he said, as he pressed his ear against the door to listen for any sounds.

Gingerly, he turned the knob. The unlocked door sprang open. He inhaled sharply, taking in the sight before him. Sharon was sprawled in the corner of the living room, blood pooled around her head. He rushed over. Kneeling beside her, he patted the wood floor next to her. The blood was dry, a sign that not a lot of it had escaped. He pressed two fingers to her neck to check for a pulse.

Detecting its beat, he gently brushed aside the hair stuck to her face. He swallowed down the bile gathering within him. The whole area around her left eye was bruised and swollen. He slowly rolled her onto her back, supporting her with one arm. There was dried blood caked to the top of her forehead.

She woke with a start, shielding her face with one hand, digging her nails into his arm with the other: "No, stop!" She pushed him away as she attempted to open her eyes, one of which was swollen shut.

"Shhh…" he whispered, gently extracting his arm from her grasp. Her nails had broken skin. "It's okay, it's okay."

Sharon's eyes fluttered, struggling to open. "Damon…?"

"You're okay, Sharon. Just stay still. I'll call for an ambulance."

"No!" Her voice came back to her as she tried sitting up. "No ambulance! You took CPR, just check my vitals or something."

"Sharon…" he implored, cradling her head.

"Do it," she whispered.

He took her head between his palms and lifted each eyelid with his thumbs to examine her pupils for signs of concussion. He got up, fumbled around the kitchen for a damp towel, and returned to wipe the blood from her forehead. He could see no deep cuts. "In my humble opinion, you'll…"

Before he could finish his sentence, she had sunk slowly back to the floor, tucked her knees toward her chest, almost in a fetal position, and returned to her own nightmare-punctuated slumber. He carefully lifted her onto the soft cream couch and tucked a throw blanket over her. Damon curled up in a felt-covered armchair a foot away. He watched her for a few long moments as the night sky bloomed into a hazy light blue. Then, exhausted, he nodded off.

* * *

He woke with a start before Sharon did. When she finally came to, Damon was sitting on the floor, cross-legged, observing her. He pressed the now-cold washcloth to her temple. She sat up and accepted the handful of Advil and glass of water he held out to her.

She tried to smile, but grimaced instead. "It's been a long night." She put a delicate hand to her head.

"Yeah, that's putting it mildly," he replied. "How are you feeling?"

"Couple of bruised ribs, a swollen eye. But besides that, I always sleep on a bloody floor while cracking a middle-of-the-night story."

Damon stared at her. He wanted to be helpful, but was totally clueless about what to do in this situation. He lacked some kind of fortitude. Marsha had always joked that he was better suited to reporting than medicine. He didn't do well with blood or pain. But he wanted to show Sharon some confidence. He also wanted to tell her everything, but couldn't. Instead, he said, "Tell me exactly what happened."

"That guy happened. The same one who came last time."

Damon remembered now: the break-in after he let Sharon run the first ITA story, the guilt he had felt.

"God, my head's gonna explode," she winced.

"Here, let me help you." He reached out to hold her hand, suddenly determined. "Did he ask you anything about the WorldWell story? I'd say we should call the police, but..." he trailed off.

"But not if there's a story here that we want to contain." Sharon knew exactly what Damon was thinking, and she agreed. "No. No police. It's fine. I'm fine." *It's not like they'd ever been a help in the past.* She balanced herself on Damon's hand and slowly stood up. She scanned her apartment. It was a mess. Dozens of folders were splayed across her desk and the surrounding floor, their former contents a thick spread of jumbled papers. Her computer speakers lay on the ground several feet away from her broken screen, their wires attached to nothing. The glass that had covered her framed *Riche$* story on ITA, a gift from Damon, now glistened like thousands of icicle fragments beneath the wall where it had hung.

She limped over to her desk and picked up the brass lamp that the brute had knocked to the floor during his rampage. Then her reporter's instinct kicked in. It gave her courage to switch her focus to the story at hand. "So what's going on with ITA? Did I miss something? And what's the WorldWell Bank connection?"

"I wish I knew," Damon shrugged. The truth was he had no idea what the connection was between Sharon's ordeal and almost getting shot at his own home. He watched her carefully restack her documents. Even after being attacked, she remained focused. He admired that. He needed to protect her. And he needed her to help him figure out what was going on. So he let her have a crumb of information. "WorldWell Bank is using some of its clients as a front to set up billions of dollars of fake loans. Then they move the cash somewhere else. And I mean billions." He watched as a look of delight took over Sharon's face.

"Wow!" she exclaimed. "And ITA is one of WorldWell's major clients."

"That's the best I've come up with," he said while scratching his temple. If she could put her attack behind her for the time being, so could he. "I was just thinking: based on your story, there might be a tighter connection."

"You decided to follow this up in the middle of the night?" she said.

Even for Damon, that seemed odd. "Well, you know I don't like to stop working. Ever," he said. He shrugged again, but didn't sound convincing. "Put me alone in a house with lots of background documents and this is what happens." He chuckled, but knew he wasn't being funny.

"But, you asked me for *my* documents." *Nothing like two reporters questioning each other.*

"Two heads, better than one. Maybe we double byline the next story," he said, offering her his signature boyish smile.

"Sure. Whatever." She thought he was sounding like a CEO, not an editor. "But what's the story? How much are we talking?"

He hesitated for a moment, but knew he needed her on board. "Forty-four billion. All in fake SEC filings."

She marched toward him. Suddenly her head didn't hurt anymore. "You mean WorldWell Bank falsified its filings to the tune of forty-four billion dollars! Wow!" That figure dwarfed her ITA story. "How did you find this out?"

Damon stared at the floor, then his feet. "You know the drill. Made some calls. Questioned some banks."

"Which banks?" No banker had ever tossed her information that juicy.

"The usual suspects: United Bank, National Bank, Silverman."

"Silverman! You're kidding me." The thought of Silverman sent a shiver up her spine. The very name. The intimate knowledge of the place and what it had done to her. And what she did while she was there.

"No, afraid not," he responded, recapturing her gaze.

"Guess it can't hurt Silverman to throw mud at their main rival. The one that's stealing all its clients."

"That's not all," he added. "They're saying the Federal Reserve knew all along."

"The Fed knows they're faking loans and is turning a blind eye? That's huge!" No matter how much experience she had watching the federal government bending over for corporations, this was a new level of complacency.

"That's right," he agreed. He was on a roll. He remembered what he had enjoyed so much as a beat reporter, before he got so caught up in the *business* of reporting. He had made his choice, probably the wrong one. But it was more lucrative to be an editor, made his parents happy. But then he spent years watching reporters like Stan Johnson grab the glory and Sharon Thomas keep the spirit that he once had in doing the real work. It was all about the story. Sometimes it was hard to keep that in mind.

He went to the kitchen to pour them both some water. Maybe together they'd uncover something amazing. He drank a sip. "The Fed's been WorldWell's most loyal friend. This won't look good for their chairman. He's given them the lion's share of the treasury bonds it issues."

"Damon, if you knew all this, why didn't you put it in the WorldWell piece?" Sharon suspected he was holding back. Reporters sensed what they were missing as much as what they uncovered.

"The timing wasn't right," he answered, picking off a strand of hair from his shirt.

"Think of the follow-up to your story," she said. "The world's largest bank and its crooked executives could go down for years. Who told you this again?" *Common reporter trick: act like you're satisfied with an answer, move on. Ask the same question with different words. See if your luck changes. Just be nonchalant.* "Hey, Damon, can you grab me some more water?"

"That's not important," he replied, handing her another glass. *He had taught her that technique.*

"The source is always important," she said, reaching. "You told me that yourself on my first day."

"Sometimes you need to protect your source," he said, as if reminding a child. "I told you that, too."

"Alright," she said, the thought of the potential story overshadowing her rising defenses. "So, my next question is— how exactly is WorldWell Bank funneling money through its clients?"

"That's where you come in." His tone became gentler.

"What do you mean?" she gulped.

"You need to go back in." At the sound of those six words, Sharon sunk back down to her knees. The night had been full of surprises, but this was the worst of all.

CHAPTER 8

Trying to process what she'd just heard, Sharon pressed the palm of her hand hard into her forehead. She knew where Damon was going with this. It wasn't the first time he'd suggested infiltration. It happened every time he got caught up in a Wall Street story. Every time he needed an edge. Or thought that she did. And in the past, she always had the same response. But usually it didn't happen after she'd just been attacked. Still she asked, "Back in where?"

"Silverman & Sons."

Sharon shook her head. "No! ABSOLUTEY NOT!"

"You have to. It's the best way," he said, cajoling.

"I can't. Damon, we've been through this. I'll find another way, go through the earnings statements of every client; I'll find the discrepancies and..."

"It's not the same as going in, you know that. Call it undercover. Call it a career shift. You need access to the WorldWell Bank documents, to their clients' documents. You need to be a part of the inner chatter. Get access to the deal information that only investment bankers know about." He lightly gripped both her shoulders.

Sharon couldn't steady her breath. It was spurting out of her in short heaves. Distance was good. Necessary. She was hyperventilating. But she still found herself discussing the unthinkable. "It's true that SEC documents only show the numbers that companies *want* to disclose."

"Precisely," said Damon. "Filings won't show the details hidden in the computer networks of banks. You know all of this just as well as I do."

"True," she said. "But…"

He leaned into her, their faces centimeters apart. "There's *nothing* that can replace *access*."

"Damon, I quit that world because I couldn't take it anymore." She backed off; that was the only reason she had ever given him. "You expect me to go back, tail between my legs?"

"I expect you to figure out how WorldWell Bank is doing what it's doing, and you can't exactly get a job there. They hate you. All those negative stories. But Silverman—you used to work there."

"And you think they'll welcome me back with open arms? You realize their CFO once called me a communist on national television."

"You said it yourself. Wall Street has no memory. Tell them you've seen the error of your ways or something."

"That's ridiculous, Damon. No one will buy it."

"I wouldn't be too sure," he said, tugging at his chin.

"Why?"

"Because Katrina Sullivan is a good friend of mine," he said as he walked to the living room window and opened the wooden blinds.

"Katrina Sullivan? The chief technology officer at Silverman…is a…*good*…friend of yours?" Katrina wasn't exactly the "friend" type. As far as Sharon knew, she didn't have *any* friends.

"Sure," Damon answered, staring out the window. "You remember that story we did on her, don't you?"

"Yeah," said Sharon, face contorting. "Two years ago, right? One of the most pathetic pieces of puff journalism ever.

What was the headline, again? "She Has it All: The Ultimate IT Girl of Wall Street"—right? God. And those long legs in their Jimmy Choos, splashed across the cover. Just ridiculous."

"I wrote that piece," said Damon, with a hint of wounded pride.

"Oh," said Sharon, containing the rest of her vitriol about Katrina, waiting for some reprimand.

Instead, he turned his gaze upon Fourth Street. His eyes fixed on a woman walking—or being walked by—a group of German shepherds and huskies. He stared at the sky, then at Sharon. *Can I really send her back? What the hell is wrong with you?* He leaned his forehead on the window pane. *The woman was just attacked by God knows whom, and all you care about is the story?*

As he kept his focus on the morning bustle of East Village life, Sharon tapped his shoulder for the third time. "Hey, Damon," she repeated. "Are you okay?"

He stifled a shudder. "Yes, sorry. I was just thinking of something. A possible lead."

"What is it?" She leaned in closer to him, re-tightening the belt of her robe, hoping he'd spill something more.

"Not sure." He looked at her, and realized she was just as eager to focus on the story and forget about her attack. *The hunt that was in their blood. That took over any other aspects of life. Convenient excuse for screwing up personal relationships as well.* "Listen, I'm going to the office to pick up some documents."

"Won't Stetson throw a fit?"

His boss was the least of his worries. "He'll be fine. I'll also call Katrina. Run our idea by her."

"Your idea," corrected Sharon. *I'm so not into this.*

"You'll be fine," said Damon. "I promise." He didn't sound like he meant it.

* * *

Sharon watched the street outside her apartment to make sure Damon really left. She watched as he crossed to his car, peeled the bright orange parking ticket off his windshield, and took out his cell phone. He put it to his ear and slipped into his Impala.

Sharon walked over to the Indian cabinet. Its dark teak was beautifully carved. It weighed a ton. Four movers had been required to carry it up the stairs of her current place after her divorce. She bought it from an old sound-guy who used to work the punk rock circuit before abandoning it to find himself. Like everyone else, it seemed, he wound up in India. In junkyards, fixing up discarded furniture and reselling it overseas. This particular cabinet was from Gujarat. It had once been used, he told Sharon, as dowry for an arranged marriage.

Apparently, the inhabitants of southern India were smart about hiding valuables. Inside the cabinet was a secret compartment, imperceptible to the naked eye. The cabinet was fashioned to appear less roomy inside than it really was. In the space between the bottom shelf and the actual bottom of the cabinet was a tiny groove. If you pressed down on it lightly, it exposed an extra panel of wood. Gently sliding it down, she accessed her secret drawer. She often wondered what the bride had hidden in it. The drawer was big enough to hide documents. Big enough to hide a laptop.

Big enough to hide the filing that marked the beginning of the trail—whatever it is, she thought.

CHAPTER 9

Sharon knew that whoever sent the brute would soon discover that the documents and her hard drive weren't what they were looking for. *He'll be back.* But not right away, her instincts told her. The brute wasn't the boss. That meant explanations would be necessary. That would buy her time. She hoped it would be enough.

She was apprehensive and still in agony from the night's thrashing. But she was also intrigued. She felt her mind searching to discern the clues, to piece together the many parts of her crazy night. Sharon had always been good at solving puzzles. As a little girl, she couldn't finish them fast enough. Her father had been a world-famous mathematician. Math was all about solving puzzles, numerical riddles, he had called them when she was a kid. Whenever he came home—always from doing something important, it seemed, at some important international conference—he'd bring her a new puzzle. He told her it was a necessary skill for survival. This was how he trained her. She'd run up to her bedroom, shut the door, and get to work. To find the answers in the fragmented pieces. To make him proud of her.

Her mother died in a car accident when she was eight. Her father became both her parents, and her teacher. She was devoted to him. But by the time she turned fourteen, she seemed to no longer exist. He took off soon afterward with a woman half his age. She was devastated, and all the more determined. She graduated high school at sixteen. Afterward, more for survival than love, she moved in with her boyfriend, saved money, and put herself through the state university.

Three years later, she graduated early with her bachelor's degree, a double-major in math and theatre. She headed for New York City, determined to make it as an actress. The drama of off-off-Broadway grew old after a few years. She hungered for more financial security, more mental challenge, more control of her life.

That was how she found herself on Wall Street. She vowed to never depend on anyone financially. Or in any other way. She easily landed a job at WorldWell Bank as a trader. She was smart and engaging. Her climb up the corporate ladder was quick. Eventually she wound up at Silverman.

Now it looked like she would be returning to that awful world. But first she had to figure things out. Just like with the puzzles from her childhood, it was time to get to work.

She would start with a phone call of her own.

A few blocks away, on a seedy stretch of Alphabet City, in a studio apartment filled with beer bottle candleholders, hundreds of indie DVDs, and the newest technical gadgets, Trevor Wood answered after the sixth ring. "Hey, what do you want, man?"

"Trev, it's Sharon," she answered, eyes darting around the room. She didn't realize how nervous she would be.

"Are you crazy? It's, like, not even noon yet," he grouched.

She heard what sounded like a stack of books crashing. "Yeah, I know. I need your techno-brain. It's about that trail thing."

"Jeez, Share—I thought you were over that like months ago. After the whole assault-and-battery of the ugly ogre thing. What are you *thinking?*"

"Just get over here, Trev. I—I kind of don't want to be

alone." She glanced at her front door, half-expecting the brute to bust in at any moment. "I'll fill you in then."

"Whatever. Cool. Let me wake up first." Trevor began patting the floor by his futon, feeling for any leftover roaches from last night. He knocked over a quarter-bottle of wine in the process. "Shit!"

"Trev, please don't get wasted right now," said Sharon. "We need clarity."

"Uh-huh. Clarity. I'm on it. I'm all about clarity, Share."

"Just get here, okay?" She opened her door a few inches and peered down the hallway. Closing it, she re-checked to make sure the bolts were locked. She took a deep breath.

"Uh-huh." And with that, Trevor hung up the phone, took a hit, rolled over, and fell back asleep.

CHAPTER 10

Sharon knew she would have to give Trevor another call shortly to make sure he was actually awake. What a lovable fuck-up he was. Within the barren landscape that passed for her personal life, Trevor was one of her steadiest friends. They had known each other for ten years, ever since he spent a few months contracting as a computer support guy at WorldWell Bank. He was a couple years younger than her and rail-thin with stringy, ginger-colored hair he kept tied back in a ponytail. The tattoos that covered his body were replicas of the foreign currency he came across in his world travels.

He never maintained full-time employment. Didn't want to be tied down—or have his fashion-style dictated. So he drifted from job to job. She admired that about him, the glow of freedom he seemed to radiate. He made money as a freelance network designer and trouble-shooter. Sometimes he spun the club scene. Every night owl in New York knew him. He rarely came home before dawn.

Trevor was a technology genius, a computer whiz. And a total pothead.

While Sharon allowed him his post-waking nap, she changed into mesh shorts and a navy blue tank top. Returning to her living room, she spread all her background ITA documents across her floor, like pieces of a jigsaw puzzle. There was a stack of them. She plugged in her hidden laptop and hooked in her DSL connection.

Next, she extracted her list of all existing tech companies from the Indian cabinet. She had painstakingly created this database, merging all her old banking clients with details from subsequent journalism coverage. Finally, she removed the March 15 SEC filing. Laying it out on the floor, she smoothed it with her hand delicately as if it was a treasure.

For all she knew it was. She hadn't examined it for months. Not since the day of the brute's first visit. Looking at it again, she remembered why she had been so confused by his anger. It didn't seem to say much of anything. The only part that was clear was the title and date at the top:

SECURITIES EXCHANGE COMMISSION
MARCH 15, 2007

INTACT TECHNOLOGY ASSOCIATED
SECURITY BROKERS, DEALERS & FLOTATION
COMPANIES [6211]
8-K

After that, it was a bunch of gibberish mixed with a few indecipherable letters; random clusters of other letters and symbols ran down the right side of the page:

```
    *&*&*&*&        or&*&*&*er*&*&*&*&*c     i^ii%
*nt*&*&*&*    *&*&*&*&*a&*&*   *&*&*&Co&*    i$v#
 *&*&   *&*mG*&   *&*a&*        &*&*     ii%
  *      &*G&*    *&*&*T&*      &*&h    i$x#
```

As Sharon sat cross-legged on her floor contemplating its meaning, she was assailed by a gigantic piercing headache. An excruciating combination of the beating her head took the night before and the incomprehensible filing in front of her. The severe lack of caffeine in her veins didn't help matters. Plus, the Advil was wearing off.

She needed Advil, coffee, and food, in that order.

The Advil was the easy part. Damon had conveniently left the bottle and glass of water on the middle of the kitchen counter. She poured herself more tap water and took four pills. Then came the matter of coffee. She hated instant, so she always kept real beans around. But after rummaging with greater and greater desperation through her bare cabinets, she realized that she was out of coffee.

It's going to be a very long day. She decided she was in no condition to go outside—not that she was concerned about what people might think of her bandage and black eye. New Yorkers kept to themselves when it came to violence. Even if they wanted to know, they didn't want to ask.

It was more the devastating sunlight she could detect even from her northern exposure window that scared her. She didn't want to deal with it. The very thought caused another avalanche of pain. She also didn't feel like ordering in. There had been enough buzzing in and out of her apartment.

She settled for the remains of a can of flat soda from her fridge. That and some milk-less Special K would have to tide her over until Trevor arrived. Swigging down the rest of the Diet Coke, she began her morning ritual of surfing the web for the day's headlines. Poring through any current news about WorldWell Bank, ITA, and the world in general. It was a force of habit on anything she was investigating, or had just published, like the ITA piece she just ran behind Damon's cover story.

A few absentminded minutes into her search, she ran across the media equivalent to World War Three. The *Wall Street Tribune's* center headline was about ITA. The story was written by Stan Johnson. A possible SEC investigation into ITA for misleading accounting.

She switched on CNN. They were running the same story about ITA, after giving an update on the WorldWell Bank scandal coverage that Damon started. Score two for the home team. Their significant news had finally bumped that serial murder piece that had been repeating endlessly for weeks. Nothing else was going on in Washington. They plastered a picture of Ivan Stark across the screen. It was happening. She knew she was responsible. She had started it.

That bastard CEO, Ivan Stark. *Let him burn.* She clenched her fists. The tension brought a sudden wave of pain up the side of her cheek. She brushed it aside.

He deserved every negative thing he got. *And then some.*

Sharon considered the timing. The visit last night. The trail. She didn't believe in coincidences, not where corporations were concerned. She skimmed the *Wall Street Tribune* story. There was nothing about a trail of any kind. Also, beyond the possible SEC investigation, there was nothing additive to the story she did months back. Typical of the press, find an old story, then reshape it to appear like news by adding a tiny bit of extra information to the front. Then, if you're Stan Johnson, take credit and win another Pulitzer.

She searched for any current news on Silverman, her potential soon to be re-employer. *God, I hated it there. I don't want to wear a suit. I don't even own stockings anymore. And, I don't want to see Sam. Not after what happened. What I did.*

Still, if something was going down involving one of the most powerful financial institutions in the world, it would be much easier to detect from the inside. People trust their own kind. It was a Darwinian corollary: survival of the best insulated.

She had discovered that when she forayed from banking to reporting. All of a sudden, doors began slamming in her face. Former colleagues were scared to speak with her. Even about their personal lives. They became suspicious. As if every detail might become her next front page story. Their own wealth depended on anonymity.

So maybe this was the only way. Maybe she could handle it. It was just undercover work—it was temporary. She could leave immediately after she uncovered whatever was lurking beneath the surface. But, if she was going back to Silverman, she needed her allies to know. Sharon made another phone call.

"Yeah, Mickey here," answered a gruff male voice.

"Hey, it's me," she answered, happy to have at least one person who immediately recognized the sound of her voice.

"Well, I'll be fucked!" he boomed over the sound of slapping his desk. "You have made my fucking year. Thought you'd left your old friends behind, kiddo."

"Never," said Sharon, staring at the ITA documents while speaking. "And guess what?"

"You finally packed it up and are moving to Ecuador to set up a dive shop with that boat boy—what was his name, Miguel?"

"Not even close," giggled Sharon. "And it was Belize. And his name was Pedro. And he was hot. Guess again."

"What's up?" She could hear him inhale his cigarette, imagined him grasping it firmly with thick fingers.

"Mickey, are you still smoking?"

"Depends what you mean by that. If you mean, am I sitting here in the middle of some back-office fucking trading room, under a fucking 'no smoking' banner sucking a Marlboro Red, then guilty."

"I thought you quit," she said, remembering their weeks

of debate on the issue. Their pact to quit together: him from smoking, her from Silverman.

"I did. Then I decided I'd rather die happy…but, I digress. Why'd ya call, kiddo?"

"I might be coming back."

"Back? To where?"

"To Silverman."

"I'll pretend I didn't just hear that little death wish."

"It's true. Apparently, as we speak, my editor is calling in some favor from the queen bitch."

"Then you're gonna need your guardian angel. I won't fuck it up this time. I promise. But why?"

Sharon's call waiting beeped. It was her assistant. "Mickey, I gotta go. I'll keep you posted."

"Morning, Sharon," trilled Amy, in her ever-light soprano.

"Hey, Amy, what's up?" she asked.

"Damon called and said you'd be working from home today. So I checked your voice mail for messages."

"Thanks," said Sharon. Amy gave efficiency a new meaning, always with a smile. "Anything good?"

"You had four calls, one from that cute guy at the SEC, Roger Francis, he said you had his number, one from WKAR radio wanting to do an interview about the second tech wave boom, and two from some woman in Washington, didn't leave a message, just a number and name, Janet Waters."

"Do I know her?" asked Sharon. New names and contacts constantly flowed in and out of Sharon's days; she relied on Amy as a second facet of her memory.

"Don't think so," answered Amy. "She's not in your contacts either—I checked."

"Okay, well, if she calls back, just ask her what she wants, and take it from there."

"Done. I'll let you know if anything else happens here," said her assistant, perky from start to finish.

"Thanks, Amy. Talk to you later." As soon as she clicked off, she realized how muddy her mind was, especially in comparison to Amy's effortlessness. She desperately needed coffee. *Where the hell is Trevor?* It was time for a second wake-up call.

"Uh-huh—yeah?" answered Trevor, not sounding at all alert.

"Trev, you need to get here, now. I'm dying. Get a quarter pound of any java beans and whatever fried food you can think of on the way. I'm buying."

Sharon knew the "I'm buying" part would work. She could picture Trevor getting up, grabbing his keys, and heading the four blocks to her place without bothering to shower or getting dressed in anything. Not that it was possible to distinguish from his usual degree of crumpledness how long he'd been wearing the same outfit, anyway.

CHAPTER 11

It was called "fuck you" money where he came from. The kind of wealth that kept all lower life forms out of your way. The kind that drew a thick white line between you and them. Between the "I have's" and the "you have not's." The kind that let you buy off anyone for anything. The kind that meant you'd never have to return to the slum you crawled out of. The kind that let you give the whole damn world the finger.

Fuck you, that's my Mercedes G500. Fuck you, that's my yacht. Fuck you, that's my Lear. Fuck you, that's my trophy wife. Fuck you, that's my even hotter mistress.

Mickey Mancuso had grown up in a decaying row house in Bed-Sty, Brooklyn, USA. It was him, his four brothers, two sisters, and perma-drunk mother. His father took off before Mickey came into the world. He never returned.

During his youth, Mickey split his time between beating up neighborhood kids and studying his ass off. He went to Brooklyn College to get a business degree and wound up a trader at Hamill Brothers in the mid-eighties. It was a boys club. Fast trading, lines in the men's room, more lines at Jeremy's by the seaport at night. Endless pitchers of beer and laughing your ass off.

Those were the days. Before structured derivative this and special purpose that made trading a fucking mess of documentation and brought in teams of quaint geeks from Princeton. You bought low, you sold high. Period. You faked out your competitors because you were smarter. You schmoozed the inter-market brokers. You fucked their sisters. You wrote a lot of trade tickets. You moved like electricity. You didn't need inside information if you used your brain and followed your gut.

During the eighties, you didn't have to piss in a paper cup to prove you were fit to whirl billions of dollars a day through dark computer screens with luminescent green type. In those days, you didn't need some fancy MBA from Harvard to land a power job. You just had to be better, smarter, hungrier, and more intimidating than the people around you.

And Mickey, at six foot four and 280 pounds, was certainly intimidating.

During the past two decades, he'd made hundreds of millions of dollars and become a legend. People who didn't know him feared him. He didn't speak much, but when he did, it was short and cutting. If you were on his good side, you were set. Mickey was all about loyalty. It was truckloads of Dunkin' Donuts at morning meetings. It was lunches at Il Mulino's where he always got a table, always tipped with Ben Franklins, and always gave Alfredo, the head waiter, box seats for whatever New York playoff game was going down. Tickets for Alfredo, his wife, and all his kids. It was $4,000 bottles of Montrachet at Boulez after work. At night, he'd sometimes let you fly out to New Jersey in his private helicopter, out to Rumson—capital of new money. Where he bought a home next to Geraldo Rivera.

But if you tried to fuck with him, you were screwed. If you were lucky, he fired you. If you were unlucky, you disappeared.

It was all a giant game to Mickey. And he liked winning games. Neutralize your opponent, move into his territory. Fake him out. It all came down to accumulating fuck you money.

The kids that came to Wall Street today—just to get a little richer than their parents—were fancy Ivy League brats to him. As far as Mickey was concerned, they slipped into the alma maters their parents donated millions of bucks to each year. Endowment fucking funds. These kids with their clean-shaven faces and parents' Upper East Side condos and Equinoxed bodies got their MBAs and easily slid through the doors of the privileged. The doors he had busted his butt to even find.

They attended bullshit two-year analyst programs where they taught you a little about finance and a lot about self-importance. He hated all of them, little white-collar wimps from multi-home-owning Connecticut WASP families with exclusive golf club memberships and easy access to everything. But they would never have the kind of street smarts, the animal instincts, he did. They would never have to. Hell, they didn't even need Wall Street for money, they were born with silver fuck you spoons in their little privileged mouths. Raised by foreign nannies who were nineteen and blonde and spoke French or Italian. Cleaned up after by foreign maids who spoke Spanish or Polish. He hated them.

But he hated Sam more. That tall, bald, turtle-like freak with his abnormally wide shoulders.

When his investment banking division started making billions of dollars out of nothing, Sam catapulted to the top of Silverman & Sons. Made CEO overnight. All of a sudden, Mickey's trading desk couldn't compete with the boys that were making a mint out of fucking air. It all happened so fast, too. Sure it was paper money—a merger here, an acquisition or an IPO there—but there was a fuck-of-a-lot of it.

Sam, in return, had no respect for the callous, grubby trading sect. In particular, Sam disliked Mickey's rogue manners, limited vocabulary, and bad fashion sense. Once he was victorious, Sam offered Mickey a way to stay on the Street. Sam wouldn't be the one to fell the mighty Mickey, just take the wind out of his sails until he disappeared.

Sam shoved Mickey into an "incubator," a dot.com think tank where he could run a small team of his own people. There, he could uncover investment opportunities in tech companies, the crumb companies that Sam's people weren't already crawling over. The inter-office memo had said "we're pleased to announce Mickey's decision to run this strategically important new area and wish him the best." The best. Fuck Sam. More like, the area where he could retire "gracefully" at fifty-two. Put out to pasture like a goddamn farm animal.

He wanted to see Sam fall. It was the only thing he craved. He wanted it so bad he could taste it.

CHAPTER 12

Trevor arrived at Sharon's apartment with a plastic bag of crucial supplies: Jamaican Blue Mountain beans, grilled cheese and tomato sandwiches, a side of German potato salad, and thick, salty pickles. He knew that she worked best on a full stomach. He often marveled at how she kept the quantities of food she ate hidden somewhere in her lean, muscular body. But he knew there were days she'd forget to eat, first too busy with the latest important bank deal, and now with whatever the new breaking story was.

After a few shuffling steps into her living room, he stopped short. "Oh man!" he exclaimed. "What the hell happened here?"

"That would be the brute's fist," answered Sharon. She grabbed the coffee beans from his hands and dumped them into the grinder next to the coffeemaker, already filled with waiting water.

"No, Share." He studied her face, then her desk. "I mean—where's your PC?"

"I think it will heal nicely, thanks for asking," said Sharon, grateful for his presence. Then, motioning to the general chaos, "That would be him, too."

"The bastard!" Trevor punched his fist into his palm, a gesture Sharon had never seen him do before. She found his anger supportive.

"Yeah." Sharon didn't want to spend time talking about

it. If she was in danger, she wasn't going to go down without figuring out why.

"I hoped you sliced up his other side at least!"

"Let's just say it wasn't one of my better nights," she responded to his way of prodding her for information.

"What else did he get?" Now he demonstrated concern, taking the cue from her opening.

"Not much really, a WorldWell Bank file with an ITA bond deal document in it that he'll figure out is pretty meaningless, and my hard drive, my password protected hard drive, which won't help him either. Oh, and I missed out on round two with Randall, who I brilliantly kicked out before the thug arrived."

Trevor grinned. "Does Randall know you go around getting beat up for a living?"

"Well, he *is* my boxing trainer."

"Right, trainer. Whatever."

"Fortunately, I had backup," said Sharon pointing to her laptop.

"Way to go, Share." Trevor high-fived her. He extracted a flash-drive from the pocket of his Diesel jeans.

"What's that for?"

"More backup," he said as he inserted it into the A-drive and began copying the files onto it. "In case the brute gets bored again."

Sharon marveled at the way Trevor performed even the simplest technological task, like downloading. He exhibited more enthusiasm for everything technical than anyone she had ever known. And flair. Not only was he downloading backups, he was searching for viruses, protecting her wireless connection from penetration, and probably a bunch of other things she was generally too impatient to be bothered with.

As she watched Trevor attending to her files, Sharon's land line rang.

"Hang on a sec, Trev," said Sharon, rushing to her desk to pick it up. "Hello?"

She could detect nothing but dim static at the other end of the line.

"Hello," she repeated to the receiver.

"*Sharon,*" said a low guttural male voice. "*You want to figure out what's going on?*"

She felt a chill. "Yes, of course...who are...?"

"*Look beneath the surface.*" His words sounded mechanical, computerized. He emphasized the word "beneath."

"Who is this? What surface?" she asked, trying desperately to place him.

"*Follow the trail. To its source.*"

"Who is this?" she said more angrily. She heard what sounded like a whir of machines in the background.

"*Find the trail. Find its source. Look beneath the surface. I'll be calling again.*"

"What? I..."

The phone went dead. Sharon's trembling fingers brought the cordless back to its cradle and turned to Trevor.

"Who was that?" asked Trevor.

"No one," she said. "It was nothing. A telemarketer."

"They should all be shot," said Trev.

"Yeah," said Sharon, looking out the window in the same direction Damon had earlier. "And I'm not even listed."

Trevor placed a hand on her shoulder. She covered it with her own. He was the one person in her life who made her feel like she didn't always have to be stuff. She remembered the first day they met. She was a young junior trader. On her first day, she walked onto the trading floor in a fire-engine-red suit, black stockings, and high pumps. She looked sexy, classy, and in complete violation of WorldWell's dress policy. If she looked out of place, his rebellious fashion sense made him look moreso. They had become instant friends.

"You okay, Share?"

"I'm fine." She took out a ponytail holder from the drawer under the phone stand and gathered her hair. She sensed Trevor's concern, but one of the reasons she'd been friends with him for so long—aside from his admirable brilliance—was that he knew when to let go, leave her be.

The phone rang again. Trevor detected Sharon's nervousness. "Should I get that?

"No, that's okay. I got it," she answered. Pressing the "talk" button, Sharon braced herself for the voice again. "Hello," she said harshly. Trevor stood behind her.

It was Amy. "Hi, sorry to bug you again, but I've got that Janet Waters woman on the phone. The one who called earlier. Says she needs you and won't let me take a message. Do you want to talk to her?"

Sharon sighed. People were always calling with stories only *they* considered important. "Put her through."

"Hello, I'm looking for Sharon Thomas."

"This is she."

"I'm...I..." the woman blurted. "It may seem like I'm calling you out of the blue, but my husband, Kevin, was working on something I think you're involved in."

"A story idea?"

"No, it—he works at the SEC, Simon Caldwell's unit, and it's...it's about WorldWell Bank..."

"Oh, you probably want to get in touch with my editor, Damon Matthews. He's doing that story."

"But my husband had your name on his files."

"Uh huh," said Sharon, debating whether to be pleasant or to blow this woman off so she could get back to her work.

"Well, now the story belongs to Damon. If you call back the main *Riche$* number—"

"You don't understand," said Janet. Sharon heard a cry in the background and then the placating words, "Sweetie, Mommy's on the phone." The cry became a screech. "He was also working on something with ITA. I'll call you back," she promised and hung up.

Sharon groaned and returned her attention to Trevor, who mouthed, "What's going on?"

The coffeemaker dinged, and Sharon triumphantly poured her long-awaited cup of coffee. She mulled over the woman's mention of ITA, and said, "Some woman with a kid. Let me just make a quick call and we can get back to work." She picked up the phone again and dialed.

"Roger Francis, SEC," answered a pleasant voice, sounding like a 1940s radio announcer.

"Hey, Rog, it's Sharon."

"Oh, hi, Sharon. Listen, I'm sorry about that Stan Johnson story—should have been your scoop."

"No problem. I understand. I could use a quick favor from you, though." She paced the room as she spoke.

"Sure, anything for you."

"Could you do a check on a Kevin Waters in the employee database?" She wrote the name on a post-it.

"Sure...do you know what area he's in?"

"No. His wife called, said he worked at the SEC—I'm just checking."

"Is he new?"

"Don't know," she answered, doodling around the name.

"Okay, I'll take a look and get back to you. Anything else I can do for you?"

"Uh, could you check out a Simon Caldwell, too?"

"Sure, no problem. Simon Caldwell," he repeated, writing it down.

"Thanks, Rog. You're the best."

Sharon hung up and turned to Trevor. "Okay, I'm not touching the phone anymore." She gulped down her cold coffee, barely realizing she was drinking it, and inhaled half a sandwich. She shoved the voice calls to the back of her mind. Survival instinct. Let things roll off. More got done that way. She had to focus. On the kitchen bar, she laid out her prized SEC file, the document that she hoped would allow her to understand the trail. "Let's figure this thing out."

Sitting on two adjacent counter stools, she and Trevor stared at the mysterious characters.

"Tell me again how you got this thing," said Trevor.

"It was simple, really," she answered. "All I did was access the SEC database, like five months ago. I was printing out all of ITA's publicly available financials for my story on them."

"So anyone could have done the same thing?" asked Trevor, to get the facts straight.

"Yeah, it's a routine story research—you find background financial data on any relevant companies. ITA stands for Intact Technology Associated. The SEC filings show the flow of money coming and going out of the company. Numbers tell stories by what they say and, more importantly, by what they leave out."

"So, that's what you were aiming for?" he asked, picking up one of the pages of the filing. "Figuring out what they might be hiding?"

"Yeah, standard reporting stuff. The story behind the story, based on the facts you gather. ITA rose from the ashes of the last telecom bust to dominate its field. Bought most of its competitors. They had this meteoric rise. I didn't buy it. And, well, Ivan Stark's a piece of work."

Trevor listened intently. He remembered when she quit WorldWell Bank to join Silverman, and how a year later, after she got out of the hospital, she spent much of their drinking time together berating Ivan. He epitomized the worst of the corporate cretins she was dealing with, according to her. "Go on," he said.

Sharon continued, raking her fingers through her hair. "Well, this March 15 filing I retrieved didn't resemble a normal 8-K or corporate exception report. It was dotted with some kind of computer code, ASCII symbols or something, with lots of gaps between them. Every few lines, there was a fragment of what I thought was some tech company name. Nothing more than a few letters."

"And?" Trevor prompted eagerly—he got off on computer symbols.

"I tried to download a clean one a minute later, but the filing had disappeared. The only relevant one I found was from a week later. A notification that Silverman's CEO, Sam Peterson, had been elected to a board seat at ITA, replacing Melvin Myers of GlobeTech."

"So you just dropped it?"

"I thought nothing of the original filing—just that it was corrupt or something. The SEC's website is notorious for being poorly supported. You'd hate it, Trev. They spend as little money as possible actually examining the financial reports of the companies under their jurisdiction."

"Isn't that, like, supposed to be their job?" asked Trevor.

"*Supposed to be* is the operative expression," she said. "In reality," she took a bite of her grilled cheese sandwich, "execs from these firms give so much money in campaign donations to politicians. They're super-valuable to the Washington establishment. Untouchable. Anyway, I decided it was just some electronic database glitch. Maybe an Internet problem. No big deal."

"You should have called in Trev," he said, grinning.

"Yeah, well, that night I submitted the ITA story to *Riche$*. A few days later, the brute barged into my apartment—said he was looking for something called 'the trail.' I had no idea what he was talking about. He was freaky, jerking like a coke addict, smelled like garlic and sweat. He was holding a jagged knife in his grubby fist over my head. We just stared at each other for a moment, then he just left. Said he'd be back."

"Right, and that's when I offered you my place for awhile and you got all stubborn and Sharon-like," said Trevor.

She smiled. "Well, I didn't see the point in running away just cause of him. I hate the idea of running away. That's why I stayed at Silverman so long, even though you kept bugging me to leave. Even when things there got...really..."

"Bad," Trevor finished. "And really scary."

"Yeah," her voice quivered, "scarier than some maniac wielding a butcher knife."

"Well, that guy didn't know he was attacking the wrong girl," Trevor said boastfully, bringing Sharon back to the present.

"I didn't expect that martial arts training to come in so handy," she said, even as she started shaking.

"Hey, Share," Trevor rubbed her back. "You did what you had to do."

"Just I–I've never attacked anyone like that. I never— sliced—into another human being. Never caused that kind of blood. Beginner's luck, huh?" But Sharon knew there were other reasons, both simpler and more complex. *After that summer, the police made me feel like it was my fault. And if the trail did exist, I wasn't going to let a police report leak the story to other reporters.*

"So this thug hadn't bothered you since?"

"No. I thought it blew over. I periodically tried to download the original file from the SEC site, but it seemed gone for good. Then, when I didn't hear from him, I assumed, I don't know, he got what he was looking for elsewhere, and I got embroiled in following stuff on ITA that I could figure out. Then, he returned. Still after the trail. He took my computer; I blacked out."

"But you are smart, and you scanned everything into your laptop," said Trevor, pressing an ice pack to her eye.

"I figured anything someone wants that badly has to be important. I've just got to focus on this trail and figure it out, before he comes back."

CHAPTER 13

Trevor was lying on Sharon's couch, feet up, head leaning on the arm rest. He took a puff of his self-rolled cigarette and held up a page of the trail document. Light streamed through the windows across the room. "What are you thinking so far?" he asked.

"Well, the first thing that popped into my mind," said Sharon, pushing his legs off the side of the couch, "was that this filing had something to do with contracts of some sort. ITA did business with lots of other tech companies. Peers."

"Why contracts?" he asked, offering her a toke.

"No thanks," she said. "A hunch. 8-K reports usually capture special transactions or activities that occur in between the regular times when companies file their quarterly or annual reports. Broadband companies exchange services with each other all the time, on paper anyway. Sometimes just to book fake fees, or hide costs. Which happens to be illegal. It's fraud." She sat down, resting her leg on the coffee table.

"Yeah, go on," said Trevor, sitting up.

"That piece I did was about ITA's numbers. ITA was booking fees from peer companies for contracts to build networks. Only it never built any networks. Those companies did the same thing back."

"Not following, Share. Come again?" His forehead wrinkled to concentrate.

"ITA made it look like they were getting money in the door, lots of money, but not paying out at the other end, as their contracts indicated. They were just swishing numbers. All companies were, but ITA was doing it more. That's why the SEC started snooping around their books."

"But, this file came from the SEC website, right?"

"Yeah."

"Why would ITA want the SEC to see their plan?"

She paused, pushing invisible strands of hair away from her puffy eye, reaching for her coffee mug. "I don't know," she said, shaking her head. "They wouldn't, I guess."

"What if you look at it from the technology angle," said Trevor, trying to be helpful. He took a blank piece of paper from the table beside the couch and began scribbling boxes and arrows.

"What do you mean?" asked Sharon, trying to focus on the paper with her good eye.

"All these firms have been expanding networks fast. So they must bump up against competitors all the time. They have a choice—build an extra network to cover the same territory or pay to use a piece of their competitor's network. It's like paying interstate tolls on a highway."

"So, you think this trail is a network highway of some kind?"

"I don't know, maybe." He took another long drag of his cigarette.

"What for?"

"I don't know."

"And why would it be with so many companies, at the same time?"

"Well, if they wanted to close a particular network circuit, they'd want to cover all entry points. See?" He drew a line circling the first and last box he'd drawn.

"Now I'm not following. Would that create a network no one else could access?"

"It would certainly help."

She paused. A closed secret network. She stared at the mysterious symbols on the confusing SEC document. She recalled how she used to solve puzzles as a kid, laying out all the pieces and looking for anything unusual before she touched them. Then she'd let the picture come to her. She studied the code pattern, looking for anything inconsistent.

"Trev," she almost squealed, her inner girl excited.

"What?"

"Look at the letters near the end of the second line, after all the title stuff."

"I'm looking."

"See, here?" she said, pointing to a line that read "*&*&*&Co&*"

"Yeah, what about it?" he asked, writing it above one of his boxes.

"'Co' could be part of the word 'com'—you know, like UniversalCom, or QualityCom, or one of those companies."

"Which one?"

"I don't know yet, but wait...wow...hey, get this." She was pointing to the next line. She circled the "*&*mG*&" combination with a red editing pencil.

"QualityComG?" he offered, clueless, but trying to help Sharon.

"No such thing, but...here, go through this." She handed him her list of over one thousand public technology companies. There were eighty-four that had a word ending in "Com" followed by one beginning with the letter "G": BrainworksComGlobal, DesignComGlobal, etc. She started checking names off and circling letters in others. Her pen whirled over the page. Soon, her scribbles looked somewhere between an Etch-o-Sketch and a Jackson Pollock.

"Share—whoa, wait a second!"

"I can't, Trev, do you know how important this is?"

"Share, 'course I do. That's why I'm here. You may have done this stuff by trial and error when you were seven, but..."

"It was *not* trial and error," she retorted, hands on hips.

"Whatever, trial and error and brains. You have like a thousand companies on that list, and mostly vowel sequences to fit. You can't do that shit in your head. You know what you need?"

"What do I need, Trevor?" she sighed, taking his cigarette and inhaling a puff.

"A program to scan this list and come up with matches to the available letters."

"And, where...?"

"Relax—you're talking to Trevor the Tech Geek. I'll take care of it. But I need my own setup. I'm taking this flash-drive—I'll scan the list of companies and I'll come up with matches."

"Okay, Trev. But be back here in a few hours. Do not smoke. Do not sleep. Okay?

"Deal," he said.

"And, Trev."

"Yeah?"

"Please don't use the word 'deal.'"

CHAPTER 14

Immediately after he left Sharon's apartment, Damon called Katrina on her private cell.

"Damon Matthews," she answered after one ring. "So nice to hear from you."

"Katrina, hi," he said.

"What can I do for you?" she asked, business-speak for "how are you?"

"Well, actually, I need to ask you a small favor."

"I'm in the middle of a lunch deal here," she responded matter-of-factly. "Here" was the posh Gramercy Tavern off Park Avenue South. Katrina was seated at a white-linen table with three Parisians. She had just informed them that Silverman would be happy to arrange financing for their private broadband network between France and Germany; in return, they would give Silverman a $25 million fee and a ten percent cut of the upside in their company.

The men were discovering that their normal charm, so effective with most American women, was no match for Katrina's hard-as-blood-red-nails business style. She had offered an acceptable fee and wasn't budging. She flashed them a gleaming, icy be-with-you-in-a-second smile.

Damon said, "It's important."

"I see. Why don't you give me a call later." And with that Katrina hung up. She returned her focus to the Euro-business-trash seated around her. Half an hour later, Katrina's lunch was finished and the deal was sealed. At her price. She never backed down from her price. *Never let them see you sweat.* At a stunningly attractive forty-two years old, she had that part down cold.

She had risen in business with a simple motto: If people want to do business with you, they will. It was just a matter of time. The sooner you were ready to walk away, the sooner you got things done. She was always prepared to get it done or walk away, to the next client and the next deal. There was always a next. She never wasted time negotiating terms. That's what made her one of the most wealthy and successful businesswomen on Wall Street.

Katrina's driver was waiting in the charcoal-grey Mercedes outside the restaurant. He stepped out of the car to open the door for her. Two delivery men whistled at her from the sidewalk. Katrina didn't respond as she swooshed into the Benz.

After polishing up her lips with Chanel's A-List, Katrina pressed one of the buttons on the mahogany armrest. She smoothed back her blonde mane of hair and popped a breath mint in her mouth. Her driver looked back at her through the rearview mirror. "Jules," she said, "Take me to 1221 Sixth Avenue, please." She leaned back, crossed her well-toned legs, and re-read the morning's business headlines.

* * *

Standing behind his cherry and walnut desk, Ivan Stark gazed out his floor-to-ceiling windows. From the forty-fifth floor, the Empire City spread wide before him. Always determined to keep up with the trends, he had competed fiercely in the real estate game. He knew how important appearances were, and as the technology and communications companies grew like weeds around him, he joined them in the search for the sleekest offices, the most authoritative views. ITA headquarters was located smack in the middle of midtown Manhattan. Right where the old-style media and publishing houses once dominated. It had taken him years to reach this point in his career. He was king of the communications industry. A powerful force in world business. He had no intention of letting it all slip away.

He was on speakerphone to his internal PR team.

"Just DO something!" he bellowed, his hand smoothing over the top of his balding head.

"We're doing everything we can, Ivan," said a male voice on the other end. "It might help if—if there weren't rumors that you were selling our stock, I mean your stock, sir. $100 million seems to stick in people's heads."

"Tim, I don't pay you for financial advice, I pay you to work the media—got it?"

"Yes, sir. It's just that these rumors are saturating the press. That we're short on the cash necessary to make good on our bond payments—"

"Thanks, Tim, I can read. What other rumors are circulating?"

"Well, it seems that bondholders are dumping ITA bonds. Wall Street traders are smelling blood, sir. They're making the situation worse. They're calling all their clients, telling them to sell ITA bonds before anymore bad news comes out."

There was an intercom beep from Ivan's receptionist. "Hang on, Tim," said Ivan. "Yes?"

"Sir—it's Ewan McPherson, in legal. We just received a Form B notice from the SEC about a pending investigation into our books. I thought you should know."

Ivan had built an empire out of little but spin. His closest circle knew it. The rest of the investors were clueless. Ivan had grown from one man and a handful of speculative bankers into a global communications money machine. His own stake in the company had exploded from an initial $20 million to over $3 billion. Counting that stake, plus the real estate and his other investments, Ivan was worth over $4 billion.

On paper.

Ivan zoomed his hand across his desk, knocking stacks of paper, pens, a date-book, and gold plaque of his name and title on the floor. "Damn that bitch!"

"Sir?"

"That little Thomas bitch over at *Riche$*. She started this with that bullshit story about our books. Who the hell does she think she is, anyway? Did she ever start a company of her own? No! Did she have to navigate everyone's personal issues every single fucking day? No! Does she have to balance cash-flow and dysfunctional networks and lawsuits?"

"Sir—uh, what should I do about this investigation request?"

Ivan continued ranting. "No! But she sure had no trouble injecting doubt about ITA into the public arena. Now the rest of the media is having a field day. At my fucking expense!"

"Sir, I need to give them some sort of response."

"Tell them to fuck off—that's my response!" He pounded his desk with his fist.

"Not advised, sir—uh, I'll try to stall."

"You do that, Ewan!" Ivan clicked to another call. "Yes, what is it?"

"Ivan, it's Trudy, in legal."

"I just spoke to your, whoever, Ewan somebody," he said, leaning over his desk, palms pressing into the smooth lacquered surface.

"Yes, I'm responsible for human resource relations," she explained. "There's a problem."

"Of course there is. What now?"

"I just received word from McDougal & Hide. They're filing a class-action suit on behalf of some of your shareholders. Sorry, sir," said Trudy.

"Damn it!" He pounded the desk again. "I'm a billionaire. Name one person in the entire fucking country who wouldn't want to switch lives and bank accounts with me. Just one. I gave jobs to 15,000 ungrateful schmucks. I gave them a piece of the pie, too. My piece. My pie."

"Yes, well, they're filing on the grounds of *improper disclosure of information.* They're saying they weren't given the whole truth about the condition of the company when they bought it."

"Well, damn them, too!" shouted Ivan. "They didn't seem to have a problem with my stock while they gave me standing ovations. No, then it was all about how great ITA was, how we would change the world, how visionary I was. How happy they all were to be on the winning team."

Call waiting beeped again. "Trudy, I'll deal with them later. Go figure it out—keep things contained."

He pressed the phone button. "Now what?" It was PR again.

"Ivan, our phones are being flooded. Reporters are calling from *everywhere.*"

"It's August, dammit. Aren't they all *supposed to be on vacation?* Some idiot journalist at the *Wall Street Tribune* gets hold of some SEC notice and plasters it all over the front page twisting the screws even tighter than that Thomas woman had. It didn't even say we did anything wrong. It was notice of a *possible* investigation into *possibly* questionable practices. Now every reporter in the fucking country wants a comment? Just—fucking field it!"

Ivan clicked off. He was sweating. His armpits were soaked. The Rogained hairs that barely covered his head were stuck damp. He skimmed his emails. Tons of them. *Dear Mr. Stark, it has come to our attention that you haven't been fully forthcoming with information about ITA.* He punched Delete. Select. Delete. Select. Delete. The same emails, over and over. Company reps trying to cancel contracts.

"Fucking cowards," he muttered "Groveled for years to get a piece of our business, be involved in our private networks, bent over ass backwards to enter partnerships. Now they all want to bail."

Ivan's secretary buzzed his intercom, "Katrina Sullivan is here waiting to see you, sir."

"Great," he said out loud. *It's about to get worse.*

But looks so good in the process, he acknowledged to himself as she appeared in his doorway. She was wearing a white Gucci suit with a crème blouse that accentuated her cleavage. A matching pair of inch-long strands of delicate diamond earrings framed her face. Signature Katrina, white and diamonds. The definition of wealth and purity encasing a hard-assed businesswoman. Innocence meets power. Her cheeks were blush with anger, her lips pursed to speak. He knew what was coming.

"Katrina, what a terrific surprise. You look gorgeous, as usual," said Ivan. He rose from behind his desk to approach her as she huffed toward him.

"What the hell is this?" she asked, flinging her copy of the *Wall Street Tribune* at him. The headline, "**Intact Technologies—Not So Intact Anymore**" lay facing upward.

"I'm fine, couldn't be better. You?" he charmed sarcastically.

"Cut the bullshit, Ivan. This isn't a social call. What SEC investigation are these people referring to? And why didn't I know about it before they did?"

"I was going to let you know today," he hedged.

"Thanks. The entire business community just beat you to it."

"I don't need this from you right now, Katrina," he attacked. "I've got my shares to worry about, and probably a gaggle of federal investigators to fend off."

"Then tell me how you lost control of this," she said, sucking her teeth.

"The SEC's just responding, slowly as usual, to old news. Our books are fine," retorted Ivan.

She shot him an I-wasn't-born-yesterday look.

"Okay, our *public* books are fine," he amended. "Not the point."

"Ivan," she stepped closer to him, capturing his eyes with hers. "I do not have to remind you how much money—personal fucking money—I have riding on this. Not to mention a little thing called *my entire career*. I chose you because you seemed capable. I thought you'd get it right. Make this go away."

Ivan inhaled Katrina's perfume, the sophisticated–sexy scent of Guerlain's Après L'Ondee.

"Darling," he said, cajoling, "don't worry, I'll make it go away. At the SEC. In the press."

"Do not 'darling' me," she said between gritted teeth. "Just deal with it."

"And what about your end?" He grabbed her elbow.

"I'll take care of what I need to take care of," she promised, pulling her arm back. "I always do."

"Sam?"

"Sam," she confirmed.

Katrina was on track to the business stratosphere. As chief technology officer at the world's most powerful investment bank during an unprecedented tech boom, she was poised for the sky. First, she was set on grabbing Silverman's CEO spot from her boss, Sam Peterson. She didn't have the political clout in Washington that Sam had. She knew she didn't have the bullshit Skeleton and Blood fraternity bond that Sam had with the vice president. But she would compensate in her own way.

She was already at the center of the whole tech industry. No important deal took place without her. She knew each CEO and what made him or her tick, every start-up, every closing firm. She chose partners carefully. Strategically. Knowledge was power. Information was power. But control of knowledge and information was even more powerful. She would not fail. She would travel the path of the men before her. Investment banker to CEO to Oval Office. No, she would not fail. Whatever it took.

"Then everything's fine," he said. He pulled her closer, placing a hand on the small of her back, running the fingers of his other hand up the back of her neck and through her hair. Grabbing it tightly. Like he was going to rip her head off. He kissed her, firmly, trying to regain some control. She kissed back harder. They clasped tensely. A mixed moment of physical intensity and mental gamesmanship.

She loosened her head from his grip. "For now."

"For always," he responded.

"I have to get back," she said, walking toward the door. "We'll talk later."

"I'm looking forward to doing more than talking." He smiled slyly after the click of her Jimmy Choos.

Ivan paced by his giant windows, tugging at his chin. He surveyed the expanse of Manhattan beyond the glass, stock price on his mind. He was interrupted by the intercom. "Mr. Stark?"

"Yes, Christine?"

"I've got Ralph Stetson returning your call, sir, from *Riche$*."

"I see." Ivan made his only facial gesture that could be called a smile. He had called the publisher of *Riche$* and demanded he send over the person responsible for the story about his company, or he'd pull all of his advertising. Immediately. Forever.

"Damon Matthews is here, as well."

"Send him right in, Christine. And tell Ralph I'll call him later." Ivan pulled out a thick stack of documents from one of his drawers.

"Yes, sir," she said.

Damon appeared at Ivan's office door.

"Damon." Ivan didn't extend his hand.

"Ivan." Damon extended his arm anyway.

"I hope you've come to apologize for fucking up my stock price and to offer a retraction." Ivan wiped a bead of sweat from between two of his hairs.

"I can't retract," Damon responded, pulling his hand back. He had told Ralph he'd placate, but not capitulate. Let Ralph do that himself.

"Wrong answer. Look, I don't appreciate bad journalism. I hate bad journalism. And still, I left that last ridiculous story you people ran alone. But this predicament is unacceptable."

"Frankly, I'm in the hot seat for today's ITA story, too." Damon charmed his best smile to alleviate tension.

"Well, *you* didn't run *this* story," sneered Ivan. "The *Wall Street Tribune* did."

"Yeah, well, Ralph sees things differently. He's upset that I didn't get there first, have Sharon run this piece, and scoop the *Tribune*. She's my reporter, after all."

"Excuse me if I don't feel sorry for you, Matthews. And I'm well aware of the fact that Sharon is your reporter. That wench has been a thorn in my side for months—no, years."

"You're not scared of her, are you?" Damon grinned.

"No, I think she's a royal pain in my ass. Starting with that story you let her run in March. Then that delusional follow-up one last week, about our impending bankruptcy. What was it called? Ah yes, "**Is Intact Off-track?**" Your choice, the title?"

"Actually, yes, it was my choice, thanks for noticing," Damon said. *Asshole.*

"She seems to think we don't have enough cash to pay our bills, or the damn bond holders. Well, she's wrong! And I'm going to release these to every nitwit journalist in the country to prove her and you and *Riche$* wrong," he said, gesturing to stacks of paper beside his desk.

"I understand you're upset," Damon went back to placating. "But—"

Ivan held up his hand again. "This *news* is unacceptable. The *Tribune* talking about SEC investigations, citing the *Riche$* story. Quoting Sharon Thomas. Unacceptable. What do you plan on doing about it?"

"Ivan, her story was correct. You *are* having some cash issues. If you want, you can write a letter-to-the-editor with your take. I'll make sure it prints."

"I can't believe you are that naïve. I have the books right here." He smacked the pile on his desk.

Damon glanced at where Ivan struck. "Okay, let me have a look," he said, patronizing. He hated the people behind the companies his magazine covered.

"Don't waste my time," replied Ivan. "You can have more than a look—in exchange for a retraction. I need a retraction running on your website. I need it sent to Dow Jones newswire and the Associated Press."

"I can't do that," said Damon, "but I'll be happy to give those documents to Sharon. She can take a look and decide..."

"You are not getting this. I don't give a fuck what Sharon decides. I don't have time to give a fuck what Sharon decides. I want a retraction. I want a big fucking banner headline everywhere, about how *Riche$* fucked up, period. Now do it!" Ivan pointed to his office door, done with talking.

Damon sputtered, "But, Ivan—"

"Now let me remind you that ITA owns majority shares in Present, Inc. As in Present, Inc., owner of *Riche$*." Ivan pushed Damon out. "Fix it," he commanded. Then he slammed the door.

CHAPTER 15

Damon required the amount of time it took to down two grande mocha lattes to collect himself after the Ivan encounter. Not because Damon was scared of him, but because of what an asshole Ivan was. Upon recovery, he called Sharon to see where her head was at, literally and psychologically.

"I met with Ivan," he offered.

"Was it fun?"

He laughed as his phone flashed Katrina's number. A text message. "Sorry, I…what were you saying?"

"I was wondering how Stark was taking to the limelight," Sharon said.

"Oh. He hates you."

"I figured."

"He hates me, too."

"I figured that, too. You let the stories run."

"Guilty," he replied. "He wants us to run a retraction."

"He can go fuck himself."

"My sentiments exactly. Sharon…"

"Yes?"

"There's something else, something I need to…" he swallowed hard, his voice trailing off.

"What else?" she asked.

"Nothing. It's…nothing. We can talk about it later."

"Okay." She had a reporter's sense of when to dig and when to give space and dig later.

"Over dinner?" he ventured. He needed to see her, figure things out with her.

"Dinner? Umm, well, I'm trying to avoid being seen. I look like a hung-over Cyclops." Suddenly, Sharon realized that Damon was the last person she wanted seeing her at her absolute worse.

"Right," he chuckled, his thoughts shifting to the sight of Sharon in her tight black robe. "I'm forewarned. But we should re-group to discuss next steps on WorldWell, ITA, and Silverman. I'll come over and we can order takeout."

"Okay," she agreed, rubbing her eye. She felt the same sense of urgency to figure things out. She crossed her arms, holding her shoulders, recalling the feeling of his hands there earlier that morning. "How about around seven?"

"Sounds good. See you then." *Good*, he thought. *That's settled.* Now he could concentrate on securing Sharon's undercover role.

CHAPTER 16

Damon thought it best to do this face to face. Katrina had agreed to accommodate him. He didn't have enough time to take a cab through traffic from midtown to Wall Street, so opted for mass transit. Like a journalist, not a banker. He arrived at Silverman's a few minutes late. After a rigorous airplane-boarding-like scan of his briefcase and questions regarding the nature of his visit at the guard's desk as if he was entering Fort Knox, he was cleared for his meeting. He walked through the brass turnstiles to the first set of elevator banks. They would take him to the fiftieth floor, where the senior executives worked.

As he entered the elevator, a mechanical female voice greeted him, "Good afternoon." He pressed 50. "Going up," the voice lilted. He scowled. *Thanks for the confirmation.* A small video screen above the floor buttons flashed updates of Silverman's stock price. Which was having a very bad day.

Stepping off, he was confronted by the set of pristine double glass doors that guarded the entrance to the Big Chiefs. He stood behind them, waiting. A number of suits walked back and forth, ignoring him. It was not their job to admit visitors, not until some administrative assistant came by. Damon spent five minutes inspecting his shoes. Finally, Katrina's trim, grey-suited twenty-something secretary, Gina, appeared.

"Hi, Mr. Matthews," she greeted him. "I'll see if Ms. Sullivan is ready to see you. Please, have a seat." She gestured toward the waiting area. It was a plush circle of light-brown leather couches surrounding a huge marble urn-like centerpiece full of long-stemmed white lilies.

Damon glanced up at the MSNBC news screen presiding over the couches. Stock tickers scrolled along its bottom, highlighting the most actively traded stocks on the day. *WorldWell Bank*, red arrow, pointing down. *Silverman,* red arrow. *ITA,* red arrow. This was the power of the media over shareholders. And CEOs.

The ticker scrolling above the stock prices pumped constant news: IBM's CEO retiring; a suspect being questioned in the Capitol murder cases; a quote from the vice president, Arthur Graceson, at a press conference restating Washington's commitment to fighting fraud. Damon realized that he missed that Monday conference because of Ralph's insistence he take time off. So far, that idiotic idea had produced an insane gunwoman and an injured reporter.

Gina reappeared. "Ms. Sullivan will see you now, please follow me," she said, turning on her impossibly high heels. She escorted him down the tan-carpeted corridor, lined with cherry-wood doors and shiny gold handles.

Katrina was seated at her desk, computer monitor and keyboard on one side. With her left hand, she was replying to email. With the other, she was signing documents. She had a head-set on and seemed completely focused on her conversation, as if she wasn't doing a hundred other things. She glanced up, noticed him, and shooed him over to the red suede couch on the far side of her office. When she finished her call, she walked slowly to him.

She gave him an air kiss on the cheek. "Damon, so nice to see you."

"Yeah, you too," he said. "I didn't mean to disturb your meeting earlier—you seemed really busy."

"It was an important lunch deal. I had to finish up to rush back here."

"Hey, no problem. You were doing what you do best." He grinned, momentarily mesmerized by the glitter of the diamond earrings dangling from her lobes.

"A character flaw at times," she replied, smoothing her perfect hair. "What can I do for you, Damon?"

"Listen, this is going to seem out of left field, but—you saw my WorldWell Bank piece last week?"

"Yes, well done. It's always nice to see negative covers on our rivals."

"Thanks. Then, you might understand this request..."

Katrina raised her eyebrows.

"I thought it might be a good idea if Sharon Thomas started working here again. Undercover. It would help my next installation...I realize it sounds odd given her prior circumstances here, but..."

"No, that's a great idea," she said, snapping her fingers like a light bulb just went off in her head.

"Really?" *That seemed too easy.*

"Yes, Sharon can gather appropriate WorldWell contracts and create a solid case against them. That could certainly give our stock price a boost. It's a fantastic idea, Damon. The timing couldn't be better."

Damon continued petitioning. "Everything would go through you, of course. We'll just get more information on WorldWell Bank, and..."

We?" Her eyebrows raised again.

"I mean you, Kat. With our help, with Sharon's help, with your guidance, with..."

"Sounds good," she said, flashing a smile.

"Okay, then. Great," he said. "When do you think she could start?"

"The sooner the better," said Katrina. "I'll have Gina bypass the human resource red tape this afternoon. Sharon should be able to start by tomorrow morning."

"Tomorrow?"

"Certainly. Why? Is there something wrong with that?" she asked, smiling at Damon's bulging eyes.

"No, like you said—the sooner the better. I'll get in touch with Sharon. Uh, do you think this will look strange to other Silverman employees?"

"Don't worry about a thing," said Katrina. "Lots of people leave Silverman and return, seeing the error of their ways. If we let them."

Damon stood hovering in front of Katrina's desk.

"Is there anything else?" she asked in a "please go now" tone. She had returned to her email, signifying the meeting had adjourned.

"No, nothing. Thank you," he said, turning to leave, wondering why on earth that was so simple.

Once Damon departed, Katrina called Ivan Stark, who picked up immediately.

"What?" he asked sharply. He apparently no longer had time for "Hello."

"Ivan, calm down. Everything's under control. Sharon Thomas will return to her old job here at Silverman tomorrow." She crossed her legs under her desk.

"Have you completely lost it? All she does is drive my stock down."

"Ivan," she spoke evenly, inspecting her perfectly manicured nails, "considering how badly you seem to be handling everything right now, you are in no position to question my decisions."

"Katrina, this will most certainly backfire. I don't see how Sharon mucking around at Silverman will expedite a retraction to the media's ITA gossip-mongering. It can only be dangerous."

"Ivan, you're so short-sighted. Sharon will do what she needs to do. That will be the end of that."

CHAPTER 17

A couple hours after Trevor returned to his place, flash-drive and tech company names in hand, Sharon succumbed to her aching head and collapsed into bed. Forty minutes later, she was ready to return to work. A steaming shower and splash of astringent aided the waking process. She threw on her comfiest pair of jeans and a white T-shirt. She poured a cup of cold coffee and added ice, to help her stay focused. Sitting cross-legged on her soft cream couch, she lifted the lid of her laptop.

There were two main things to figure out. The first, of course, was the trail. She had a hunch it had something to do with tech company contracts between ITA and other firms. The second was the nature of those contracts.

She got back online and surfed for anything new that might have broken on ITA. The Associated Press had a follow-up story to the *Wall Street Tribune* one, repeating most of the same facts and adding a "no comment" from an SEC spokesperson. The *New York Chronicle* had a profile of Ivan Stark as its lead website business story.

They ran an old picture of him from when the firm went public. She froze on the picture, searching for anything in his expression, his body language, his smirk, that gave away the fact that he was hiding something. She enlarged it in Photoshop, studying his eyes. They were stone cold, even as his face registered a victorious smile. She remembered how his stock soared 600 percent by the close of business that first day. *No wonder he was smiling.*

She zoomed in on the background faces behind Ivan on the stock market exchange podium. Two in particular caught Sharon's attention: Sam Peterson and Katrina Sullivan, CEO and CTO of Silverman. *Silverman had taken ITA public.* Silverman's shares were slipping too. She could see the headline now: "**Silverman, Losing Its Silver Touch?**" *It couldn't happen to nicer people.*

She knew she would have better access to information on ITA and all the other tech companies from inside Silverman. She'd just have to be careful. Silverman functioned like Big Brother. Senior management watched and knew everything. She had discovered that her first time around. Sharon froze the frame on Ivan and Katrina. Katrina had steered Silverman into taking hundreds of tech companies public around the same time. Which brought her back to the trail. She wondered how far Trevor had gotten.

"Yeah?" he answered.

"Hey, Trev, what's going on over there?" she asked, still inspecting her screen.

"I've got each line in this trail thing down to a maximum of ten possibilities, with a probability confidence interval of at least ninety percent."

"Could you repeat that in English?"

"I'm almost there, Share. Another hour and I'll have these little guys nailed."

"Fine. Hurry up though," she said, biting her thumbnail. "Wait. Trevor?"

"Yeah?"

"I just remembered something. There was a part of the document we didn't talk about, the characters to the left of each company name. I can't figure out what they stand for."

"Share, one thing at a time. Let me finish this up, then we'll try to tackle that one," Trevor replied, rushing her off the phone.

"Fine," Sharon conceded. "One more thing..."

"Yeah?"

"I was looking through some old photos of ITA's IPO, and it occurred to me..." She gasped for breath.

"What? What is it, Share?"

"They went public exactly two years ago." Her heart slammed against her chest.

"And?"

"It was on the same day that...that I was shot." The last word lingered in the air. *Shot.*

CHAPTER 18

Sharon ran her fingers up and down her left side. The wound had healed, but would never disappear. She lifted her T-shirt. The ugly, discolored indentation looked like a tattoo gone wrong after an intense night out. Today it itched, like it knew something was up. She rubbed the spot to alleviate the taunting tickle. She drank more coffee, checked her office voice mails and emails, and then clicked on the TV.

The vice president of the United States was on CNN, preaching that fighting corporate corruption was a major administration priority in the wake of the WorldWell Bank scandal.

"Asshole!" Sharon middle-fingered the screen. His former company was under a $7 billion fraud investigation.

Her land line rang. It was from a 202 area code—D.C.— but not a number that she recognized. "Hello?" she said.

"Hi. Sharon, it's Janet Waters, again."

"Oh. Hi, Janet. I didn't recognize your number from before." She wondered how Janet got her home number, but didn't ask.

"I'm at a payphone. Please, just listen to me. My husband's missing. He was working on a case—I think on WorldWell Bank. It's been almost twenty-four hours..."

"Maybe you should call D.C. Metropolitan police. They'll be able to help more than I can," Sharon suggested, almost too curtly. Missing information was her thing, not missing people, and she had things to figure out.

"I've called them. They say it's too early to file a missing person's report. Look, I'm not crazy."

Sharon eyes were glued to the TV set. The woman sounded desperate, but Sharon couldn't focus on her right now. "I know you're not. Listen, why don't you give me some numbers to reach you at? I'll call you back." Sharon jotted down the numbers Janet reluctantly gave her.

Her heart went out to Janet Waters. But she needed to address one thing at a time. And right now, she needed to figure out the appropriate story angles to follow with her editor. She would get back to Janet after, she promised herself.

Leaving the TV on for background noise, she went to change into something more presentable. It was a quarter to seven. She stepped out of her jeans and threw off her shirt. She went into her bathroom and switched on the flourescent light. It was the first time all day she let herself examine her face in a mirror. What she saw was not pretty. The patch above her eyebrow was swollen, a mixture of dark purples, navy blues, and muddy browns.

Lovely, she thought, reaching into the medicine cabinet for some L'Oreal peach-pink cover-up. Several applications were necessary to make a dent in the angry color. Wiping the latest crust of dried blood off the top of her forehead, she applied cover-up there as well. She brushed her hair over as much of the affected area as possible. She padded beige eye shadow on both eyebrows and lids, wincing at the touch of the tiny brush. *I look absolutely hideous.* Adding mascara didn't seem to help matters much.

She hoped brick-red lipstick would counterbalance what was going on at the top of her face. From her closet, she selected a black knit summer dress. Attractive, but not too revealing. She continued refining her appearance until the buzzer sounded, promptly at seven.

He stood at her door holding a flower bouquet. After agonizing for long minutes over what kind to bring, Damon went with pale violet tulips; roses seemed too romantic. Clutching them in his hand, he now wondered if they were inappropriate, but decided to be glib about it.

"For you," he said, handing her the tulips. "A get-well and find-the-scoop kind of thing."

"Thanks," she said, taking them from him. "They match my eye." Then, realizing that sounded callous, she added, "Come in, come in. Can I get you a drink? Some wine, perhaps?"

"Sure, that'd be great. Thanks." He positioned himself on her couch, leaning back.

"Red?"

"Always," he grinned.

Sharon extracted a bottle of Côtes du Rhône from under the sink. Peering into the cabinet, she told him, "The only thing I have to nibble on in here is Paul Newman's finest popcorn. I can nuke it. I find it goes great with red wine."

"Real classy, Thomas." He strolled to the kitchen, hands stuffed in his back pockets while she opened the popcorn packaging.

"Hey, lay off. Microwave popcorn and red wine go together like peanut butter and jelly."

"Sure," Damon said. She stuck the popcorn bag in the microwave. "So here's what I was just thinking," he continued. "Well, wondering. What do you know of the relationship between Katrina Sullivan and Ivan Stark?"

"Not much," she said, and uncorked the wine bottle with suddenly unsteady hands. "Silverman is ITA's banker. Silverman's CEO, Sam Peterson, is on ITA's board as of this March. Helps getting deal approval without questioning the details."

"What about Katrina?"

"Don't know. She *is* Silverman's chief technology officer. ITA *was* a powerful tech company. Until now, anyway." She poured two glasses and handed one to him, all the while awaiting recognition for her contribution to today's disclosures.

"That's all you know?" He sipped his wine. "Pinot Noir?"

"Côtes du Rhône," she corrected. "Basically. I mean, they could be sleeping together, even though he's kind of short and dumpy," she said, half-jokingly.

Damon stiffened. "Isn't it unethical to sleep with clients when you're that high up the pecking order?"

"We're talking about an unscrupulous investment bank and a fraudulent broadband company. I don't think ethics is a factor."

"So Katrina may be sleeping with Ivan to get his business?" He walked over to the kitchen bar.

Sharon hastily gathered the trail documents into a pile as he approached. Something in his suddenly sharp tone alerted her latent self-protective instinct. "I don't think Katrina needs to sleep with *anyone* to *get* business," she replied, elbows resting on the stack of papers. "If anything, it's to get information from him, keep him close. Or maybe..."

"Maybe, what?" He grabbed one of the bar stools and sat opposite her, planting his own elbows on the countertop. Leaning toward her.

"Maybe it's to feed *him* information." Sharon scooped up the documents and placed them in the junk drawer beneath the counter, along with a pair of pliers, refrigerator magnets, Scotch tape, and various takeout menus.

She grabbed the menus and spread them across the counter. Holding one up, she said, "This place on Seventh has awesome sesame noodles, a bit more substantial than popcorn. You game?"

"Sounds terrific. I'll have an order of sweet and sour chicken."

"Done." She picked up the cordless to place the order.

After two bottles of wine, several emptied cartons of Chinese food, and a discussion of all major WorldWell Bank, Silverman, and ITA transactions over the past two years, Sharon discovered that alcohol trumped Advil to reduce pain. She and Damon were sitting on her Iranian carpet, leaning against her couch. SEC documents and news stories were spread out around them.

She could tell something was gnawing at Damon. Something beyond WorldWell. He was barely focused on the story, most uncharacteristic of him. Finally he spilled it: "Sharon, why didn't your marriage work out?"

Her eyebrows jutted up. She stood and walked to her desk.

"Sorry. That was out of line. It's personal, I know," he said, picking up a 10-K annual report for WorldWell and examining it.

"That's okay. We've been working together long enough, it was bound to come up at some point, I suppose," she replied, the wine working overtime. "Well, my husband had an affair."

"I'm sorry." He put the report down.

"No reason to be. It was the wake-up call I needed to get out of the marriage." She walked back to the couch, picked up her wine glass from the coffee table, and took a long sip. At this point in her life, she didn't feel like she ever had been married. Like it was another person she was speaking about. She returned her glass to the table. "We were going our separate ways, anyway." She crossed her hands and pointed her fingers at opposite angles to illustrate. "Or had already arrived there."

He remembered, after his wife had informed him that their marriage had fallen apart, long after he had stopped paying attention, his way of dealing had been to pretend it wasn't happening. That lasted a couple days. Then he got the call that his wife was gone. Forever. "But—it must have been painful for you." Damon saw a distant look come across her dark eyes. *That was a real dumb question, Matthews.*

"It's all in the past now." Sharon waved her hand, emphasizing "in the past," and knocked her wine glass onto the rug. They looked at each other for a moment. Then they burst out laughing. She rose to get some paper towels from the kitchen. When she returned and began dabbing the red puddle, she said, face blushed, "You know what the most painful part was?"

"What?" He had never seen so much naked emotion in his reporter before.

"It was how stupid it made me feel. Like, how could I not have known right away, you know?"

He nodded. He knew. It was that feeling of having been duped that made you insane.

"I mean, you live with someone for years, you learn their habits, you know their patterns, and they can pull the wool right over your eyes, just like that." She snapped her fingers. Her anger was self-directed. "And what's worse, I'm an investigative journalist—I mean, I piece stuff together for a living, but I miss what's going on right before my eyes, in my own bed."

"I know exactly what you mean." When he got the news, he had been as angry about Marsha's betrayal as he was shocked and saddened that she was dead. He beat himself up over that for a long time. "How long was the affair going on before you found out?"

"Maybe a month," she replied, shrugging. "I'm not sure. I guess I was focused on my own thing."

He had only ever been focused on his own thing. Hard as he tried to shake that habit. He went to a grief therapist for three months after Marsha's murder, but in the end, fell back on old patterns. He didn't have time for sorrow. "How did you find out?" he asked.

It wasn't like Sharon to disclose so much about herself. *The wine was prying it out*, she thought. *And our common experience.* "Email. Capturing IM's. Once I suspected, I couldn't rest till I was sure. I'm not good at letting go of something I don't understand. But I guess you know that."

"That's why you're a first-class reporter," he said. "And, I guess everybody leaves some kind of trail." But he had never found the slightest bit of evidence in their home. He hadn't recognized the negligee wrapping her body when she was strangled, nor the diamond jewelry that adorned her toe.

Sharon looked at him. *Did he know something about the trail?* She searched his eyes for an answer, but only found Damon's same-old focused gaze. "What do you mean?" she asked.

He drew himself back to the present, forced his thoughts away from his wife's body. "Well, I thought IM's were instant and not traceable. How did you do capture them?"

"With software that took snapshots of everything he typed. I..." she looked toward the kitchen.

"You?" he prompted.

"Nothing," she said, adrenalin suddenly flowing. "Listen to me going on. Sorry. Look, I'm exhausted and a bit tipsy. I should probably get some sleep before tackling this stuff again tomorrow."

Sharon's disclosures evoked mixed emotions in Damon. He felt sadness at the end of this revealing look into her and curiosity at the lengths she went through to spy on her husband. "Oh, that reminds me. Speaking of tomorrow...this is probably not a good time to tell you this, but I spoke to Katrina today. She agreed to give you your old job back at Silverman, to dig into WorldWell Bank. You'll report directly to her." Damon hoped that—in the few hours since their conversation that afternoon—she had accepted the inevitability and importance of re-entering Silverman.

Sharon's face drained to white. Damon added the clincher. "Tomorrow's your first day."

She stood up too quickly. The room spun and she felt dizzy. She dashed to her bathroom, slammed the door shut, gathered her hair back, and threw up. Collapsing on the cold tile floor, she cradled the rim of the toilet with her arm, kneeling at its base. She tried to steady her breath.

She willed the nausea to subside. Willed her past to stop following her around like a probation officer. But the heaves returned. A combination of Chinese food and memories flooded the bowl again. Two minutes later, Damon knocked on the door. "Are you alright?" he asked.

"Yeah. I'm fine. Be right out." She wiped her mouth off and brushed her teeth. Feeling embarrassed and less drunk, Sharon emerged. The impact of Damon's height before her, the angle of his determined face, his penetrating blue eyes, all made her breath quicken again. She smoothed her dress.

"Sorry, that was rather shocking news," he apologized, reaching toward a misplaced piece of her hair.

"That's okay. We talked about it this morning. You're fast, Matthews!" She reflexively tucked the hair behind her ear and play-punched his shoulder.

He smiled. "You'll be okay."

"I know I will."

He took her hand, surrounding it with both of his. She looked up at him, leaned in closer, and covered his top hand with her other one. "Damon," she said softly, "I know about Marsha."

CHAPTER 19

Damon changed the subject and left abruptly after Sharon's mention of his wife. Sharon had never seen the solemnity that instantly overcame him. Different from his usual impatience, his aggravating perfectionism. She assumed his reaction had something to do with her lack of tact regarding all things emotional. Her way of dealing was to move past emotion to action.

It was getting late, anyway. His departure afforded her more time alone. She shivered and glanced at the front door. *To think.* While recounting her ex-husband's affair to Damon, she'd been struck by a thought: maybe the same technology she used to prove his affair could come in handy at some point. Maybe with the trail. At Silverman, where passwords were layered so thick, getting to anything real could be tricky.

Installing screen-capturing software was the computer equivalent of bugging telephones. Trevor had hooked her up with Spectator software last time to catch her ex-husband. It was created by his former tech-buddy-turned-Seattle-software-company-CEO. It was virtually undetectable by any other kind of spy-ware. She realized Trevor hadn't been in contact the whole time Damon was over. She called his apartment. No answer. Same with his cell.

She didn't know if her head was reeling from the previous night's blows or from the unimaginable but all-too-soon reality of her pending start at Silverman. She had no interest in remaining there a second longer than she had to. The place ignited disgust. It was oppressive when she left. It would be oppressive when she returned. Plus, there was the guilt. The guilt that wrapped her in a permanent chokehold. That would never let her be free. She had always shunned dependencies, but she discovered there were some responsibilities that were permanent. Her time at Silverman had taught her that.

After leaving Trevor messages on both his numbers, she returned to her laptop. To the pictures of Ivan and the stock exchange opening. To Katrina standing beside him. To the pack of suits at the podium. She pondered a deeper relationship between two of the business's most powerful people. She shivered, though it wasn't cold.

The words of her mysterious caller pelted her. *Look beneath the surface.*

She tried to place the voice, but couldn't. His words were measured, like they were constricted in his throat, trying to simultaneously escape and stay contained. His sound was low. Slightly hoarse. There was an unmistakable air of learnedness in his tone.

She had no idea if it was someone she had met before or not. Not knowing was maddening. She resolved to tape all new calls with her reporter's mike on speakerphone. It was designed to eliminate background noise and concentrate on primary sounds. The idea gave her a bit of peace. Outside, the quiet of the August night was marked only by the occasional sound of honking horns and people stumbling out of bars.

It felt like she was the only one in her building. Doubts simmered through her thoughts. Maybe this trail was nothing. *Maybe the damn filing is just what I originally thought—a corrupt document with random names on it.* But that couldn't be. Her encounter with the brute wasn't *nothing*. It was real. She had the bruises to prove it. And there was the gunshot wound from two years ago. Two years ago today.

After her release from the hospital, after enduring two months of physical therapy, she undertook her own therapy. She trained to protect herself. Yet, last night, that whack to her head could have killed her. She rubbed her hands up and down her chilled arms, over the standing hairs.

She shook her head. This wasn't about street fighting. White-collar crime went into the millions or billions of dollars, not quite small-scale back-alley mugging. The stakes were higher. Much higher. And different. Or was it all the same game, just a different approach? Upper-class thieves dressed up in limos, towering skyscrapers with gold-gilded elevator banks, and Armani suits.

Past and present swerved around in her head. She had come so far. Aside from that, she was quick on her feet and with her hands. She'd be okay.

CHAPTER 20

The Waters lived on a well-manicured Georgetown street, among D.C.'s wealthiest and most fashionable. It was a neighborhood they shared with the most notable senators, ambassadors, and their lawyers and lobbyists. Homes cost well over $2 million. Inhabitants were discretely labeled: "arrived" or "established." No other categories mattered.

Tonight, trappings of wealth offered no comfort. Janet wandered around her living room, stopping at a silver-framed photograph of herself, Kevin, and their daughter Britney that was taken that spring. She picked it up and gently wiped away the thin film of dust. Janet had cancelled the cleaning lady for this week. They were standing under one of the cherry trees in Potomac Park. Britney had on a bright orange and yellow sundress. She was sitting on top of her father's shoulders. Janet and Kevin had their arms around each other's waists. Everyone was beaming smiles. Everyone was so happy.

Janet recalled how peaceful that day had started, the beginning of the annual Cherry Blossom Festival. She and Kevin looked forward to the event every year. Thousands of locals, innumerable tourists, all converging around the Jefferson Memorial, all celebrating a simple tree blossom. Treetops blanketed in balloons of pale pinks and enamel whites, explosions of blooms all around the tidal basin of the park.

They'd bring blankets, toys, and picnic food. They'd coordinate with friends, many of whom they hadn't seen since the last festival. Kids played games. Parents played politics.

Somehow, it was the one time when Washington seemed hopeful, optimistic. The weather on that particular spring Sunday was perfect. Glorious blue skies replaced months of gloomy ones. Wafts of laughter and conversation mingled and rose from the colorful blankets dotting the great lawn.

A shiver ran up Janet's spine as she remembered how that day ended. That was the day the second body was found. A young girl, not much older than Britney, discovered it. She'd been collecting blossoms by the side of the river. She had waded into the basin to scoop up bits of petals with her petite hands.

The little girl had reached across the water surface for a particularly beautiful crimson blossom. She was standing ankle-deep in the river. A small current temporarily threw her off balance. Her mother, engrossed in conversation with a lobbyist's wife, noticed her by the river's edge and raced toward her. She watched her daughter try to steady herself by placing her hands on a mossy rock. But it was soft and spongy, causing Taylor to further lose her balance.

And as she pressed down on it, her free arm flailing, she realized it was no rock. It was a badly decomposed, blue-green body, more a moldy oversized loaf of bread than a man. The man was drifting face down, tan pants billowing like a river-kite around his legs, his asparagus-colored Lacoste shirt melding with the river's green.

Moments later, officials swarmed onto the scene. D.C. river police and the U.S. Coast Guard extracted the body. Homicide cops questioned the crowd. Kevin was concerned. He told her he wanted to stick around, see what happened. Janet wanted to get herself and their daughter away as quickly as possible.

But Kevin was adamant. He stood mesmerized as the body was carted away from the river, wrapped up, placed on a stretcher, and shoved into the waiting ambulance. It was the second body to be plucked from the same spot in two days.

Janet had stood far away, behind a tree, shielding her daughter and angry at her husband. When Kevin finally walked back to them, he didn't apologize. All he said was that the police referred to drowned bodies as "floaters." The press soon dubbed the person responsible "the capital killer," or sometimes "the yuppie shooter." Someone who stalked junior lawyers or Senate aides, the media had reported. Each man had been shot twice, once in the right hand, once in the left eye—straight through the skull.

In her living room, Janet felt another chill run up her spine. The TV didn't help matters. It felt like she was stuck in a time warp. In the corner, the nightly news was reporting a breakthrough in the serial murder case, going through all the background. The police had apparently found a viable suspect after months of nothing, but the news gave no further details.

She shuddered at the story and turned the TV off. She caught sight of her pale face in the silver-rimmed living room mirror. She looked like she hadn't slept in weeks. Her blonde hair was unkempt. Normally it was neat, tied back in a tidy ponytail. But her appearance was the least of her concerns. Her thoughts drifted to the night before. Just twenty-four hours ago. How routine it had all been. Janet was struggling to get her young daughter to go to sleep. Teeth brushed and hair combed, it was story-telling time.

"But I want Daddy to read me a story tonight," three-year-old Britney had whined, with an emphatic swing of her own pale-blonde ponytail.

"I know, sweetheart," replied Janet, "but Daddy's working late."

"You said that yesterday!"

"I know I did, but your daddy's working on a very important job—for the government."

"He's always working!" cried Britney.

"Not always," said Janet in a quiet monotone. "Now, come on, what shall it be?"

Britney hopped under her pink floral sheets in her white four-poster bed, folded her arms, and shook her head no.

"Britney," her mother admonished gently.

"Ham!" Britney finally relented, handing over *Green Eggs and Ham*.

"Excellent choice," said Janet, taking a position beside her daughter. She managed to get Britney off to sleep with only one rendition. At the soft rise and fall of her daughter's breathing, she rose, switched off the light, and climbed down the crème-carpeted stairs.

As she reached the bottom, the phone rang down the hall.

"Is she asleep already?" asked Kevin. "I wanted to say goodnight to my little girl."

"Yeah, I just left her room," Janet replied. "She missed you. I don't do Sam-I-am's voice like you do."

"Tell her I love her," Kevin replied, his voice tight.

"Um...sure. Are you okay?"

"I'm fine, just another late night at the office. I'll give you a call later, darling. Love you."

"Love you, too."

Now Janet stood alone, twisting her sweaty hands. *So, where the hell was he?* Her head pounded. Desperately, she eyed the bottles of Johnnie Walker Gold, Tanqueray No. Ten, and their impressive collection of Russian vodkas in the glass cabinet across the living room. No, she contained herself. She would not go there. She'd been clean for five years. She would not go there. She poured herself a glass of orange juice instead.

The bottles continued to beckon. She needed some semblance of calm. She walked over to the cabinet, gazing at the shiny crystal glasses inside it. She took one out, ran her fingers up and down its stem. Those glasses were a recent addition to their home. She hadn't had a relapse for so long. Kevin suggested the cabinet for entertaining.

She put the glass down on the silver platter that cushioned the bottles and moved to the couch. Her body doubled over as she sat holding her head in her hands. She couldn't let herself succumb to the budding thought. *He is NOT the next floater.*

CHAPTER 21

That night, Sharon's alcohol and stress-induced dreams turned more sinister than usual. Instead of her Upper East Side attacker, she was confronted by the brute. He was pointing his gun at her heart in the middle of her apartment. Nowhere was safe. Standing over her, he had the PC tucked under his arm before he made his getaway. Just as the shot fired, she looked straight into his face. His black eyes turned reptilian. His face became that of Sam Peterson, CEO of Silverman.

She bounded into consciousness and a cold sweat at the sound of her beeping alarm clock. It was 6:00 a.m. These were banker's—not writer's—hours. The old days of ridiculously early mornings. Coffee at the corner deli, because there was not enough time to become alert and make your own coffee and get to work by seven. She doused her face with cold water, applied a quarter-inch of foundation, and got dressed in the suit she'd laid out the night before. Now a foreign outfit to her. One she had not missed. Pausing on her front steps, she inhaled the early morning air, for balance. It would have been financially prudent to walk over to the F train and switch to the E at West Fourth. It was too damn early for that, so she hailed a cab. She'd start taking the more fiscal route tomorrow.

Sharon's re-entry into Silverman occurred with little fanfare amongst the rank and file. Half the people in the elevator banks or lobby didn't seem to notice she'd left. Others recalled her departure, but bought the story that she missed the money.

They never understood why anyone would leave a job with the potential for a multi-million dollar bonus, anyway, unless it was to climb further up the ladder of inflated salaries.

Katrina Sullivan greeted her personally, summoning her to the fiftieth floor as soon as she got word Sharon was back in the building. "Sharon! It's been too long," Katrina cooed in a face-to-face at her office doorway. "Welcome back to the family."

Sharon shot her a "Please, spare me look," which she quickly adjusted. No point in burning remaining bridges. Plus, there were people around. "Hoverers," as she used to refer of them. Investment bankers striving to get Katrina's approval or attention on some deal they were working on, so they could remind their bosses at bonus time that she liked them. Sharon recognized Katrina's outpouring of affection as part of the grand show. *What the hell?* She had acting training, too. It was show time.

"Thanks for the opportunity, Katrina!" she beamed. "I'm really excited about getting back on the wagon."

Katrina beckoned Sharon into her office and asked her to take a seat in front of her desk, shutting the door on the hoverers. They'd spread gossip about Katrina taking Sharon under her wing around the firm within minutes. For Sharon, that would come in handy. She definitely didn't miss that part of investment banking. The type-A personalities who never missed a chance to suck up to authority figures who could help them race up the pecking order.

"Let's get something straight between us, shall we?" Katrina's tone turned immediately cold, her eyes pierced Sharon's. The two women held each other's gaze. There was no love lost between them.

"Yes, Katrina," replied Sharon, her voice laced with equal amounts of sweetness and venom.

"I know you're here to snoop around. We don't need to pretend otherwise. So understand one thing. I will allow you access to anything that can bring WorldWell Bank down. To anything that may help your editor with his story. You're annoying, but you can manipulate numbers into telling a story better than anyone I know."

"Thanks for the compliment," Sharon interjected.

"You know how it works here. Everything is password-protected. You will *only* have access to what I want you to see. Any questions?"

"Yes." Sharon was prepared. "I assume by access to anything that can hurt WorldWell Bank, you mean any deals for which both WorldWell Bank and Silverman were joint leads, but where only WorldWell Bank may have acted illegally."

Katrina sniffed. "Yes."

"Well, over the past year, that would mean mostly tech and broadband company deals."

"Yes, of course, that's my focus. What's your point?"

"My point is I'll need access to *all* those transactions," Sharon laid down the gauntlet.

She awaited Katrina's reaction. Katrina may have had her reasons for wanting Sharon around, but she had also read Sharon's damaging ITA stories. Still, they were both in dangerous territory.

"Fine," she said. "But I watch everything. Screw up—just once—and you're gone."

"Got it. And, uh, thanks for letting me work on the WorldWell situation from inside," Sharon said. *Might as well let her know I know what's going on.*

"Then we understand each other."

Sharon nodded. It was too bad Katrina was such a bitch. She respected her more than Sam, or Ivan. In another situation, she might have even liked her. They both knew about fighting in a man's world. They just chose different paths to do it.

"Oh, by the way," said Katrina, softening as Sharon opened the door, "make sure you come to the weekly tech meeting this afternoon. It's at three in the conference room on the thirty-first floor. You're back on the team now."

"I wouldn't miss it for anything."

Sharon surveyed her new office. Her temporary cell. It wasn't the same one she had occupied before she quit, but it was only three doors down and had an identical appearance. Turquoise green carpet, a desk facing the hallway, not the window, positioned to ensure maximum concentration on work, not outside scenery. There was one fake plastic palm plant in the corner of the room.

Situated on the desk was a speakerphone with headset and four different lines. A flat widescreen monitor stood at the corner. The PC hard drive beneath it possessed no disk drive, a construct key to ensuring no information could be downloaded. Everything would have to be emailed, leaving a trail. Knowing this, Sharon had her own drive handy to install, though she knew that might take some technical maneuvering, possibly with Trevor's guidance, later.

Touching the keyboard by the screen, the computer immediately flashed to the Silverman homepage. Her ID was sharon_thomas@silverman.com. Her initial password was her social security number. As she typed it in to start surveying what was available to her, the phone rang.

"Hey there, stranger!" trilled a friendly voice.

"Nina!" acknowledged Sharon. "Wow, it's been ages! How are you?"

"Great, fine. Still hanging around this dump. You know: usual boring meetings and fights with the old men assholes.

Geez, Sharon. You were my idol for giving this place the finger a couple years ago. What are you doing back?"

"I don't know, Nina. I guess I got sick of comparison shopping for shoes. On sale."

"Does the money suck that badly in magazines? It must be so cool to see your name out there, in public."

"Let's put it this way, it barely pays utilities. When I'm lucky I get cheap take-out."

"Yeah, but come on. You must have socked away a bunch while you were here."

"I did, I guess, I don't know, maybe I miss the thrill of closing deals, or something, maybe the dependability of knowing whose ass to kiss. I dunno."

"Well, I'm glad you're back," said Nina. "I missed you tons. There are so few normal people left around here. We must go out for drinks so I can fill you in on all the bullshit."

"Sounds terrific—I'd love that. I really would love to catch up," replied Sharon, feeling that familiar tug of camaraderie that had kept her in banking for so many years, the fact that there were some decent ones sprinkled amongst the sharks.

"Great. I'll check with the other girls, get a good crowd to welcome you back in style. Like old times. We'll start out flaming Harvey-asshole-Philips and work our way through the powers-that-wanna-be."

"Cool," said Sharon, "let me know the plan. Talk to you later." Her cell phone rang in her purse.

"Hey, Share." It was Roger from the SEC. "You're a tough lady to track down. Anyway, I wanted to get back to you about your request from yesterday."

"Oh, right. Kevin Waters and the SEC? So, what's his deal?"

"Well, actually, I couldn't find any Kevin Waters here. I even checked the new employees list. Checked over in the

Justice Department, too. Maybe it was a name mix-up? But Simon Caldwell, the other guy you asked me about, he does work here. Started two years ago. In Special Fraud."

"Interesting. Thanks for getting back to me, Rog." She pushed her hair behind her ear and mulled. *No Kevin Waters at the SEC, but a Simon Caldwell. That's weird, why would Janet tell me he worked there? Yet she was right about Simon, so she couldn't be lying. One of them was lying—either Janet or her husband. It was strange.* Strange enough to warrant a follow-up call.

Janet picked up on the first ring.

"Hi, it's Sharon Thomas. Sorry I was so abrupt yesterday. I can't imagine what you're going through."

"A weird kind of hell," sniffed Janet Waters.

Sharon knew plenty about hell. "Do you mind if I ask you a few questions?"

"Not at all," answered Janet.

Sharon heard a long sigh. "First, can you tell me a little about Kevin's work?"

"Okay. I guess I'll start from the beginning. Before he even took the position, Kevin told me there'd be sacrifices. But they'd be small and temporary compared to the big picture. I understood his career was important. I supported him." Janet glimpsed out the window at their Lexus SUV in the driveway. "That life of canned food and balancing the phone against the electric bill seems light years away now."

"So, you live in Georgetown?" Sharon asked, having Googled the woman's phone numbers.

"Yeah, in a townhouse. Part of the package Kevin received. At first, I didn't understand how a government regulatory agency funded by tax dollars could foot the rent bill for such prime property. Kevin explained that this house was wired specifically for access into some highly confidential network."

Sharon's ears perked at the word "network." She was jotting notes. "Go on."

"Kevin's group was responsible for investigating the most complicated frauds at the highest echelons of corporate America. Lately, he was working around the clock on some top secret corporate scam."

"When did you realize he was missing?"

"At about six o'clock yesterday morning I rolled over and realized he wasn't there. He didn't come home that night or the night before. He's pulled all-nighters before. But usually he calls. And with this yuppie murderer still on the loose, I just...I couldn't bear it if..." her voice broke into sobs.

"I hear you; I'd be freaked out myself. So what did you do?"

"After I couldn't reach him on any of his numbers, I phoned Simon and..."

"Simon Caldwell?" Sharon interrupted.

"Yeah, he's Kevin's best friend and boss. We used to hang out all the time in college. They went to law school together, Simon and Kevin."

"Got it. Okay, go on." Sharon replied, scribbling furiously.

"I asked him where Kevin was. He told me they'd been really busy the last couple weeks and Kevin was probably out getting coffee. He told me to relax and he'd call later."

"But, he didn't."

"No—three hours of nothing. So, I called 911. They said it was too soon to file a missing persons report."

"Yeah, that is technically protocol." Sharon didn't know what else to say. Her experiences with the police had never been that satisfactory.

Janet coughed before she continued. "The police have been completely useless. They're all tied up with this serial killer thing. I've left tons of messages. I had to take Britney over to my neighbor's because I didn't want her to see me like this. Kids pick up on everything."

"Let me help you out. I'll give Simon a call this afternoon. See if I can get anything out of him." Shifting gears, Sharon added, "Where did you say you found my name, again?"

"Oh, right, the file in my husband's office had your name on it. It also had a date."

"What was it?" But somehow she already knew. No such thing as coincidences.

"It was March the fifteenth."

Sharon stopped writing at the mention of the trail date. Before she could press Janet for more, she was interrupted by a call from Sam Peterson's office. "Shit! Janet, I'm sorry, I have to go—let me call you back later."

* * *

Seeing Sharon Thomas at the technology bankers meeting threw Mickey Mancuso into a time warp. Sharon knew about fuck you money. She knew what it meant to claw herself out. Even though she was a woman, and damn hot, her reputation as brilliant and stone-cold calm was well deserved. He had to admit it, he respected her. When she used to walk across trading floors full of coked-up guys checking out her legs, she never flinched, never blushed. She gave it all back. They never knew what hit them.

Once she broke a trader's thumb after she politely asked him to remove his hand from atop hers. She bent the thumb sideways and then straight back, some self-defense move she'd learned somewhere. The guy was ridiculed for months afterward. No one ever laid a hand on her again.

Mickey had met Sharon in the early 1990's, a few years after she crawled out of some state school in some God-awful cold climate town in the bowels of upstate New York and pounded the pavement for bit parts in off-off Broadway plays. He hired her to work on his floor. For years, she rode the Street wave. She was on the brink of making it big. Really big. She was a great trader who transitioned into creating these newfangled high-profit products that everyone was so thrilled about. She was a rare combination; thought like a rocket scientist, acted like a real person. Everyone knew who she was. When she landed at Silverman a few years back, she was on their super fast-track.

But she didn't fit in there anymore than Mickey did. She got messed up with the wrong boys club. Internal politics. You need a godfather on Wall Street, and he needs to stay in power, otherwise you're fucked. Her godfather lost his battle to one of Sam's boys. One of Sam's boys wanted her out. So she was fucked. She cut her losses like any good trader should. She left the business and decided to become, what the hell was it, some reporter or something. Write poetry. Whatever. *What a shame*, he'd thought at the time. *What a waste.*

Which reminded him of how much he hated Sam.

He always thought Sharon knew what she was doing. Even though he thought she was insane for the amount of money she left on the table when she quit. When she left the Street, people got scared. She knew how it worked. She was a finance mechanic. She got numbers like nobody's business. She got a glimmer of what was going on with WorldWell Bank and ITA and that crowd before she left. They knew she wasn't afraid to talk. It was just a matter of time. They watched her. They tried to shut her up. They left no tracks. He was off inspecting a new microchip center in Texas when it happened. He wondered if she knew about the connections, knew what dangerous territory she was getting into. He even discussed his suspicious with her after she came out of the hospital, but she wouldn't go there, brushed them completely aside. Then, that ITA piece she wrote a couple months ago raised some blood pressures.

Now she was back in the pit. Why? She said she would never come back. Jump without a parachute, she told him on her last day. "Mickey, I gotta do what's in my heart, you know? I can't live like this anymore." That's what she said. So, what the hell was she doing back here? It didn't make any sense. He didn't know why, but he was going to find out.

Feeling more alive than he had in years, Mickey stormed into Sharon's office. "Well, what the fuck?" he greeted her, walked in, and shut the door behind him.

"Hey there, Mickey." Her smile was genuine. In her heart, Mickey was the replacement for her own father, the man she barely knew and hadn't seen since she was a teenager. Before she could contain herself, her eyes brimmed with tears.

He didn't know what was going on, but gave her a giant bear hug.

She held up her hand in a tiny "stop" gesture. Her eyes averted upward to a small camera. She knew Mickey was Sam's nemesis. She knew she was not Sam's favorite person, either. Grand displays of affection between two of Sam's enemies on camera was probably a bad idea.

He acknowledged her apprehension and stepped back.

"You look fantastic, kiddo!" he exclaimed.

Sharon brushed her hair away from her face. *Well, not quite fantastic.* "Thanks," she said.

"Welcome back," said Mickey, turning to leave. "Oh, me and a bunch of the boys are meeting up for drinks tonight at Jerry's Bar—join us if you can. And in case you forgot the address while you were away or something, here it is." He took a post-it from her desktop and scribbled on it.

"Thanks. Good to see you again, Mickey," she said.

He tipped his head, turned around, and left her office.

She nonchalantly glanced down at his note.

Things are breaking fast, meet me tonight at 8

She took a deep breath, feeling admiration and all the old feelings of respect for this bear of a man. Mickey knew what was really going on. She could always count on him. Plus, there was no such thing as Jerry's Bar. She would meet Mickey tonight at eight, at the back of Jeremy's at the South Street Seaport. Like old times. With new stakes.

CHAPTER 22

Sam Peterson's office was considered the most decadent on Wall Street. Its walls were adorned with real Monet's and Picasso's from his personal collection. An entire wall held the largest flat screen TV in the world, courtesy of SONY, Inc. one of his closest clients as he rose up the ranks. Rumor was that the screen had to be air-lifted through his office windows because it couldn't fit into the freight elevators.

He greeted Katrina with his agenda. "I heard that Sharon Thomas was back," he fake-grinned. "I called her in for a five o'clock 'catch up.' Before that happens, tell me what the hell she's doing here."

"She's helping us expose illegal contracts between WorldWell Bank and most of our clients," said Katrina, circling a diamond earring with her index finger.

"Speaking of which, what are you doing to contain our stock hemorrhage after the ITA announcement?" He stood in front of a second screen, also a gift from SONY, Inc. He clicked the remote that controlled it, flashing second by second snapshots of Silverman's stock price.

"Funny you should mention it, Sam. That's one of the reasons Sharon's here." Katrina didn't bother looking at the screen. She smoothed her ivory Dior suit jacket.

"As I recall, it was you, Katrina, that made the rather unfortunate decision for us to take ITA public, and invested a lot of Silverman's money in its expansion plans."

"In return for a hefty chunk of their stock," she fired back, stepping between Sam and his stock screen.

"Which is plummeting," he added, clicking again.

"Sam, we need to prove WorldWell Bank is knee-deep in fraud, get them out of the way. This ITA business with the SEC, it's just bad timing. You're on their board, you know the real deal."

"Exceptionally bad timing," he said, breezing over Katrina's comment. "And how exactly is Sharon Thomas going to help us distance ourselves from a company that's thick in the line of media fire—which she started?"

"Irrelevant," Katrina waved her hand. "She's here to focus on WorldWell Bank, that's all. She can reverse engineer the deals between it and other companies. We close them down for good."

"Reverse *what?*" Sam asked, seating himself behind his mahogany desk, unique amongst the partners. It was an antique, but its gilded handles had been replaced with shiny metallic coded locks, which opened by thumbprint identification.

"*Reverse engineer,*" she said slowly, like talking to one of her junior assistants. "You know, work backwards from money flows to figure out what deals were struck and on what terms."

"You're trying to tell me that we need *her* to get this thing done?" He rose, opened the glass-plated humidor across from the flat screen, and extracted a cigar.

"Yes, Sam, that is exactly what I'm telling you." Katrina planted her hands on her hips, nose crinkling at the smell of its sickly sweet smoke.

"*No one else* here can uncover and feed the proper information to the SEC or the press but her?" he puffed again.

"That's right, Sam," replied Katrina, turning her head away from the smoke.

"Why is that, precisely?" He puffed a ring directly at her.

Katrina picked up Sam's remote and clicked to ITA's ticker, one of the few stocks falling faster than Silverman's. "Because Sharon created the template for those contract deals. No one will know how to find the numbers that violate federal securities regulations like she will. That's why."

"Sharon created those deals?"

"That's right, Sam. Surely you remember that." She shifted toward the door.

He puffed smoke rings at her back.

"You caused her to resign, Sam. I've hired her back to fix what you did. And get our bank back on top. Are we done?" added Katrina.

"For now," he said, reptilian eyes placid.

"Excellent." She turned and left Sam's office. Smiling to herself, she strutted down the hall back to hers.

* * *

Sharon's stomach was a yarn-ball of anxiety. Internal politics had a longer memory than the stock market. There would be nothing pleasant about a face-to-face meeting with this CEO. In the privacy of his fiftieth-floor office, Sam Peterson rose from his desk to greet her.

"Sharon, I want to welcome you back to the fold." He captured her gaze. His stare that evoked legendary apprehension. He extended his hand.

"Thank you, Sam," said Sharon, shaking it, then discretely rubbing her hand on her navy skirt.

"We are happy to have your expertise on our team again," he gushed, in his reserved way.

"Good to be back," lied Sharon. Sam's clear green eyes and

beaked nose were sterner than she remembered. She thought he resembled an erect turtle, a well-bred one.

"Well, I'm sure you have settling in to do," said Sam. "Let me know if there's any way I can help."

"Yes, sir," said Sharon. *Like you did last time? So we're all pretending that didn't happen?*

With that, he subtly motioned to his door.

That was it? Sharon took the hint and left. Sam commanded without exuding outward effort. It was all part of his breeding. He never gave anything away.

CHAPTER 23

Simon Caldwell arrived at the SEC building twenty minutes after Janet's 6:00 a.m. Tuesday morning phone call. He zipped his BMW 526 into a choice spot in the lower level of the garage, one reserved for government officials. As usual, his was one of the first cars there. He grabbed his briefcase from the passenger's seat and got out, locking the door behind him with his key-click. It emitted a sharp beep, reverberating through the otherwise silent lot.

Briefcase in his left hand, he headed toward a set of double-glass doors. He inspected his appearance in the glass. His blue-grey eyes mirrored approval as he smoothed his full head of light brown hair, fingered his maroon Brooks Brothers tie, and straightened his charcoal pin-striped suit.

Looking good, Caldwell. As usual. He punched in his security clearance code with his right index finger. The doors opened. A tiny ULTRA Pro-series camera above them recorded his presence. A mechanical voice greeted him—"Good morning, Mr. Caldwell"—as he entered the bottom floor of the SEC.

He continued straight down a hallway to a set of elevator banks. A security guard standing by the end of the hallway greeted him with a second "Good morning, Mr. Caldwell."

Simon stepped inside the farthest elevator and rode it to the third floor. There, he got out and headed toward another bank of elevators to his right. Then down another hallway. He entered a second elevator and took it to the sixth floor.

The labyrinth continued on the sixth floor, where Simon got out of the elevator and walked to a stairwell down another hallway on his left. He punched a different code into a second security pad. A steel industrial door opened, revealing another set of stairs that he took back down to the fifth floor, one not accessible by elevators. This floor, as far as most SEC employees knew, was closed for renovations. The building was over two hundred years old; renovations were constant and common.

He wasn't sure where Kevin was. All he knew was that he had seen Kevin leave the office in a rush around eleven o'clock two nights before. At the time, he assumed from his manner, it was family-related or something.

He dismissed the idea of Kevin having an affair as quickly as it came to mind. It was unfathomable. Simon knew Kevin well. When you study together for four years, spend every waking moment cramming and debating all facets of the law, you get to know a person. The man was annoyingly devoted to his wife.

Simon himself had gone home sometime after two a.m. the night before, for a quick nap and change of clothes. Maybe his pal was slumped over his desk, asleep from his workload on the WorldWell case. After all, Kevin hadn't been asking any questions that Simon knew about.

Simon paused by the door at the bottom of the stairs. He stood motionless as a tiny fiber optic mirror reflected a picture of his eye to a hidden retina scanner. The scanner took an imprint of his eye and checked it against its stored graphic image. It matched. The door popped open. Simon entered the latest, greatest unit of the SEC.

He glanced down both sides of the hallway before cautiously entering Kevin's office. Quietly, he shut the door behind him and walked over to Kevin's desk. Uncharacteristically neat. Simon leafed through some files on its surface. They were each labeled with some household-name company to be investigated. Kevin was doing his job.

* * *

Later that same day, Sharon re-mapped the events of the last forty-eight hours in her mind. She was walking back from her meeting with Sam. Her stomach was weak. The brute, Kevin's disappearance, Janet, March 15. It was *too* coincidental to be a coincidence. She had to dig deeper. But where to start? Once she got back to her office, she punched in the number that her SEC contact had given her.

"Simon Caldwell."

"Hi, Simon, I'm Sharon Thomas. I work for..." she paused to figure out which hat would get her the most information, reporter or banker. She opted for "...Silverman & Sons."

"What can I do for you, Sharon from Silverman?" asked the smooth young male voice, wondering just how she got his number.

"I'm working on a deal with WorldWell Bank. I needed to get a sense of how they're doing, in the investigation pipeline, you know with all the bad press out and everything. Don't want to lose money on this deal. My boss'll kill me." She realized she was blurting. *Very bad technique*, she thought. *I sound like a first-day junior reporter's assistant.*

"I can't really comment on any pending actions."

Of course, you can't, you're the SEC. Party line. It's always no comment. "Thanks, Simon. No problem—just thought I'd ask. Oh, by the way, do you know a Kevin Waters?" *Too abrupt, Thomas. Relax. Or at least, pretend you're relaxed.* What she couldn't understand was why she wasn't.

"Kevin Waters? No," answered Simon. "Why?"

"No reason—an old friend of his works at the SEC now, Roger Francis, said he went to law school with you guys. You probably know Roger—medium height, brown hair, blue eyes. Small world and all."

"Wait a sec," amended Simon, "yeah, that name does ring a bell. Kevin took international law with me at Harvard."

"But, you weren't really friends."

"It was hard to be friends with anyone, with the workload."

"Yeah, must have been tough. Anyway, so Kevin didn't follow you to the SEC."

"That's right," Simon replied, his voice grating.

"Do you know where he went to work after you guys graduated from, where was it again?"

"Harvard, I said Harvard."

"Wow, I gotta say, I really admire you guys. I mean, I barely finished undergrad, I hear law is gruesome; the hours, must have been pretty competitive?" said Sharon. Reporter trick: ask a question, leave some space, change the subject, come back later, put it differently, see if you get a different response.

"I guess you could say that."

Another reporter trick: don't dwell if you get a better response, continue like it didn't happen. "So, you guys kind of lost track of each other the last couple years."

"Pretty much," said Simon. "Look, I don't mean to be rude, but I've got a lot of work to do.

"I hear you," she said, going for empathy. "Anyway, thanks for your help. Take care."

At the SEC building, Simon got off the phone and returned to Kevin's office. Sharon's call had made him curious all over again. He continued raking through files. He knew Sharon Thomas alright—he and the rest of the SEC were all very familiar with her. She couldn't be as smart as she was made out to be if she used her real name. From inside Silverman. The thought didn't keep his fingers from trembling each time he picked up another piece of paper to examine. What did she know about Kevin? Too many questions were never a good thing. Extracting his cell, he made a call. To his godfather.

"Yes, Simon?"

"Sir, uh, I don't know how to say this, but, well, I'm a little bit, uh, confused."

"About what, son?"

"Well, I thought I did a good job with, you know, that other thing and..."

"Yes, you did. I was proud of you, son."

"Uh, that's why I should have been...I mean I thought I was responsible for, you know, problems..."

"Yes, you handled those spring threats most efficiently."

"Thank you, sir. I had no choice. Things could have become messy."

"You did well."

"So, I mean, I should have for—for K-Kevin."

"You've been very valuable, Simon," he said.

"But, this should have been, been...my responsibility."

"This...?"

"Kevin. I warned him, I did, really. I...I'm sure he didn't— he was my...best friend," Simon stammered.

"Simon, we don't have anything against Kevin."

"What? What are you saying, sir?"

"We don't know where Kevin is."

Simon was stunned. He couldn't think of what to say to his godfather. He wasn't used to being speechless. He checked his watch, realized he was running late, and made a hasty goodbye.

Simon had a dinner meeting that night with Adams, the Republican senator from Mississippi, regarding a chemical conglomerate the senator felt was being unduly scrutinized by the SEC. The company in question was also his largest campaign donor. Though Congress was on summer recess, the senator was working overtime to raise funds. There was an election coming up in a few months.

Over juicy steaks, a bottle of merlot, and sautéed potatoes at a discrete restaurant near the Capitol Building, Senator Adams loosened his belt a notch, dabbed the corners of his mouth with a napkin, and got right down to matters.

"Simon, this is a very important election for me, as you know. Dowage Chemicals has been a loyal supporter. There's got to be some way you can clear up this little investigation mess, isn't there?"

"Certainly, sir," Simon assured the senator. "You can count on me."

The dinner ended with an agreement and a handshake, but all the while Simon's mind was on other matters. On Kevin. *"We don't know where Kevin is."*

Simon had an obsessive-compulsive, anal personality. Every detail of every matter was of equal importance. Things had to be in their place.

Knowledge was control. Knowledge was money.

Simon had left messages for Kevin everywhere but his home. He didn't want Janet knowing he was concerned about Kevin's whereabouts, too. Not because he cared about her feelings, but because if Kevin didn't show up, he might need access to Kevin's home files. For that, he would need Janet's help. On that steamy August night, Simon's brisk walk back to the SEC building soon turned into a jog.

Back at the unit, Simon navigated through the greetings of his colleagues, all working late because he was. He brushed them aside as he made his way back to Kevin's office.

Kevin's junior assistant, Julian, approached him. "Simon, have you seen Kevin today?"

"Why does everyone keep asking me that?" demanded Simon, wiping the sweat from his forehead.

"Well, it's just that I need to speak with him. Is he out on a research-gathering call?"

"Yeah, Kevin's out on research," said Simon, brandishing his briefcase as if to say, "can't you see I've got a week's worth of more important business in here?" "He'll be back later."

"When? I need to speak to him about something urgent, regarding new reports on WorldWell Bank." Julian patted the folder he was carrying.

"Tomorrow," replied Simon curtly. "Could you just get back to work and stop wandering the halls?"

"Sure. You're the boss," said Julian. He turned and headed down the hall.

Once Julian had returned to his office, Simon pressed his thumb to the entry pad. Kevin's office door flung open. He entered and shut it behind him.

"We don't know where Kevin is." What if his godfather was lying? Simon never trusted anyone, never took anything at face value. His whole career, his whole life, revolved around altering, or casting doubt on, face value. He seated himself at Kevin's desk, glancing at the door to make sure it was shut. *"Relax, Caldwell,"* he told himself. Years of his father's advice came rushing to his head. His father, an international trade lawyer, was making nowhere near the money Simon was making. But he had taught Simon well. *Confront tense situations with placidity. Otherwise, you lose focus. You make mistakes.*

CHAPTER 24

At 8:00 p.m., Sharon pushed through the revolving doors of Jeremy's and walked straight to the back corner. That's where Mickey's table was. Always had been. A mark of respect from the owners. Mickey wasn't there every night, but when he was, his table was ready. When he wasn't, no one else touched it.

She sat in front of Mickey at the old wooden table riddled with etchings, shellacked by years of spilled Heineken and Budweiser. Some of the markings were fresh. Some were dulled by time and beer. They all told tales. Taken together, they offered up decades of Wall Street escapades. In the markets. In trading. In dreams. In broken hearts. In broken wallets. They told war stories. Of winning. Of losing.

"You first," Sharon urged, sipping from her mug of beer. "What's going down?"

"No way, Thomas. You don't get off that easy. First, tell me—what the fuck are you doing back in this hell-hole?"

"How much time do you have?" she asked, leaning back in her chair.

"For you—all the time in the world."

Sharon told her former mentor everything. About struggling as a freelance journalist, of having her stories relegated to back pages, or worse, not run at all because the companies involved had arm-twisted her editors. About her divorce. Getting beat up. About her determination to figure out what was really going on behind all those vaulted exteriors—ITA, Silverman, WorldWell Bank. She needed a pillar to lean on.

One of the reasons she trusted Mickey all these years was that she never sensed he wanted anything in return. When she had no experience in banking, not even a checking account of her own, he gave her an opportunity and the benefit of his experience. He was there for her now, just as he had been through her years of doubts about Wall Street, the years of navigating through the daily drudge.

One of the reasons she had chosen to leave the industry, besides her own internal devils and enemies, was watching the slow destruction of Mickey. By forces he couldn't control. Like Sam. She had watched him slowly rip Mickey apart. The rules of the game had changed over the years. It wasn't any longer about being better than your competition, inside or outside the bank. It was about cutting them down. Killing them. It wasn't about skill. It was about planting the right crop of lies. Maneuver over matter.

She knew Mickey held on from the depths of that pathetic incubator because it allowed him at least some semblance of connection to the old world. He didn't know what else to do. He was nostalgic for the simpler days of Wall Street. Couldn't let go.

Mickey listened with the attentiveness of a loving parent. She told him everything she knew about the trail: when she first came upon it in March, the call from Damon in the middle of the night, her vague ideas about what the hell it might be. Every so often, he'd interrupt with a characteristic Mickey-ism. Like when he motioned to her black eye, and she told him about the second encounter with the brute.

"I'll fuck him up," he said, with utter seriousness. "Say the word, he winds up at the Staten Island dump—one-way ticket."

She knew he meant it. She hadn't thought of Mickey as being able to help her with the stuff on the outside, her world after banking. But now that her worlds were overlapping, the idea comforted her.

"It still hurts, doesn't it?" he whispered, knowing what was always there, beneath the surface.

"Yeah, well I got pretty beat up the other night." She touched her rib cage instead of her eye.

"I wasn't referring to last night." Mickey moved in closer, leaning over the table, his hand covering hers.

Head bent, she traced a groove on the table with her index finger. "I still feel so guilty."

"It wasn't your fault, kiddo. You had nothing to do with it."

"Try telling that to his dead kid. It was my financial genius that scared her father into gassing himself."

"He didn't know she was in the backseat. You know that. You have to let it go."

"She was four! It's not that easy!" She wiped her eyes. "Excuse me a sec, Mickey." Sharon pushed her seat back and headed toward the ladies room. Once inside, she faced the mirror, turned on the tap, and watched the water swirl down the drain.

Banking was supposed to be a game, a way to make money. It was never supposed to be the difference between life and death. *She was never supposed to be the difference between life and death.* She would never forget the look of sheer sorrow in the eyes of the girl's mother. Her life, suddenly void of husband and child, would never be complete again. Sharon almost felt guilty that she dared feel bad about her own role. That woman's loss was magnitudes greater. Since leaving Silverman, she had gotten good about ignoring this part of her life. Leave it to Mickey to bring it all back up, with all of his good intentions.

She turned the tap off and exited the restroom. Changing the topic, she asked Mickey, "Now, what's going on at Silverman?"

"I fucking hate that fucking cock-sucker Sam Peterson!"

"Me too." She laughed. "Now, tell me something I don't know."

"Katrina hates him. She wants to send him down. Forever. My money's on the broad."

"What's she up to?"

"She's using that prick, Ivan Stark, over at ITA, to create a trail of offshore partnerships that all have Sam's name on them. His footprint."

"You mean ITA is involved in these partnerships?" Mickey nodded, urging Sharon on: "And since Sam's on their board now, he and Ivan can easily approve them, with no one else asking any questions. Which means..." Sharon stopped.

"Exactly," said Mickey. "Katrina's maneuvering to take 'em both down. My guess is that when the time's right, she's gonna pull the plug on the money they're funneling around illegally, and emerge lily-white with a nice offshore cut stashed somewhere. Maybe head both empires."

Sharon pondered Damon's latest story about WorldWell Bank's financial woes, and what he had told her yesterday morning. A light year ago. WorldWell Bank was making illegal loans to most of the technology industry, disguising them as trades. She was thinking about the connection between WorldWell Bank and ITA. ITA and Silverman. Ivan and Sam. Ivan and Katrina. Sam and Katrina.

"How is Sam not aware of this?" she asked. "Wouldn't he know the nature of those partnerships?"

"That's where Katrina's brilliance comes in. See, when the idea of the partnerships was first brought up, she picked a fight with Sam over them. Said they were a money loser. That she didn't trust Ivan or ITA. I got to witness the whole exchange before Sam dropped kicked me to financial oblivion."

"And, let me guess, Sam, the ego-maniac, didn't want her telling him what to do."

"You got it, kiddo. And guess when that all went down."

"Right before Sam got on Ivan's board at ITA." Sharon knew how Sam played: it was all about control.

"Bingo. See, Katrina cast enough doubt to make him think she was hosing him, but not enough to make him drop the idea. She's a good actress, that broad."

"Have to be in this town," Sharon consented. "Kat knew that Sam's best vantage point was being on ITA's board."

"Yup, and she convinced Ivan that it was a great idea for the two firms to link arms that way, show the world that Silverman believed in communications technology. The perfect match."

"Wait a minute. And all that press buzz about Sam Peterson joining ITA's board came just a day before ITA filed an 8-K with the SEC," Sharon said, piecing together the chronology. "The 8-K said that their former board member, Melvin Meyers, CEO of GlobTech, would be replaced with Silverman's CEO, Sam Peterson. And that was a week after I discovered the trail document!"

"Can't be a coincidence," said Mickey, tucking in the shirt that was hanging over his belt.

"Yeah, and the partnerships?" added Sharon, tucking away the hair falling over her face behind her ear. "They've all been going through, right?"

"Absolutely," replied Mickey. "And all of them are loosely disguised as investment opportunities. Profit contingent on new fiber-optic contracts between ITA and other tech firms. Really, though, they're a way to hide money. Lots of money."

"And WorldWell Bank?" she asked, taking another sip of beer.

"WorldWell Bank is funding the tech companies, especially ITA, but hiding how much money's streaming out to these bogus partnerships and a select group of very rich fucking people. Maybe it's getting a cut."

"Makes sense. So that's what Katrina wants me to find out?"

"Probably." He slugged what was left in his beer mug and motioned the bartender for another, and another shot of whiskey.

"She already informed me I'd only have access to WorldWell stuff."

"Sweet of her. How'd you respond?"

"I told her I needed access to all the tech companies' contracts, too, the ones connected to WorldWell Bank."

"Which—let me guess—she hesitated on, then agreed to?"

"Yup."

"This way, you help her take WorldWell Bank down. She stays clean for the cameras and the courts."

"Yup."

"This smells, kiddo."

"What do you mean?"

"I don't like it. She's not going to want to be connected to these discoveries. She's gonna want the power to resurrect these companies from the ruins of their former CEOs. She's gonna want to stay clean. That means..." he frowned.

"That means what?"

"You've got to watch your ass."

"I can take care of myself," she offered, defensively. "I need to find these partnership documents to get an idea of where money is being farmed out, how much, and to whom and by whom."

"That'll be the easy part—the documents showing WorldWell funding. That stuff, Katrina will let you get to. The partnership documents about the contracts with Sam's name all over them will probably come your way, too. Gotta admit, I like that part myself."

"And the harder part?"

"The harder part is connecting Katrina to this scheme. And the more dangerous part—until Sam discovers what's going on. Then, they're equally fucking scary."

"Great," said Sharon. "How am I going to get to those documents?"

"You're going to rely on your old friend, Mickey."

"That I can do. Thank you." She got up to leave, and then asked, "Mickey, if you know all this stuff, why aren't you blowing the whistle?"

"I don't know all the details, kiddo. Something's going down in Washington—that's not my area. Besides, it ain't my thing. Luckily, it is yours."

"Oh, that reminds me, one more thing I wanted to tell you, the oddest thing happened today." She chugged the rest of her beer.

"More odd than this shit?"

"Well, yesterday I got this weird call from some woman in Washington—said her husband, Kevin Waters, worked at the SEC with a Simon Caldwell. She knew about the fifteenth, the trail date—it was in one of his files at their home."

"Sounds like you need to pay this chick a visit at some point soon."

"Thing is, my friend Roger said there wasn't anyone by that name ever employed at the SEC, but that Simon was.

Then, when I talked to Simon, at first he acted like he had no idea who Kevin was, then he told me they were law school classmates, but had lost track of each other. Any idea what all that could mean?"

"Means someone's lying to someone. Let me do some digging for you." With that, Mickey swallowed the last swig of his whiskey, chased down by a half mug of beer. "Good luck, kiddo. And be careful."

CHAPTER 25

It was only 9:45 when Sharon left Mickey to head back uptown, but it might as well have been midnight. She was frazzled. It had been a mercilessly long day. A day in which her new life as undercover journalist and old life as Wall Street banker collided. She was surprised at how quickly the dread she felt about entering the empire of Silverman dissipated. It almost felt normal. Like returning to some kind of dysfunctional home. As much as she detested the executives at Silverman, regardless of her disdain for their lack of integrity, their greed, and their shallowness, she enjoyed reconnecting with the people she liked, people like Mickey and Nina.

In truth, she had to admit that investigative journalism could be a lonely endeavor. Most of the leads you followed went out of their way to shake you off. The more critical your articles were, the more criticism they threw back at you. And death threats. And violence.

Then, there was the money. Money. That precious commodity that inspired endless actions and emotions. It meant so many different things to different people. To Sharon, it had once meant independence and security. Insulation. But, she ultimately discovered, it really meant collusion, suppression, guilt, and pain. She had struggled her whole life to define herself. The more she rose on Wall Street, the more disgust she felt—for the petty power struggles, for the sense of lavish entitlement.

She emitted a sigh of too much beer and not enough sleep, unsure if she would ever really fit in anywhere. Still, she felt compelled to expose the rot that was Wall Street and corporate America. Even though she knew the rot was endless. That it defined the boundaries of the entire system. That it *was* the system. When she worked in banking, her way of dealing with it was to ignore it. Until she found herself in too deep. Everyone had some blood on their hands.

She didn't have a choice but to resign when she did. She wasn't a crook. But it wouldn't look that way to the outside world, to her peers, to the federal regulators. Sam was very clear on that point. She would have become the center of a global investigation. They were going to throw her under a bus. Sam offered her reputation for her job. She accepted. Partly because she didn't have the political capital within Silverman to fight. Partly because fighting had drained her like nothing in her life ever had. And then there was that ever-present guilt.

It took everything out of her. She resigned. The investigation into those tax shelters miraculously disappeared. Another example of corporate power run amuck. Now, her mission was to expose the heads of Silverman, ITA, WorldWell Bank, and any other company or executive that played fast and loose with the law. To expose the criminals they were. That's why she became a reporter. Even if some things were forever unchangeable, she'd do what she could.

But right now, her legs felt weak under the weight of the rest of her. She had to be at her most alert with Katrina and Sam. Mickey was right. She needed to watch her ass.

She stood on the subway platform waiting for the train that didn't seem to be coming. Mickey once again proved his endless support. She was so young and innocent when she first met him. It all washed over her. Combined with the half pitcher of beer she drank on an empty stomach and the dull ache that persisted from her two-day-old thrashing. All she wanted to do was go home, take a bubble bath, and sleep. She would deal with the trail and Silverman tomorrow. Maybe it would make more sense then. She leaned her head back against the subway window and spaced out.

She called her cell phone voice mail the second she surfaced from the subway. While she punched in her code, she listened to her stomach rumbling. She craved carbs. Pizza. No—potato chips. No—Fritos. She hadn't been to the gym in days, though she was usually maniacal about working out. Especially her recent boxing training. She was fit. Strong for her stature. Still, she worried about keeping her tiny figure. She'd get a bag of carrots and munch on them the rest of her walk home. She crossed First Avenue and headed toward the Korean deli on the corner of her block.

She had five messages. She hoped for at least one from Trevor, since she hadn't heard from him since last night. The first three were from Damon. Give him a call when she had a chance. How did her return to Silverman go? He wanted to apologize for leaving so abruptly the night before.

She'd call him back when she got home, to have a proper conversation with him. Meanwhile, she stared, mesmerized, at the colorful packs of junk food. She loved Fritos. It was her ultimate comfort food. *I'll work out tomorrow*, she promised herself, and reached for two bags, at 420 calories a piece, and a Diet Coke. She paid the wrinkled Korean woman behind the counter.

The fourth message was from Nina, suggesting they go out for drinks Friday night at a new bar opening in the Lower East Side, maybe go see a band Nina's boyfriend was playing in afterward. Sharon had no idea what Friday had in store. The last forty-eight hours had been life-altering. Still, it sounded like fun.

She headed toward her apartment building as the fifth message began.

It was the same low, guttural, chilling voice that called her home phone the day before. Her hands turned clammy-cold. Her pulse quickened. She dropped the white plastic bag of groceries on the sidewalk as a tingling of terror raced through her.

"*Sharon,*" he said. "*It's me, from yesterday. You're doing well. You're getting closer.*"

Shaking fingers pressing against her cell phone pad, she replayed the message several times, listening for any sounds that could identify the voice's whereabouts or identity. But there was nothing, only a click immediately following the word "*closer.*"

"Sharon," a male voice called from behind her, quickly approaching. "Remember me?" She felt a hand cover her shoulder. She stopped still. Then instinct took over, as she spun around to elbow the man, up to his esophagus. Down to his groin.

"Share, whoa, it's me, Randall. Remember? The guy you kicked out of bed the other night?"

She breathed a sigh of relief and faced Randall, her trainer and sometimes lover. It seemed a year had passed since she last shared her bed with him. In reality, it was just two nights.

"Randy, I was just…just listening to an upsetting phone message."

"Musta' been," said Randall. "If I was anyone else, you would have knocked me out of commission."

"Sorry, Randy, I just kind of lost it for a second there," she answered, straightening her skirt.

"I'm impressed." Randall flashed the whitest teeth. "I wouldn't want to get on your wrong side, lady."

Looking at him, she became self-conscious about her black eye, still covered in L'Oreal concealer. She could tell he noticed. But he didn't say anything, which only made her more defensive. "I'm in a rush, Randy, I gotta get home."

"You sure you don't want some company tonight, Sharie?" He closed in on her, gripping her wrist.

She brushed him off. "No, I'm fine."

"You sure? You don't look that fine," he replied, his grip tightened, almost crushing her bone.

"I said I'm fine!" she snapped, spinning her arm away from his grasp. She picked up her bag and stomped away, heart pounding.

At her stairwell, she ripped open the bag of Fritos and started munching as she climbed the steps, only vaguely worried about her carb intake. As she approached her hallway she listened for any abnormal sounds. There was only a TV blaring from the adjacent apartment and a mother yelling at her kids on the floor below. Slowly, she undid the locks of her front door. She pushed it open and immediately turned on the living room light.

A message light flashed on her answering machine. No noises; nothing else. She pressed play and stepped away from the apparatus like it was an explosive. But it was just Damon asking her to call him on his apartment line when she got home, no matter how late it was.

"Sharon," he answered after half a ring. "How are you? How was your first day back?"

"Long," she began, but first she wanted to clear something up. "Hey, listen—"

"Yes?"

"I'm sorry if I upset you last night, about Marsha, I didn't mean to; I just wanted to let you know that I understand that finding out about an affair, under any circumstances, sucks."

"I know you meant well, it's just—the whole thing still makes me so mad. Which is crazy considering it wasn't the worst part of..." He trailed off.

"I understand," said Sharon. She jumped with panic, "Hang on a second, Damon." There was a crunching sound coming from under her desk. The crackling, fluttering sound of papers being rattled. She tiptoed over to inspect the area, bringing the cordless. The culprit was a window left slightly ajar. A brewing rainstorm, preempted by a growing breeze.

She breathed in deeply. "Listen, Damon—"

"What?"

"Would you mind, maybe coming over here...to...to talk...about today?"

She interpreted his silence to mean he thought her suggestion was ridiculous. He'd been there last night. And the night before. She would handle her jitters herself. "Sorry, Damon, I know it's late, never mind."

"No," he said, "I'll come over. I'll be there in twenty minutes, okay?"

"Okay. Yes. Thanks."

"Do you want me to bring anything?'"

"Yeah—I would love a pizza," she replied without hesitation.

CHAPTER 26

The antique oak and bronze grandfather clock that sat in the dimly lit hallway of the Harvard Club chimed ten o'clock. Two CEOs, Sam Peterson and Ivan Stark, sat in a remote corner of the downstairs lounge. Dark was the most popular color of the club's interior. The cavernous space on West Forty-fourth Street had only recently opened its doors to Harvard's female alumnae. Women, however, rarely bothered showing up. The décor accentuated their absence.

It was a stern locale. Forest green paisley carpet gave way to high-backed mahogany arm chairs with gold-plated trimmings. Designer-suited executives, comfortably in their middle age, sat around low tables of solid wood carvings. Nondescript bartenders hovered about inconspicuously. They were paid to serve drinks and leave the clientele alone. The burnt-cigar smell of old money permeated fabric and furniture equally. Sam Peterson fit in perfectly

Ivan Stark had a bit more trouble. Unlike the more ostentatious, new money-types who wore their wealth like neon lights strung within an ancient castle, Ivan spent years doing everything he could to morph into an impression of old money.

Old money smelled different than new money. It was a genetic trait more than a commodity. Passed on from father to son. It separated those born into fortune from those who came by it organically, through work, luck, fraud, or a combination of the three.

Old money protected old money. New money competed with new money. Old money mingled with new money, but never meshed. It didn't want to become tainted. Old money was forever. New money was fleeting. Old money surrounded itself with old money. New money coveted that relationship, but would never be accepted or trusted the same way, no matter how hard it tried. New money that tried to behave like old money was particularly suspect.

Tonight, old-money-Sam and new-money-Ivan were worried about the same thing. The stock price of their respective companies. For two days, shares in their companies had taken a significant pounding. ITA stock was down 27 percent since the *Wall Street Tribune* article suggested an imminent SEC investigation, on top of the *Riche$* article against the company that Sharon Thomas wrote months earlier.

As ITA's lead banker and investor, Silverman's stock was down 11 percent. Guilt by association. All signs indicated more of the same pounding in tomorrow's market.

Sam leaned back in his armchair and inhaled a deep puff of his Cohiba Cuban cigar. Smoking, banned throughout New York City, was a permanent fixture of the Harvard Club. Cuban cigars, banned throughout the United States, were as well.

"What are you doing about damage control, Ivan?" he asked.

"I made some calls into the SEC yesterday afternoon."

"And?"

"I was told it'd be taken care of—that there'd be a press release negating the allegations."

"Who did you talk to?" Sam inquired, crossing his legs.

Ivan shifted to the side of his chair. He squinted at his business partner and board member.

"It's not important. I spoke to the right people."

"I'm not playing this game. My Washington connections are more influential than yours will ever be."

"Your ties are well known, Sam."

"Well, I'm not having Silverman take anymore of a beating for your screw-ups."

"My screw-ups?" Ivan leaned forward, forehead crinkled.

"Yes. You know it and I know it," Sam said, extracting his cell phone from the inside pocket of his double-breasted suit. The first number he dialed went to voice mail. The second number brought a response.

"Yes, boss?" said the young man.

"I'm sitting here at the Harvard Club, opposite Mr. Stark, from ITA. As you must know, it's not been a very good day. In fact, it seems that between the two of us, we've lost about $18 billion of market cap today. I don't like to lose market cap, you understand?"

"Yes, boss," he said.

"You'll take care of this, correct?"

"Yes, sir."

"Immediately, correct?"

"Yes, sir."

"Excellent, my boy, excellent." Sam terminated the call, folded his cell phone, and put it back in his pocket.

Ivan sniffed and motioned to a nearby waiter. "Two scotches, on the rocks," he ordered, no please, no thank you. As soon as their drinks arrived, Ivan raised his glass. "To you, Sam, for knowing how to get things done."

Sam nodded and took a sip of scotch without meeting Ivan's glass or eyes. The next day the *Wall Street Tribune* would run a retraction to their Tuesday article, based on an early morning press release stating that upon a thorough SEC examination of ITA's books, there was no foul play to be found. That, in fact, the company was in excellent health.

CHAPTER 27

While waiting for Damon to arrive with the fresh pie, Sharon chose to stave off exhaustion with work. As she pondered the meaning of the trail document and the meaning behind it, Mickey called.

"Kiddo, you're not gonna like this," he said, in a gentler-than-usual tone for him.

"Like what?" She braced herself for another piece of Silverman crime or something about Kevin Waters.

"Your friend from the SEC. Roger. He's..." Mickey sounded like he'd just ingested a pack of Reds.

"He's what?"

"In a body bag."

"Oh my God!" Sharon almost dropped the phone, "How?"

"Shot twice —in the hand and through the eye. I'm sorry."

"No!" Sharon cried. "No!" She slammed shut the laptop cover. "Mickey, it's all my fault. I know it is! I was the one who...who got him into this."

"Sharon, you don't know that. You don't even know what 'this' is. Stop beating yourself up. Whatever's going on—it's bigger than you. We'll get you to D.C. tomorrow. We'll figure it out."

"But this can't be a coincidence. *Not again!*" she sobbed, both hands raking through her hair.

"Hey. Kiddo. Do you want me to come over? You shouldn't be alone."

"No, I'm…Damon's coming over. I'll be okay. I'll call you later, Mickey. I promise."

After she hung up, she decided to call Janet Waters. She needed answers. And needed to make sure Janet was okay. To her relief, Janet answered on the first ring. "Thank God you're there," said Sharon, breathless.

"I'm waiting for the police to call. Digging into more of Kevin's files," she replied.

"Listen, there's something I need to tell you."

"What?"

"You said your husband worked at the SEC for two years.'"

"Yes, that's right."

"Well, I called to check, just routine background with a friend there, and…"

"Yes?"

"Your husband doesn't work at the SEC. There's no record of his employment. What's going on, Janet?"

After a long pause, she said, "I don't know. What are you saying? Why? I thought you were someone who could help. Sorry I bothered you…" Her voice turned defensive.

"Wait, Janet, I am someone who can help. Look, I have a friend at the SEC. Known him for years. I just asked him to do some routine checks on Kevin and Simon. Just a reporter's reflex. Like Googling."

"Well, your friend was obviously mistaken. Maybe you should ask him to check again." Janet fought her instinct to hang up on Sharon, knowing this woman could be her only remaining hope.

"I can't do that, Janet."

"Why not? Who is he?"

"His name is, was, Roger Francis. He's dead."

"What? Oh my God—Sharon!"

"Janet, he was killed after I spoke to you and to Simon."

Janet's voice was tight, "But I don't understand! What do you mean *no record?* Kevin was always talking about the SEC. If he wasn't working for them, who was he working for?"

"I don't know, Janet. All I know is Roger's dead."

"And Kevin's still missing."

"Janet," said Sharon, her voice sounding distant to both of them. "We need to talk. I'm coming to D.C. tomorrow. Maybe, maybe you shouldn't stay at your home alone tonight."

"I'll be okay," said Janet, her voice wavering. "See you tomorrow, then."

Hanging up the phone, Sharon returned to her laptop, still shaken, hungry for news. There it was, the press ever-eager for fresh blood—literally. The breaking red banner topping the MSN headlines read: **"Capitol Killer Nabs Third Victim."**

She clicked to the full AP story. The police were saying that this was the first identifiable male in the chain of killings that began in the spring. The police connected the killings because each of the men was shot twice, once through the right hand and once through the left eye, straight into the skull. This time, the victim was found in his car below the SEC building. Her heart stopped beating as she read the name in the text. It was SEC employee Roger Francis, age thirty-one. Her friend. Contact. And source.

A chill ran up her spine and through her head. Sharon didn't know how big a can of worms she was dealing with. But someone was playing for keeps. And none of it felt random.

CHAPTER 28

Kevin Waters knew he was taking a huge risk with his marriage and his wife's psyche. It couldn't be helped. If you turned, you died. It was that simple. He had no intention of contributing to the body count. But he couldn't keep quiet, either.

So he made his choice. The only choice he could make—to do the right thing. After contributing to the wrong thing for too long. He spent months gathering information, hacking into the secret corners of the network, developing his case. Now, for the first time, he needed help.

He could only hope he had chosen the right ally. He knew time was running out.

What he had to discuss was too important. It had to be done in person. So here he was, waiting for the appropriate moment. On the corner of East Fourth Street and First Avenue, opposite the apartment building of *Riche$* reporter and former banker, Sharon Thomas.

He knew she was home. He had watched her arrive from his window table at Three of Cups, the neighborhood Italian joint. Kevin motioned for the check, paid in cash, and headed to the corner payphone to make the call. He assumed her phone was tapped, but if he could make the call short enough he could dodge a trace. Since it was a payphone, he knew it couldn't be longer than twenty seconds.

Payphones were property of the conglomerate old-world phone companies; in the case of New York City, they belonged to Verizon. Verizon was less high-tech and more cost conscious than network or specialty broadband companies. Its tapping devices didn't extend to common street phones. He dialed.

"Hello?" Sharon answered on the second ring.

"We've got to talk." He had already started counting the seconds.

"Who is this?"

"I haven't got time to explain. Please. Meet me at DBA's," he urged. He had seen the nearby bar on his way over and parked around the corner from it. "It's about the trail," he added. Nine seconds remaining.

Sharon stiffened. She went with her gut. "I'll be there in two minutes." She knew it could be a trap or an informant; either way, she couldn't afford to leave an ounce of data unturned. She didn't have time to worry about safety. She assumed Damon would be over in twenty minutes, maybe twenty-five if he took the subway. He'd probably pick up a pizza at Joey's on his way. He would understand if she was late returning.

Grabbing her cell, microphone, purse, and notepad, she dashed down her stairs, out the door, and turned left toward First Avenue.

She didn't get very far. At the corner, a man standing by the newsstand, his head buried in a *New York Post*, clutched her arm. He had been waiting for her.

"It's me," he said, pushing her forward. "Let's go."

She tried to get a read on him. He was young, clean-cut, handsome. His kind and intelligent blue-grey eyes were tinted with desperation. Her radar with men she found attractive was notoriously poor, but in this case, she had to follow her professional gut. She decided to trust him.

"Okay," she said.

"Follow behind me," he directed, adjusting to a slow jog. She did as he said, dropping a pace behind.

He slowed at a white Ford Taurus parked slightly up the avenue. His head stayed motionless while his eyes darted around the street to check if someone had spotted him. He unlocked the doors electronically. "Act like you're hailing a cab," he said, "then get in." She walked around to the passenger side and raised her arm to hail a cab driving up First Avenue. There were plenty of empty cabs that time of night competing for fares. Immediately, one scooted in front of another, stopping on the passenger side of his car, shielding her. While facing the taxi, she quickly opened the door of the Taurus and edged in backward. The taxi sped off into the night to find a real fare.

The man switched on the ignition as she slammed her door. The car screeched off the curb and headed uptown. "I should probably introduce myself," he said, extending his right hand while his left firmly gripped the wheel. "My name is Kevin Waters."

"Sharon Thomas," she responded, shaking his hand. "Though I'm guessing you already know that."

"Yes. You must be wondering what's going on."

"I sure am," she said. "Your wife called me. I spoke to her a couple times."

"I left your name for her to find. She's no dummy," he said. "Just in case anything happened to me."

"She said you work for the SEC. But you don't. Do you?" She fingered the door lock.

"I couldn't compromise her. I work in Washington, at an organization fronted by the SEC."

"What do you mean, fronted by?" she asked.

"Long story, but basically our unit was created to scrounge info on the biggest corporations."

"Go on," said Sharon, switching on the mike inside her purse. "Why haven't I heard of your department?"

"Because its activities are not public. Been in the works for years."

"What activities?"

"It investigates the largest corporate frauds," Kevin replied, peering into the rearview mirror.

"Why wouldn't the president want it broadcast?"

"Because that's not what it really does."

"What do you mean? Is it a ruse to make us think something's being done against white-collar crime?"

"Not even." His grip tightened on the wheel.

She processed this for a split-second. The co-dependent nature of politicians and corporate executives meant everything came down to money. This was just another puzzle to be solved. "So it's a group that shields corporations from investigations and bad press—in return for a steady flow of campaign money?"

"Close, but no cigar."

"Is it part of Special Fraud, where Simon Caldwell works?

"How do you know Simon?" He turned his attention from the road to Sharon for a moment.

"Your wife mentioned you were friends. I called him. Roger Francis, my SEC connection, told me you didn't work there. Simon did. But now..." her voice trembled, "Roger's dead..."

"That means Simon knows you're onto him. Damn it!" Kevin swerved the Taurus in front of an oncoming city bus, and then jerked onto a side street. The car's tires screamed.

Sharon's body smashed against the car door. "Hey! What the—!"

"We're being followed," he informed her. "Hang on!"

Kevin wove the Taurus around the double-parked cars lined up along the curb. The car behind them kept tight on his tail. Sharon gripped the dashboard to brace herself as Kevin roared the car through a yellow light. They sped down Second Avenue. Sharon craned her neck to see who was following them.

"Hold on!" yelled Kevin. He shot left onto Houston Street, through a red light, as oncoming cars screeched their brakes. All the while his eyes remained glued to his rearview mirror. He continued zipping in and out of the stream of cars headed toward the FDR.

A maroon Oldsmobile bumped the back of the Taurus. Sharon's body jerked forward. She saw her knuckles go white, felt her throat constricting.

Kevin stepped on the gas to dash through another light just gone red. The Oldsmobile did the same.

Sharon searched for the car's license plate and a view of its driver. She could make out a large man. The top of his head almost disappeared into the roof of the car. But it was dark, and they were driving too fast, and she couldn't make out any of his features. Then, with an abrupt chill, she recognized him.

"Oh shit!" she exclaimed. Her heart leapt into her tightened throat.

"Friend of yours?" Kevin asked, his chin tucked into his neck as his eyes stayed pasted to the road speeding past them.

"Only if you consider people who try to kill you friends." Her mouth went dry.

"Should we take the FDR?" he shouted. "Quick!"

She mulled the possibilities. "If we're being followed and the FDR has traffic—"

"Quick!" he repeated, foot pressed hard on the gas pedal. "Yes or no?"

"No! You'll get stuck. Turn onto Allen Street. Make a right, there!" She pointed to a broad street three lanes of traffic over from where they were driving.

"On it!" Kevin jerked the wheel. Other cars were honking and slamming brakes all around him.

"We're not going to make it—too much traffic!" she screamed.

A shot fired from the Oldsmobile.

"Yes we will!" yelled Kevin, flooring the gas.

Another shot fired. The second bullet shattered their back windshield and streamed through the center of the front windshield. Right between them. Sharon shielded her face with the back of her hand.

Kevin cranked the wheel all the way to the right. Sharon slid further down in her seat. Somewhere in between, she thought she stopped breathing. Kevin maneuvered the Taurus across the lanes of traffic, amidst more car horns, more swears. Two more gunshots rang out as the bullets flew by the driver and passenger windows. From a falafel place on the south side of Houston, two cops jumped into their parked squad car and cranked the siren.

The Oldsmobile was tailing close. A fifth shot rang out, kissing the passenger side door handle. It was separated from Sharon by three inches of metal and vinyl. Sharon ducked her head further toward Kevin, clutching the arm rest. Sirens were blaring.

"Drive on!" she screamed.

He complied. At that moment, the clang of shattered glass and the crunch of metal broke the air. Sharon looked back. The Oldsmobile didn't make the last turn.

The Olds halted on impact as it railed with a spectacular crash into a FedEx truck. Kevin didn't look back. He kept focused ahead, driving away. The cops had called in reinforcements. A group of squad cars were circling the Olds. One sped off to follow them.

"No! We can't stop now!" yelped Kevin, hearing the siren near their car again. He maneuvered the car into a narrow side street with a sharp yank of the wheel. Sharon turned around and watched the Olds blur into the distance. She wondered if it was bad karma to hope the guy gunning for you wound up dead in a heap of twisted metal. She wondered if it was her duty as a human to call an ambulance. She decided it wasn't—there were tons of other people around, anyway. And tons more cops.

The wail of the siren started to recede. Kevin took a deep breath. "Sorry about that driving demonstration. I got my license in Ohio," he said, as if that were all the explanation necessary. "I think we lost him."

She laughed nervously. "For now. The man has amazing resilience. He's kind of like the Terminator—just substitute the bad Austrian accent for a middle-Brooklyn one, and worse hygiene."

Kevin laughed in spite of himself.

"Pull over at the next corner, on the left." She pointed. "There's an old kosher coffee shop on Delancey. It's been there forever. We can sit in the back. Talk. No one will see us." Then she thought of Kevin's wife, Janet. "In the meantime, are the cops watching your house?"

His face turned ashen. "No. No cops. Let's talk. I need to get back. This whole thing's gonna blow."

CHAPTER 29

Kevin slowed the Taurus and squeezed into a tight spot. The two walked together to the coffee shop. The owner knew Sharon. She often brought contacts there if they didn't want to be noticed. They took a back booth and ordered two Diet Cokes.

"So, where exactly did you learn to drive like that?" asked Sharon, sipping hers to calm her nerves.

"My dad was a cop; he taught me the ropes."

Sharon nodded. "He taught you well. So..." She changed the subject. "You were about to tell me I was wrong about campaign contributions."

"Not wrong," he said. "It's just that it's bigger than that—much bigger." His hands gestured a globe.

"In what way?" She leaned forward in the booth.

"The unit's not looking to keep corporate contributors lined up for campaigns." He leaned toward her over the table. "It's looking to redesign how firms compete."

"Meaning?" She leaned in to meet his eyes, gauging the credibility of his words by his focus.

"It's taking in large chunks of money from some companies to put their competitors out of business."

Sharon pulled her hair back with both hands. "What kind of money are we talking, exactly?

"This year—so far—over nine billion dollars."

"Wow! Are you kidding?" From his eyes, she could see he was not. She tried to make sense of the figure. "Corporate campaign contributions for the last ten years combined barely total four billion. This is a shitload of money. It's massive fraud and collusion and...how do you know about this?"

"I know because I am an 'enforcer.'" He looked her squarely in the eyes. Full frontal credibility.

"A what?" Her eyebrows rose.

"I'll explain," he said, "and tell you about Simon Caldwell. First, did he say anything about me?"

"No. He said you went to law school together then lost touch."

"This is worse than I imagined. At first, I only suspected he was involved. Now that he's outright lying, I'm sure of it."

"Tell me about him, about *it*." She took out her notepad.

He placed his hand over hers. "No notes—please. Just listen."

She folded up her pad and stuck it back into her purse.

"Simon had been an enforcer for six months when he suggested I join. When he explained about the unit, I was confused. I mean, I always thought the SEC already did that. You know, checked public company books to make sure they reported honestly, indicted white-collar criminals who break the rules."

"Well, they pretty much suck at that," said Sharon.

"Anyway," Kevin's face grew more animated, "Simon assured me we'd be handling the most intricate cases, the biggest corporations. He said the area was so important that it was created by a special White House order, and has a reporting line up to the Oval Office."

"You mean not to the head of the SEC?" queried Sharon.

"No," Kevin shook his head.

"Then to who?" she asked.

"To the vice president."

"Oh my God!" she exclaimed, suddenly understanding the size of the can of worms before her. "This is bigger than huge!"

"And more dangerous. The group has its own computer network and office space only accessible by individual fingerprints and retina scan. I asked Simon how they funded it all when he recruited me, said it seemed fishy."

"What'd he say?"

"He said, 'Kev, if we're gonna bust the biggest cases, we've got to fit in with the big boys, the mega-CEOs. We need to make friends with them so we can gather extra evidence before other federal investigative bodies get involved and screw things up prematurely.'"

"Nice company line," grimaced Sharon.

"Uh-huh. This conversation took place at an expensive French bistro in Dupont Circle. Simon picked up the tab with his black AmEx. A month later, I joined. I thought, how could an operation with such a high calling be anything but crucial to the integrity of corporate America? Particularly if it was under the watch of the vice president."

"You thought wrong."

"I discovered that," said Kevin. Then in a whisper, "There's more."

Sharon fingered her mike to make sure it was still on. "Keep going."

"The worst part was *how* the specific ones our group focused on were selected. That was key. Simon used to say, all companies commit fraud. They all cook books. Some just get away with it. And some don't pay the SEC enough money to stay away from them."

"How Machiavellian," said Sharon.

"Yeah, everyone won that way. The companies that 'commissioned' us got away with cooking their books. For a fee. The public got to feel like the SEC was watching out for corporate crime because some companies were passed back to the main SEC office for prosecution."

"Which is why Simon is listed in Special Fraud, which really exists, but you..."

"Aren't listed anywhere. Neither are the rest of the enforcers, except my assistant, Julian Elliot. He runs errands between units. Unofficially, we're the Enforcer Unit. Officially, we don't exist." Kevin paused, letting this sink in. "To top it off, the best enforcers even got a cut of the value of the fraud in question."

Sharon's eyes grew wider. "So the enforcers get *paid* to look the other way?"

"Exactly," Kevin responded. "Occasionally, they'd have to come down on a company. Make it look like they're doing a 'public service' job. Then the company's rival points a finger, provides some misleading data, and secretly pays the fee to the unit—to enforce the law *against* its competitor."

"This is surreal. Does every enforcer know about all this? Seems a lot to keep under wraps."

Kevin shook his head. "No, most of them think they're protecting the public. They look for fraud and bring it to Simon's attention. Simon brings it to the attention of the vice president. That's when the fee negotiations start in earnest."

"The vice president," Sharon said slowly, "Did he...? I mean, does he...? How involved?"

"In the background, hard to prove, but very directly," said Kevin.

"I can't believe this," said Sharon, "And, of course, if too many people knew what was going on, someone might blow the whistle."

"I'll get to that in a second, but yes, that's why it's crucial to keep the flow of fees secret. It would be a national scandal if anyone discovered the SEC—funded by taxpayer dollars to monitor companies—was making billions of dollars by deciding who and who not to monitor."

Sharon shook her head. "Wow…"

"I've been piecing together the trail of these so-called enforcer fees. They started with a company here and there. Enforcers would investigate certain companies—like the SEC is supposed to do, and then when cases got solid, hand them over to the SEC. Like I said, not every enforcer knows that's just a cover."

"But you do?"

"Mostly. Not all the pieces, but enough. That's where you come in. I need your help."

"Why me? Why not Stan Johnson from the *Wall Street Tribune*?"

"Because you understand how phony numbers tell stories."

"So?" she asked. *Stan knew how to spin numbers into stories.*

"I think you'll have a particular investment."

"What are you talking about?"

"Your old company—Silverman—and your old nemesis—ITA—are both involved."

Sharon stiffened. "How?"

"There's a contract between them that's the cover for a giant fee transfer." He unfolded two sheets of crumpled paper and slipped them across the table to her. "Here."

She scanned the contract before her. It was one she had designed while at Silverman. Her thumbprint. "Oh my God," she covered her mouth. "This is just like the original one between Silverman and the old ITA, the one that went bust. This was going to set up a whole offshore scam. Before any regulators sniffed around, it was shut down. The old CFO even killed himself, thinking an investigation was coming. You must know all this, right? But then the weird part was that no investigation ever took place."

Kevin nodded his head. "It gets worse."

"How can it?" Sharon clutched her stomach, feeling anxiety rise.

"The enforcers who've tried to talk before have disappeared."

Sharon inhaled deeply. She knew where this was going. "You mean the capitol serial killer?"

Kevin nodded. "The first two guys were enforcers."

Sharon cringed, felt her fingers dig into the linoleum table. She dug for another connection. "Was Roger Francis an enforcer?"

"No. I know the name, but he wasn't in our unit."

"This doesn't stop, does it?" Her eyes welled.

"No, it doesn't. But the group is getting nervous," said Kevin. "Which means they're trying to seal up all the holes, plug any leaks. I've been on the run for days. These people know everything. Or find out eventually. As it is, I need to get back to D.C. now. My wife, Janet. Help me."

"What can I do? I can't run a story to expose the unit. Enough people are...dying."

"We need more proof," he said. "See, none of the actual money touches the SEC—or the White House. We need to find out where the fees are going. Where pay-outs happen."

Sharon's heart sank. "But without an actual money trail, this could all be conjecture."

"Tell that to the dead men." Kevin's hands shook, and Diet Coke brimmed over the lip of his glass.

"We need conclusive proof of this fee trail." As she heard the word come out of her mouth, her mind spun. *Trail.* Could the document she had downloaded fit into all this? Was the trail a set of instructions? A way for companies to deliver fee money? Hush money. Payoff money. *Murder money.*

"Listen," Kevin said, seeming to sense Sharon's wandering mind. "There isn't a lot of time. As far as I can tell, something big is going down next Tuesday."

"Do you know where?" Sharon asked.

"Belize, I think."

She smacked her hands on the table. "Of course! That makes sense," she said. "It's the only offshore banking setup that asks no questions. Money flows in and out all the time. With no documentation. It's been a hot spot for money-laundering drug dealers since the early nineties."

"Then even if we could trace the money changing hands, there might be no records of it?"

"Right. No records, no numbered accounts, nothing. You'd have to be there in person to facilitate any transaction. And grease a lot of palms in the process."

"Is that possible?"

"It is now," said Sharon. "I just rejoined Silverman yesterday. No, wait, today actually. It's been so eventful, I'd forgotten."

"Why did you go back?"

"I wanted to dig into the connection between WorldWell Bank and Silverman, though now it seems—"

"It's an enforcer project," he interrupted.

Her jaw dropped. "You mean Silverman?"

"Yep! Paying the enforcer unit to smear the WorldWell Bank."

"Damon has no idea."

Kevin held his hand up. "And he can't know now. This is too dangerous. It must stay quiet." He had to emphasize this. She was, after all, still a reporter.

"Got it." Sharon nodded. She would have to take this risk, even though she didn't like it. "If you can get me any documents that show intended money flow and to whom, I can try to intercept it. But I probably won't be the only one. If so much fee money is flowing to Belize, others will want to make sure it winds up in the right hands."

"Here's information that should help." Kevin was prepared. He handed her a manila folder.

"Thanks," she said, opening the folder and surveying its contents. She was looking for any document that matched her March 15 8-K report, but found none. Still, what he gave her would help with access down in Belize. He included source bank account numbers for many of the companies.

"Thank you, Sharon." His smile exuded gratitude. "Thank you. I'll drive you back."

"No, that's okay," she said. "I'll grab a cab—you need to get home. How can I get in touch with you?"

"Here are two cell phones," he said. "They're Canadian-based and can't be traced through the usual wireless networks. I'll keep one. You, the other. Numbers are on the back. Memorize and destroy them."

"Thanks," she said, pocketing the phone. They walked out of the diner. She had so many more questions to ask him, including how he knew to give her the two new cell phones, but let him go home to his family.

"I'll be in touch." Shutting the car door, she examined her own cell phone. Two missed calls. One from Damon. He was on the stoop of her building with a cold pizza. One from Trevor, which she returned.

"Just where the hell have you been?" she asked when Trevor picked up the phone, her tone sharp.

"Uh, I kind of fell asleep," said Trevor, bracing himself for her wrath.

Sharon sighed. "Have you put the trail pieces together at least? Matched the companies?"

"Done and done, Share. I'll come over with everything right away."

"No, that's okay," she said.

Trevor voice was worried. "'That's okay? *Okay?* Whatdya mean? I'm, like, a month late!'"

"Yeah, I know. I'll pick it up from you tomorrow morning, on my way to work."

"Way to work? Whoa, what else did I miss?"

"Trev, things happen while you sleep. I'll fill you in tomorrow, say around seven."

"Seven? In the *morning?*"

"Trev, don't give me that—you're a month late, remember! I gotta go. Damon's coming over to–to talk about a piece."

"Got it. Enjoy—your piece," he clucked, as she ended the call.

***

As Kevin hit the New Jersey border, the summer storm that had been brewing all evening opened fire. It started pouring relentlessly. A barrage of rain pelted his Taurus and shifted his concentration to the road. The sloppy weather would lengthen his journey.

He could only hope that the man in the Oldsmobile was sufficiently detained—by impact or otherwise—and that if anyone else was following him, their task would be rendered impossible by the storm. Another thing his father had taught him from years in the police force: rain makes it hard to find people, and easy for them to get away. Water serves many purposes.

Kevin desperately wanted to call his wife, hear her voice.

The moments away from her were unbearable given the magnitude of what he was doing. And how close he was to its epicenter. The danger of getting caught. But he knew it was safer for Janet if there was no contact that could be traced between them. The rest of the enforcers had no families. He wasn't taking any chances.

CHAPTER 30

By midnight, most of the enforcers had left the unit. But Simon sat at Kevin's desk, occasionally glancing at the door to make sure it was shut. *Relax, Caldwell,* he told himself. *Hopefully,* he thought, *Kevin's made some mistakes.*

Simon methodically opened each of Kevin's drawers, all by thumbprint. He combed through notes about Wal-Mart, McDonald's, and IBM. He rummaged through Kevin's pen drawer. Flipped through the calendar on his desk. He turned on Kevin's computer, logged onto the enforcer's network, and went through its firewall to access the Internet. There would be URLs of the last places Kevin had visited. He scrolled down the list. All the sites that appeared made sense given Kevin's case load. They all related to the companies he was investigating. Besides that, there were a number of WorldWell press releases and some PDF files of its recent board meeting minutes.

So far, so normal. There were more sites visited for news on WorldWell Bank and Silverman. *The Wall Street Tribune,* ITA's home page, and *Riche$* magazine. Simon recalled that *Riche$* had done a cover story in their last issue on WorldWell Bank. How their earnings were declining and more trouble lay ahead, possibly related to cooking the books. *If they only knew.*

It wouldn't have been Simon's preference to run that story yet, but he stayed out of the media strategies of his clients. He was just interested in making an airtight case against whatever company was on the line, and then collecting the fees. Curiosity took him to the *Riche$* website to peek at their

WorldWell story. He clicked on the *Riche$* URL in the list of Kevin's recently visited sites. It directed him to the August story on ITA by Sharon Thomas. No, he realized as he looked more closely, this was a story from last March. *Kevin always was particularly thorough*, Simon thought, and moved on.

Simon continued his search into Kevin's emails. He scrolled through recently sent and received messages. Nothing seemed out of the ordinary. They were mostly requests for further information from companies, sometimes from their lawyers, and the replies to those requests. All part of building the enforcer case. All sent from Kevin's email address, kwaters@sec.en.gov.

Simon was about to close Kevin's email account when he decided to take a quick look at the recently deleted ones. Data requests, setting up appointments. Nothing personal. Simon had strict rules about using the network for personal reasons. Nothing he found in the deleted items explained where Kevin was or what he was doing. There were no listed appointments over the last two days, either.

Finally, he exited the email account and turned his attention to the rest of Kevin's computer. He scanned the recent documents that Kevin had accessed or written. All related to the companies he was investigating. He went into DOS to access Kevin's cache files, the ones that traced all of a computer's activity, tagged by date. Simon was used to poking around other people's computers. The good stuff rarely showed up in the main Microsoft Office screens; you had to go beneath the screens.

There, in a cache of recently printed documents, he found something outside Kevin's case load. Not an SEC filing, but something else. Simon opened the file, an ITA document. It appeared to be a contract of some sort. Some kind of a swap deal. ITA would provide Silverman access to the finances of all its clients that used ITA networks in return for—Simon's eyes bulged as he read the figure—*one billion dollars!*

He examined the date on the document. April 15. Tax day. Did that mean anything? He didn't know if this contract was accounted for in either Silverman's or ITA's regular SEC filings. Somehow, he doubted it. It was signed on Silverman's side, not by their chief financial officer, which would have been normal, but by their chief technology officer, Katrina Sullivan.

What was Kevin doing with this document? And how did he get it? Why was Simon not aware of it? More importantly, was Kevin getting a cut of *a billion dollars* of fees to look the other way? Simon leaned back in Kevin's chair, his blood pumping overtime.

Then he noticed something else he hadn't thought to examine. Kevin's wastebasket. Casually at first, then with increasing scrutiny, Simon rummaged through the trash. He waded through stacks of printouts of SEC filings for Kevin's investigation list. And, there at the bottom, between stacks of white paper, opened envelopes, and cellophane wrapper from a lunch sandwich, Simon noticed something.

A crumpled yellow post-it. *A mistake.*

He reached into the basket and grabbed it like it was a lost jewel. Unraveling it, he stared at the almost indecipherable scrawl: *March 15*th.

He would need to make a house call to the Waters' residence. Immediately.

CHAPTER 31

Simon printed out the contract between Silverman and ITA, then folded and stuffed it in the breast pocket of his suit. The stiff wool, mixed with his nervous perspiration, was causing a heat rash that Simon could feel spreading across his abdomen. Even in the height of summer, Washington's government employee dress code was formal; there could be no deviation from suits, ties, and jackets.

His head wouldn't wrap around the contract's sum. *A billion dollars.* It went way beyond any fee ceiling he'd ever seen before. What kind of information was that important, that *expensive*? And why did Silverman have to *pay* ITA for it? Weren't they already one of the key bankers for all of ITA's clients anyway? Couldn't they get that financial information directly?

Unless...unless that money was a personal gift from Silverman to ITA, disguised as a business contract. Simon had seen that kind of thing many times before, but not for anywhere near that type of money. What kind of gift does a billion dollars buy? What was ITA going to do with that money, or the more apt question, what was ITA's CEO, Ivan Stark, going to do with that money?

And why the hell didn't he know about any of this? And why did Kevin?

Feelings of betrayal made Simon's blood boil. It was the same feeling his father had dumped on him growing up, of not being quite smart enough. Cutting corners. Letting others do his job. Kevin was the one guy in the entire world he ever let himself trust. Was that bastard undercutting him? After all he had done, after hooking him up with the enforcer job, making sure he got all the best perks, keeping him away from the life of a low-salaried public defendant that Kevin was about to settle on...Hiding *a billion dollars* from him? And from his own wife? Janet didn't know where Kevin was. Or *did* she? That recovering alcoholic bitch. Was she in on something with Kevin?

I'll kill him, thought Simon. *I'll kill him myself.*

He bolted out of the enforcer offices, through the barren hallways and flourescent lights. He headed for the parking lot. In the world where corporate America and Washington collided, there was no time to waste. He jumped into his BMW and headed for Georgetown.

As he approached the Capitol Building, he ran into traffic. There was some midnight vigil or demonstration. *Fucking radicals,* thought Simon, clenching his fist as he sat in lines of traffic watching Washington riot police, dressed in full robocop garb, attempt to break up the crowd. The protesters were marching about ending U.S. occupation in Iraq.

Why couldn't these people just go find jobs like the rest of us? Let the government do its job, for fuck sake. Simon laid on his horn, but it was useless. He could do nothing but watch and wait for the cops to evacuate the protestors.

He switched on the radio and flipped through channels, settling on business news. The lead story was on ITA. He turned up the volume. The announcer was talking about the *Wall Street Tribune* piece and how ITA's stock had made an amazing rebound a day after dragging the markets down.

It had recovered half of its lost value. As ITA's prime banker, Silverman's stock had taken a hit as well, but a more modest one, and was now on its way to full recovery.

That's the kind of thing that happens, Simon thought, *especially in the summer when trading volume is light. The slightest piece of bad or good news can make the markets go crazy. Exaggerating moves that would be less dramatic during a more active time of the year.*

Either way, their stock was still down. That had to hurt. *On paper.* Simon wondered if that little Silverman-ITA contract was struck in cash, not stock. If it involved stock, it was now worth eight percent less than a billion dollars. He extracted the contract from his breast pocket and studied. It was in stock.

* * *

When Simon pulled into Dumbarton Street, there were no available parking places. *Perfect*, he thought. He considered double parking, but was especially protective of this latest automobile purchase and didn't want to risk his Beamer getting towed. Nor did he want to spend the time tracking it down. D.C. was crawling with cops, many of whom disliked those who could afford the best cars. Hence, they were the cars that usually got towed first. He didn't feel like dealing with that tonight.

Instead, he circled around for another twenty minutes before securing a spot four blocks away. He had called Janet several times from his car on the drive over, but got no answer. This only served to stroke his paranoia. Kevin was clearly not going to be in contact with him, and Janet wasn't answering his calls on her home or cell phone.

Typical, he thought, *she had no problem speaking to me this morning and throughout the day, when she was looking for her precious husband. She has a young daughter, for God sakes, where the hell could she be this late at night?*

He parked across the street from the Waters' home. After looking up and down the street, he crossed to their front door.

Simon's entire body was clenched and dripping. He knew that the Silverman-ITA contract was the culmination of other prior negotiations that had to have a paper trail somewhere. He assumed the document had something to do with Kevin's disappearance. He just didn't know what. He found nothing else suspicious on Kevin's work computer. Now he'd check his home PC.

He'd deal with Janet. Maybe convince her to take a walk or something, while he searched her husband's study. Or tell her that he heard from Kevin that morning, that he was hot on a corporation's tail. That he took the latest flight out last night to the West Coast and didn't have time to get in touch. He was sorry and had asked Simon to go over and check on her and hoped she'd understand. Or some such bullshit. He knew Janet wouldn't buy it, though. Hell, he wouldn't buy it either.

He ascended the three steps to their front door and pressed the buzzer. And waited. There was no answer. As he buzzed again, he strained to hear inside noises. Peering through the living room window, he saw only the sky-blue curtains, completely shut.

Now where the hell could she be? he wondered again.

CHAPTER 32

As Sharon stepped out of the cab and onto the curb, the skies opened with a torrential late summer shower. Damon was sitting on her front stoop. As she dashed through the swirling rain, she could see that Damon wasn't happy. Roger's death, the conversation with Kevin, the Enforcer Unit. These had pushed all thoughts about WorldWell Bank to the back of her mind. But she was convinced there had to be some link. She just needed to think it through.

He rose to greet her. "You had better have a damn good explanation for this, Thomas."

She gave him a kiss on the cheek and a brief hug. "Boy, do I," she replied.

"Good, 'cause this," he gestured to the pizza box, his eyes twinkling, "is very cold, my friend."

Sharon clutched Kevin's folder of documents close to her chest, having slipped it beneath her blouse to protect it from the storm. The clouds flashed bolts of lightning, followed by thunder, emitting a heavier, solid sheet of rain. Damon held the pizza box over their heads as a shield. They were drenched in the time it took for Sharon to dig out her keys and unlock the front door.

"Let me edit that," Damon amended. "Very cold. And very wet."

Sharon didn't know how long she could keep events of the past hour away from Damon. Upstairs in her apartment, Sharon removed the folder and casually slid it beneath a stack of business magazines on her desk. Meanwhile, Damon dried off in the bathroom.

She didn't know where to begin with him or what to tell him. It was good to see him. And when she kissed him, he placed his free hand around her waist, part hello, part like it belonged there. The physical sensation it evoked startled her. The pizza hadn't been the only thing getting wet. She sniffed the air. A rather erotic male cologne had followed Damon in.

Then she looked down at her hands that were still shaking, and thoughts about Damon were replaced by those from her earlier game of car dodge.

Her mind was all over the place. She had to re-examine the brute's role in all this, the same giant oaf now trying to kill or scare both her and Kevin Waters. And the role of whoever was sending him out. Or maybe the brute was after Kevin the whole time, not her. Maybe her trail belonged to Kevin? But how did ITA and the brute fit into the work of the enforcers?

The trail? The fee trail? Enforcers? Corpses? Where did it all begin? *Look beneath the surface.*

Damon emerged from the bathroom drying his hair with a towel. He was wearing an old gree "Ralph Nader for President" T-shirt, the biggest article of clothing she had been able to find. It fit him tightly, revealing arms more defined and muscular than Sharon had expected. Her eyes fixed to his upper chest and outline of his biceps.

"Hey there," he pirouetted, "how do I look?"

Like a radical," she answered, noting his flat stomach and runner's build.

"Thank you. Now, you must do two things. First, tell me why you almost stood me up in the pouring rain, and second, get out of those sopping clothes. Actually, maybe reverse the order."

Sharon thought talking about Mickey was the safest thing

to start with. It wouldn't exactly explain why she was late, but it would focus the conversation away from the other subject. As for the clothes, she glanced at him with a glimmer of flirtation. Then quickly looked away.

"Can I get you a drink with that cold pie?" She opened her refrigerator.

"Sure. What do you have?" He followed to the kitchen bar and took a stool.

"Diet Coke? Or wine, same kind as the other night?"

"Wine's good."

"Okay," she said, uncorking a bottle and pouring two glasses over the counter.

Their fingers touched briefly as she handed him a glass. The pizza remained on the counter. "Maybe I should heat it up?" she said, motioning to the wet box.

"Heat what up?"

"The pizza, Damon." She turned on the oven and inserted the pie in two halves.

"Sure. So, about your evening?"

She sighed. "Let's sit down for this, okay?" She walked over to the sofa and seated herself on the corner, one leg bent and crossed at the knee, the other dangling. She had removed her wet stockings, but hadn't changed out of her damp blouse. The folder was too important to leave alone, but she couldn't risk Damon noticing if she tried to move it somewhere else.

Damon sat down on the other end of the couch, facing her. Their arms draped over the couch's back, their fingers inches away. She began by recounting her first job, the legend of Mickey Mancuso that had once permeated the Street, in the 1980s, his move to Silverman, his slow destruction by Sam Peterson. She painted him larger than life because, well, he was.

Damon sat mesmerized by her story, by the way she told it, her passion, her animation, her experiences. It scared him. It seemed that he could never be that directly inspired by his life. He tried: with stories, with his marriage. But he just couldn't get there.

Sharon always seemed enraptured by everything, positive or negative. This Mickey fellow and her years with him were no exception. Sharon had never really talked about him before. When she and Damon first met and she pitched her first story about a corrupt former client, she offered minimal description of her Wall Street background. Frankly, he wasn't very interested. But he was interested in the story and offered her the opportunity. He edited her writing heavily when she submitted it, but was impressed with her attention to detail; her use of financials surpassed that of any other business reporter he knew of, including, he had to admit, himself.

She stopped and faced him. "Are you listening to me, Damon?"

"I'm listening to everything, I am."

"Okay, well, so that's why I was late," she lied.

"What?"

"Because we were talking about old times—you know the times where everything was possible, where everything was immediate, good or bad." *Before you had to worry about what things actually meant.*

"It isn't like that now?"

"I don't know. I just mean that those were really good times. You'd like Mickey. He's warm. Smart. A real character."

"I'm sure I would, if you say so."

"I say so."

Their finger tips were touching now. Both of them were aware of the heat tingling through them and butterflies in their stomachs. Neither moved their hand away. Sharon needed the moment to take a break from the mounting surprises, from the feeling of something deeply sinister engulfing her. Damon needed the moment to remind him that he was human. That he might have screwed up his marriage and caused his wife to stray. But that despite all that, he could still feel.

The moment was interrupted by the phone ringing. Sharon jumped. It rang once. Twice. Sharon glanced over. She didn't want to answer. Because she had been quite comfortable exactly where she was. Because she was scared.

The third ring killed the mood. "Aren't you going to answer that?" asked Damon.

The fourth ring. She had promised herself she'd use her mike to record the next intrusive call from the voice. That would involve explaining. She wasn't ready. "Uh, no, that's okay, I don't have to..."

The fifth ring.

The sixth.

"Well, maybe..." She hesitated to grab the phone.

Her voice mail picked up as the ringing stopped. She kicked the phone table leg, "Dammit!"

"Are you okay?"

"I'm fine. There's this prank caller. He's been bugging me the last few nights. Kind of creeps me out; probably some kid with nothing better to do."

She checked the kitchen clock. It was almost midnight. "It's getting late," she said. "I have to hit Silverman at a ridiculous hour tomorrow morning."

"We haven't had the pizza yet—smell that fresh re-heated scent," he said, exaggerating a sniff. "Plus, you haven't told me what happened at Silverman today, and if you found anything worth digging into yet."

"Okay, one slice and some recounting," she agreed, smoothing her blouse and taking the pizza out of the oven. "Then I gotta get some sleep."

"Makes sense. Banker's hours. Sorry about that," He hadn't move off the couch.

"Yeah, that certainly was your doing." She placed their paper plates on the coffee table in front of the couch. Her shoulder grazed his.

CHAPTER 33

Simon stood at the Waters' front door, waiting for someone to answer. He was already irritated from the ride over. By the time he finished tangling with the awful combination of any-hour D.C. traffic and worthless protestors, Simon couldn't keep his breathing even.

On top of that, he had the sinking feeling that his best friend was screwing him over. What else could explain Kevin's complete disappearance and the $1 billion contract that only he seemed to have access to? The last thing Simon needed was the vice president thinking he wasn't fit to keep tabs on the operation.

He hated being put upon. He hated when others had the upper hand. It was particularly annoying with Kevin. Throughout law school, Simon was propelled by two things. The first was to earn his father's respect, or at least his support. The second, to get better grades than Kevin, who reminded him of his could-do-no-wrong brother. He had always been inferior to his older brother, now one of the country's leading international trial lawyers, following in Dad's footsteps.

When Simon was selected by the vice president to lead the enforcers, his father had barely reacted. All he offered Simon was a lukewarm, "Congratulations, but is being involved in a regulatory agency that challenging?"

Thanks, Dad, thought Simon. *Thanks a whole fucking lot.* Simon realized he couldn't begin to explain the magnitude of his role to his father. He had sworn most of it to secrecy as per the vice president's wishes. But if he only knew the importance, the influence, the power that his son wielded. Then—maybe— he'd register a modicum of pride.

At least the vice president had faith in him. *Take that, Dad. If you only knew.*

Shrugging off his internal demons, Simon contemplated entering the house. He didn't like the idea of entering without permission, though he had no problems justifying far greater transgressions. But breaking and entering seemed too gauche, beneath someone of his stature.

Nevertheless, he had to know what Kevin had on his home computer. He knew the alarm code to the Waters' home. Kevin gave it to him when they first moved in, in case of emergency. *Well*, thought Simon, *we seem to have ourselves a little emergency here.* He punched the code into the alarm. No response.

Simon realized the security system was already disabled. All he could think was that wherever the Waters had gone, they had left in a hurry. Kevin trusted enough of the neighborhood and regular brigade of cops that passed through it to leave without setting the alarm. But Janet was too hysterical to do the same, no matter what the circumstances. The woman checked every door of her SUV individually even after she power-locked it, every time.

Simon concluded that they were probably off trying to figure out how to spend *his* fee money. He tried the door handle. It was locked. He extracted his set of keys, fingering the one that belonged to the Waters' home.

He inserted the appropriate key in the lock, turned the knob, and slipped open the door. He stood still, listening for sounds. Maybe of the couple and their daughter upstairs, not having heard his thirty-odd buzzes at the front door. He heard nothing. He turned on the light with the nearest switch and shut the front door behind him.

Actually, he thought, this was kind of perfect. A free ride into the house. He tiptoed toward his best friend's study. He didn't know exactly what he was looking for, but reasoned that it would be on or near Kevin's computer. He sat himself behind Kevin's desk and powered the computer on. All the enforcers had computers with the same security devices as the ones at the SEC building. This meant that the password was a thumbprint, and Simon had the master thumb.

He pressed it to the screen. Then, he started digging. For over an hour, Simon penetrated the deepest corners of Kevin's cyber and file worlds. What he found surprised even him. Kevin knew far more than Simon thought. Or that Simon himself was aware of. Simon had a newfound respect for his best friend, even as his anger and jealousy swelled. In a very quiet, methodical, and organized fashion, Kevin had pieced together a puzzle far larger than Simon could ever have done. And all the while maintained his regular work load. Engaged in normal relationships with his colleagues. Without a hitch.

Simon was engrossed in his findings. The silence of the Waters' home served as a cover for his inspections. Every so often, he paused to wonder where Kevin was. He looked over his shoulder, growing more certain that Kevin was alive somewhere. He just didn't know where. Nor did he know where Janet was. He popped a flash-drive into the side of the computer.

Simon began copying the puzzle of files onto the tiny flash-drive. Some were located in folders with monikers that began with the word "stuff": stuff01, stuff02, and on and on. Simon shook his head. Everyone made one mistake, and this was Kevin's. Folders with non-descript labels like "stuff" were flashing red lights that screamed "Critical information in here!"

Simon was fishing around the "stuff15" folder when he stumbled upon the most important document of all. He went into the stuff15 directory, then into the sub-directory, and clicked on the one titled "TRAIL."

Kevin Waters, you idiot, he thought.

CHAPTER 34

Sharon could feel the skin on her arm tingle where it had touched Damon's. She dismissed the sensation as soon as she distinguished it, and changed the subject. "So, how did you get Katrina to let me back in, again?"

"She owed me one," Damon said tersely.

"Why?" asked Sharon

"Hey, reporter, what's with the barrage?" He shifted upward on the couch and reached for the slice.

"Just curious. She's poisonous, you know. And she's got a lot of enemies."

"I'm aware of her reputation, Sharon. I'm the one who did that cover you called fluff."

"Yeah. *Vanity Fair* meets high finance."

"Everyone wanted a piece of her at the time." He folded his slice and took a large bite.

"I remember. I was there. Inside Silverman. The word was she needed the positive PR to up her deal fees. Star quality isn't a usual trait of investment bankers."

Damon took another bite. "It's getting late. Let's fast forward to today. What's happening in there, since the *Wall Street Tribune* piece? And all the WorldWell stuff?"

"I don't know yet," she answered. "Unfortunately, I spent most of today in 'welcome-to-Silverman' red tape—human resources, internal meetings, same old shit that gets in the way of doing anything real. I got into their system though, extracted their tech company clients and current activities. I'm going to check the money flow for all these deals tomorrow, and then match it to money flow in and out of WorldWell based on their filings."

"What will that show?"

"Hopefully, the timelines of all the deals, so I can see when they happened and what money has slipped out around the edges. Particularly around the bank advisors."

"I'm impressed, Thomas. And what do you hope you'll find? I mean, what's your theory about the money flow? Who's hiding what?"

"Damon," Sharon responded, a glint in her eye, half-smile across her lips. "I'm shocked."

"About what?"

"I don't have a *theory*. I'll let the numbers talk. There are things we know. WorldWell Bank is loaning money to companies under the guise of trades, so neither WorldWell Bank nor the companies are accounting for them to the Federal Reserve or the IRS—you told me that the other night. Separately, I know that ITA fudged numbers around quarterly and annual reports, because I've followed those changes for years. Other companies are probably doing the same thing. Somehow it's all connected. Whether through WorldWell Bank, Silverman, or ITA, I'm gonna let the numbers talk," she repeated.

"You seem to have a plan, as always."

"Someone very wise taught me to have a plan and let the story unfold for itself."

"Who, Mickey?"

"No," she laughed. "You."

"Right, I remember. Our first meeting."

"Fifteen minutes in your office," she added.

"I didn't know you were listening that closely. You seemed to have your own ideas of how to do things."

"Still do, but I need advice along the way. Anyway," she stepped toward the door, "thanks for coming over, and for the pizza."

"Anytime," he replied, rising in response. "You think of cold pizza, you think of Damon Matthews."

"I will—promise," she said, grazing her thumb over her lips to wipe away any remnants of crust.

He stood opposite her, towering over her. The fragrance of his cologne permeated her nostrils. She opened the door. "Well, good night, then," she said quietly, her eyes fixed on his.

"Good night," he replied, leaning down. He kissed her left cheek. Then her right. Her hand gripped under his elbow, moving him closer to her. He pulled her gently but purposefully toward him, cupping her face in his hands. Their lips brushed.

They backed their heads away, eyes transfixed on each other's. The second kiss was a firm meeting of lips. Her head dipped slightly sideways into the warm of the palm of his hand cradling her cheekbone. Her breath quickened and she backed away slightly. "Damon," she whispered, "we shouldn't. You're my editor. We..."

Their third kiss was passionate. It felt like exploration. His tongue probing her mouth, melding with hers. Hers circling his, pressing herself closer into him. Sharon felt herself melting into Damon as she gripped the back of his head tighter, weaving her fingers into his thick brown hair. It had been a long time since she'd had this kind of a kiss. It was dangerous territory for her. She could have no romantic entanglements in her life.

The kiss continued into the early hours of the morning. As they undressed and found each other's bodies, their lips never stopped touching. An intense mixture of anxiety and emotion engulfed them as he entered her. He held her tightly in his arms; she wrapped her legs around his body. They each were spurred by a personal cocktail of internal cravings and even deeper demons. Passion and fear. And guilt.

CHAPTER 35

By the time Kevin reached his Georgetown home, it was well past two in the morning. There were no lights on in the house. Nor shining from any of the other houses on Dumbarton Street.

Before he reached his front steps, he noticed copper-colored spots along the walkway. They speckled the grey cement that outlined each pale red brick. He knelt down to get a closer look. Patting the grout with his fingers, his heart skipped a beat. They were droplets of human blood. He clutched his stomach. He stumbled to his feet like a weightlifter trying to straighten his legs under an over-the-limit load.

No, no, he thought. *Not Janet!* Then he was assailed by a more sickening possibility. His throat constricted. His mouth went dry. His beautiful daughter. *Oh my God, Britney!*

He should have left it all alone. What was he thinking? You can't mess with the vice president and come out the winner. He should have kept his head down. Did his job. *Janet!* He quickly punched in his home security code, willing his trembling fingers to hit the right numbers. The disarmed alarm system was the second clue that things weren't in order.

The door pushed open too easily. It was barely leaning against the frame. That was the third clue. He rushed through the door and switched on the hallway light. What he saw in front of him stopped his heart. And sent a flood of chills through his spine.

He gasped at the war zone before him. Blood was splattered all over the living room carpet, the murky maroon accentuated against the plush cream. His chest heaved in its cavity. He couldn't breathe. He saw that the trail of blood came from his study. He raced toward it. His body was moving for him, on behalf of his frozen mind.

The shock of the room's condition ripped through his gut. He had never seen anything like it. The blue curtains behind his desk were a collage of hideous fall colors, muddy browns, damaged reds, decayed oranges. He stepped towards the center of the chaos, his desk. The tiny hairs on the back of his neck stood in nervous attention.

On his desk was a pool of sticky, brick-red blood. The hard drive under his desk was knocked on its side. The place reeked—a combination of human damp and iron-tin. He stumbled around the room in the slow motion of a vivid nightmare, hoping he would wake up and everything would be in its rightful place. That's all he had ever wanted.

Kevin doubled over, staggered by the smell of death and thoughts of Janet. Her body wasn't in the study. *Who did this? Where is she?!* Frantically, he ran in and out of the downstairs rooms. He had to find Janet. And Britney. He checked the kitchen, the closets, and returned to the study. Besides the copious amounts of blood, there were no signs of anyone around. *What had he done? And for what?*

Enough was enough. *I have to call the police*, he thought as he raced toward the steps, too clean in contrast to the rest of the place. He tripped up the steps, his legs moving faster than his brain. His coordination was off. As he dug into his pocket for the back-up cell phone, he heard a muted knocking coming from upstairs.

He stopped everything. He heard it again. A faint thud. *Janet? Britney?* He dashed up the stairs. The first room at the top of the steps was Britney's. It was a mesh of bright pinks and purples. Stuffed animals and dolls. A happy room for a sweet child. The room was untouched and empty. *He would never forgive himself.*

He heard the thumping once more. It sounded like it was coming from the bedroom. Was the killer still in the house? No, he wouldn't give that kind of a warning. *Janet. God, please.* He didn't know what to pray for anymore. On the off-chance this was some kind of trap, he moved carefully toward the bedroom and slowly opened the leaning door. He switched on the light. The bedroom was untouched.

He heard the thumping again. It was coming from the master bathroom. He sprinted to the bathroom door, yelling his wife's name.

*   *   *

She had been sitting at a round iron table in the food concourse of Tysons Center, a Virginia shopping mall. Just far enough outside the jurisdiction of the D.C. police. Janet sipped a mocha frappuccino opposite her husband. He warned her that her life was in danger. He told her that she would have to leave their home for the time being. He nervously peered around his shoulder as he spoke. As if someone was stalking him. As if he might have to bolt any minute.

She could stay with her mother in North Carolina, he told her, though that would probably just be a temporary measure. Britney could be taken there, too. Kevin told her how to make those arrangements. She was not to use her cell phone for any of it. She was not to use anything in their house to communicate with: not email, not the land-line phone, nothing.

"What's going on Kevin?" she pressed. "What are you involved in? What kind of trouble are you in?"

"Honey, I wish I could tell you more. I just can't right now. You've got to trust me. Please, I love you. I'm doing the right thing."

Janet was quiet, gripped by an overwhelming suspicion.

"I love you, too," she told him, almost inaudibly, not sure if she still meant it.

Janet wasn't sure if she believed her husband. She believed this was a dangerous situation. That much was obvious from his temporary disappearance. She knew it was big, but if only Kevin had confided in her about what was really going on. If she only could keep her faith in him.

"Please, believe me. This will all be over soon. Everything will be back to normal soon," he said, but she wasn't sure that he meant it.

Still, she nodded a faint-hearted yes. She would do as he asked. For Britney. For now. She would re-group mentally at her mother's. She looked deep into her husband's eyes, searching for a sign, hoping that he would tell her what was really going on.

"Okay, then," he said, pecking her cheek. "I have to go now. I love you."

"Will you call me?"

"I can't call you, for a while. But I'll keep in touch. I promise." *He placed his hands on her shoulders.*

"Okay," she said, but it was most definitely not okay. Suddenly, she couldn't breathe. She was gasping for air. She couldn't move. She was trapped. She had to escape. She had to break free. She...

Janet Waters awoke drenched with sweat, roused by shouts moving through her house. She didn't recognize her surroundings at first. As things came into focus, she realized that she was lying on the cold hard tiles of her bathroom floor.

Kevin shoved open the bathroom door and instantly sank to his knees. There she was. His beloved wife, bound by rope, with her mouth taped shut. It was both the happiest and most enraging sight he had ever seen. He leaned down to pick her up.

She tried to jerk free from the ropes binding her wrists and ankles, but couldn't pry them loose. She didn't recognize the hands of her husband slipping around her. She tried to scream, but couldn't. Her vision was blurry, too, like she'd been drugged before she fell asleep. Her tongue was dry. The cotton mouth was reminiscent of mornings after drinking binges.

Kevin gently peeled the duct tape from his wife's mouth. "Oh, Janet, I'm so sorry, about everything. he tried to calm her. "I love you so much!"

He squeezed her tightly. He still wasn't sure if she recognized him. Lying next to her was a pair of tiny nail scissors. Kevin realized that his wife must have tried to cut her way through the ropes. As he held her, Kevin untied the knots.

"Kevin." Her voice was scratchy. He untied her arms and she eagerly wrapped them around his body.

"Where's Britney?" he asked, his brain flicking through horrible scenarios, realizing his wife had been bound for— almost an entire day?

Janet's puffy red eyes struggled to full attention. Then she remembered dropping Britney off at the neighbor's yesterday, saying that she and Kevin were going through a rough patch, needed a bit of together time. Could she watch Britney for a few days?

"She's fine, Kevin. She's with Cathy."

He was relieved that Britney was safe and had not witnessed whatever transpired in the study. He gathered his wife closer to him. The two struggled to their feet together. There would be words, soon. Explanations. Both of them had processed thoughts of extreme loss, of the dread of living a life without the other, or not living at all. For now, the silence of relief would suffice as they clung to each other. He caressed her hair; she buried her head in his chest.

"I'm so sorry. I should have never kept any of this from you."

Their embrace was interrupted by the screaming sound of police sirens blaring through the quiet Georgetown night. Approaching. Screeching to a halt. Stopping at their house.

There hadn't been time yet for him to ask Janet what had happened downstairs, or to her. Now there certainly wasn't time. He could hear the police swarming through the open front door. The couple, arms entwined around other's waists, staggered down the stairs. Janet's steps were strained, her legs weak from the lack of movement.

Janet surveyed her living room. The trail of blood. The overturned easychair by the couch. What must have occurred while she was knocked out on her bathroom floor. She could barely stand. She buckled against her husband. The nausea streaming through her was overwhelming. She swallowed down the bile rising toward her mouth. She stifled a cough.

Two police officers stood at the base of the stairs. Kevin wasn't sure how to react. The state of their living room would require explanation. The policemen assessed the living room and study from where they stood. The burly red-headed one nodded to his partner, a heavy-set Hispanic man, who turned to Kevin.

"Kevin Waters?" he asked.

"Yes," he replied.

"You're under arrest for the murder of Simon Caldwell."

Kevin couldn't believe what he just heard. The blood was Simon's? Could Simon be dead? There was no body in his study. It was all too much. Too many people were dying. If Simon was really dead, it must all be blowing up sooner than he had thought. He gaped at the police officer. He had heard the words so many times: as a little boy when his father explained his job, on television, in the movies. But never *to* him. This couldn't be happening. "No, officer, you've got the wrong man."

"You have the right to remain silent. Anything you say may be used against you in a court of law..."

Kevin stopped listening. He looked hard at his wife. Her eyes implored him to make this all go away. Then a different look came across them. Of distrust. Could she be wondering if he was a murderer?

The officer separated him from his wife and cuffed him. He continued to protest as he was escorted toward the door.

The red-head approached Janet. "Officer O'Harris, ma'am. I'm deeply sorry. Truly, I am. But, you can't stay here. It would be a good idea for you to check into a hotel nearby. We're going to need to ask you some questions later. Meanwhile, don't talk to anyone, especially the press. We'll dispatch an investigation team here immediately to assess the situation. This place will be closed off."

Janet stared at him, heard his words, but couldn't make herself move or speak. *What is happening to my life?*

The dark-haired officer walked over to her. "Janet," the officer used her first name now, softly, lightly gripping her upper arm. "My name is Officer Rodriquez. I can understand how you must be feeling right now. I've got a squad car on its way. Some of my finest officers will escort you to the Patriot Hotel."

She nodded from a place far away, a place where the world wasn't losing its center.

"Do you want to put together some things to take with you—clothes, a toothbrush?" he continued.

She shook her head and whispered, "I'll take my purse." It was still hanging in its place around the stairway banister. *What just happened?* Memories of the intruder dangled in her head, blurry. She became aware of the burning in her wrists and ankles. Had Simon Caldwell been in her house? What had happened to her? She knew one thing for sure.

"Kevin didn't do this!" she screamed as the officer moved her husband through the door. "There was a man—a beard, he had a beard, he..." She held her arms up so they could see the rope burns around her wrists.

Officer O'Harris slowly held up two items. A wig and a beard. "Would this be the beard?"

Janet was silenced. She knew better than to say anything more at the moment. She understood what the sergeant was insinuating. Kevin could have been the man wearing the beard.

She felt the neighbors peeking through their curtains, watching her husband being dragged off by the police. She had to get away from here. She succumbed to their suggestion of the hotel. She had no choice.

It was the first time in her life she'd ridden in a squad car. And the only person she felt she could turn to was a woman in New York City she had never met. She ignored the officer's warning about talking to the press. On her way to the Patriot, she dialed all of Sharon Thomas's numbers. They all went to voice mail.

As soon as the cops dropped her at the Patriot, Janet succumbed to something else, the only thing that could help her now. She moved toward the mini-bar and poured a shot of Jack Daniels.

CHAPTER 36

Kevin spent a sleepless night at the D Street jail. Pacing his tiny holding cell, he prayed that Sharon was doing her part. That she was finding the evidence they needed. Tuesday was approaching quickly. Something was going to happen. He knew it. Time was playing wilder and wilder tricks. He was sitting in a jail cell accused of murder. His wife was stranded in some hotel. Exposed to the world, while he was out of contact with everyone.

Murder. In the better moments, if they could accurately be described as such, he told himself that whoever had killed Simon would be found. That the truth would come out. But what if it didn't? Janet would know something; she was probably there when it took place. But what if she didn't? And how could he protect her from where he was?

Poor Simon. While he was gathering the condemning data, Kevin came to understand that more sinister players operated above Simon. He was a pawn—a willing pawn to be sure, but no more than that. Or was he? Kevin now realized that Simon had been spying on him. His best friend. Correction: his dead best friend. And, more importantly, who turned on Simon? In his house? *Because whoever it was, was still out there.*

* * *

Sharon awoke in a puddle of cold sweat. She and Damon had eventually moved to her bed, where they remained entwined as they drifted from the intense haze of passion to the liquid warmth of sleep.

She didn't remember having any nightmares as she lay wrapped in his arms. Damon was still asleep, breathing quietly. She bent her head toward his and gently kissed his forehead, each of his eyelids, the tip of his narrow nose. Settling on his lips again, she parted them awake with the tip of her tongue. She wedged herself tight against his body. His erection was firm against her thigh.

Dawn slowly brightened the room. Her fuzzy feelings of post-coital, waking tenderness lasted precisely eight seconds. Unanswered questions and loose ends, temporarily evaded by the night's desire, hovered impatiently in the morning air. The enormity of the tasks ahead of her took over. She shot up in bed, causing Damon to almost roll over onto the floor.

"Morning," said Damon, his eyes brushing over her naked body.

"Morning, yourself." Sharon felt immediately self-conscious, not about her body, but about what to do next.

Her alarm clock said six a.m. She had to gather the documents Kevin gave her last night, make sure she took the Canadian cell phone, get to Trevor's to pick up the trail company list, and rush down to Wall Street in time for a seven o'clock sales meeting at Silverman. For starters.

Damon sat up and reached out his hand for hers. She wondered how she was supposed to act. She figured this wasn't a casual encounter, but knew she was ill-equipped to manage anything more than that. She didn't want to deal with the possibility of a real relationship.

She settled on the easiest route. Avoidance. "Uh, I have to get going."

"You should probably get dressed first," he responded. "I hear Silverman is pretty strict about that kind of thing—wearing clothes and all," he said, kissing the top of her shoulder.

"Very funny. I'm on it." She extracted a suit from her closet, a soft ruby color with thin pale grey stripes and a short-sleeve white blouse.

"I should probably be going, too," he replied, as his gaze settled on her ass.

Damon's glance followed Sharon out of the bedroom. He snuck out quietly while she was in the shower.

A few minutes later, Sharon towel-dried her hair as she walked into the bedroom. When she called out his name, Damon didn't respond. The comforter on the bed was folded over. On it she found a note:

"Have a good day. I'll call you later. xoxo, Damon."

Sharon didn't have time to analyze Damon's stealth departure. So she decided to shelve it, and headed toward Trevor's apartment. Knowing it was unlikely he'd be awake, she called several times on her way over. He didn't pick up. She imagined him cursing the phone from his futon, or incorporating the rings into some hazy, drug-induced dream.

When she knocked on his door, he opened it quickly, fully clothed. Or at least, fully clothed for Trevor. He was wearing nothing but tattered jeans and a wide grin. "Morning," he greeted her.

"Wow! You're wide awake."

"Ye of little faith," he twinkled. "So, how did that 'piece' you were working on last night go for ya?"

"No comment," she responded, a smile escaping.

Trevor picked up on her grin right away. "You hooked up! You dog, you!"

"There will be no discussing of—the piece—this morning," she said, eyes glittering. "I have the most boring meeting in the world to get to in a half an hour."

"Hey, no problem, Just making some morning conversation here."

"Thanks, Trev. Now, the trail, the companies." She extended her hand for his computer wizardry.

"Got it all right here, Share." He held up a disk and an envelope. "Fifty lines of the pseudo-8–K document matched uniquely to fifty tech companies. They were cross-checked with your old client list and with the latest Google news for each firm."

"You are the best!" exclaimed Sharon, taking it from him and turning to leave.

"Not so fast—there's something else I did for you."

"What?"

"I added a column for where they are all headquartered, so you could check out legal jurisdictions, or whatever it is you do."

"Good work, Sherlock. Let me guess: none are officially headquartered in the United States?"

"That would be correct."

She nodded. "Makes perfect sense; if you're going to move money around illegally, best to start as far away from the federal regulatory agencies and tax authorities as possible."

Beneath the surface. Sharon opened the envelope to inspect his list. The names were familiar.

"Yeah, they have to be all the firms dealing with ITA," said Trevor.

"Exactly—the same firms I'm going to find contracts for in Silverman's database today." Her plan was to uncover the dates of these contracts, which might help figure out when the money for them would be changing hands. And just how much money was involved.

"Have fun," said Trevor.

"This is fantastic. Thanks, Trev," she told him. "Oh, one more thing."

"Yes?"

"Were those characters on the end of each company line a code for the headquarter locations?"

"No, why?"

"I don't know, there's just a missing piece then, at the end of each line." She brushed her hair back off her face.

"Any ideas what it could be?"

She shook her head. "No. I'll think about it today, and let you know what else comes up," she answered, still examining the list of headquarters and company subsidiary locations. "Wait, this is odd."

"What's odd?"

"ITA, headquartered in Belize—I thought they were Bermuda."

"Maybe they wanted better beaches."

"As if anyone ever visits these places! Oh, God, Tuesday!" she exclaimed suddenly, remembering all that lay ahead of her. "I gotta go, Trev. Call you later." She dashed out of his apartment.

He called after her, "Wait, Share! You forgot your laptop!"

But by then she was on the curb hailing a cab downtown. Maybe all the pieces were falling into place. Forget WorldWell Bank. Maybe this list of companies doing secretive business with ITA was related to the enforcer fee ring. Belize. The timing of everything.

* * *

As he did every morning on his way to work from his Upper East Side penthouse, Sam Peterson checked his stock price. Early morning trading figures on his Blackberry indicated Silverman shares were up five points, or eight percent. Analysts were predicting even more positive movement throughout the day. Sam scrolled through the headlines.

There it was. The SEC had called off investigations into ITA's practices, no conclusive evidence of foul play. *Wall Street Tribune. Serves those journalist bastards right,* he thought smugly.

He breathed a sigh of relief and reclined in the back seat of his limo. Having friends in D.C. always came in handy. What an idiot Stark was to think he had anywhere near the same connections. His private cell phone rang just as he congratulated himself on averting the crisis.

"Yes?" he answered.

"We've got a problem, my dear friend," said the vice president.

When Sam finished the call, he re-directed his driver to the private strip at JFK airport. He called his secretary to make sure his plane would be fueled and ready. He was going to Washington.

* * *

By the time Sharon slipped into the sales meeting, she was ten minutes late. All eyes followed her entrance. *Come on, get a life, people, it's ten lousy minutes.* These sales meetings were always a complete waste of time anyway. Particularly today, when she had to get to D.C. and check in on the Waters. But she sensed that she had to make a show of being at Silverman to not raise undue scrutiny. She needed to keep her access. So she sat, bored out of her mind, as a parade of egos droned on about how great they were at manipulating their clients, all the while munching on bagels and cream cheese:

City Life Insurance is looking to buy a large chunk of the Microsoft deal for their bond portfolio. The New York State Pension Fund is looking to increase their derivatives exposure. They'll buy any crap we sell them. Etc. Etc.

As head of sales, Harvey Schwartzman ran the meetings while continuously checking his Blackberry and interrupting repeatedly to answer "crucial" cell phone calls. All designed to make him look more important. Sharon noticed he'd gained weight since she left Silverman. Tubby rolls were bulging from beneath his suit jacket. She scanned the room, at the salespeople seated around the cherry-wood conference table.

She wondered if anyone else noticed. Her eyes caught Nina's. Nina had to attend these meetings because she worked on the analytics behind the trades. When salespeople needed someone to explain numbers to their clients, they called on her.

Nina mock-stifled a yawn, and Sharon giggled softly. Sharon noticed tiny puddles of sweat emanating from Harvey's armpits. She nonchalantly placed her thumb under one of her own armpits to point this out to Nina. Nina laughed out loud. Harvey shot her an evil glare.

Sharon knew, from the look of disdain in Harvey's eyes, that he was not pleased she was back in his boardroom. She told herself not to let him bother her. This was temporary. She was there to get information and get the hell out.

Patience.

Like in Aikido, don't expend any more energy than you have to for any given situation. Don't let your enemy antagonize you. It will upset your focus.

Besides, there were other things to focus on this morning— like the trail, and the documents from Kevin waiting in her briefcase. She was itching to get to her office computer and dig into whatever Katrina had given her access to in Silverman's database. She had fifty names. Her gut told her that they all related to Belize somehow. And Tuesday. She had to find the company that would be easiest to intercept. And then figure out how the hell to do that.

* * *

While the morning sales meeting was in progress, Katrina Sullivan made a call to Ivan Stark.

"Hey, babe!" he answered Katrina's call joyfully.

"Do not call me babe," she replied.

"A slip of the tongue, my dear, won't happen again. It's just that I'm in a fucking great mood—ITA stock is up. And every newspaper has run the SEC press release stating our books are A-okay, no thanks to you."

"Or you, probably. Anyway, that's not why I'm calling. Are we set for next week?"

"Yeah, all systems are go. I'm looking forward to it."

"Excellent." Katrina hung up. A tingle of excitement swept through her. The titillation of anticipation. The expectation of winning. Within less than a week, she'd be sitting on top of the world.

CHAPTER 37

After the morning sales meeting, Sharon called Mickey from the internal phone in Silverman's lobby. Dozens of bankers were milling about, checking cell phones, Blackberries, running up the escalators from the cafeteria with paper trays of coffee and croissants.

"Hey, I'm going to Starbucks, can you get away?"

"Done," he responded.

At the Starbucks on Broad Street, Sharon ordered two double espressos and headed to a back table. It was not protocol for a banker to leave the Silverman tower during the day, except for a client meeting. It was like a daily jail sentence that way. No time out for good behavior.

As Mickey sat down, he wiped away beads of perspiration on his forehead with the heel of his hand. Sharon cut right to the chase. "Last night after we met, I got this call." She had received more than one call, but wasn't sure what to say about the nameless man yet.

"Go on."

"From Kevin Waters."

He leaned in. "And?"

"He drove up from D.C., said he worked for a group called the Enforcers Unit. Know anything about them?"

"Not exactly—well, sort of. Maybe. See, I know there have been corporate payoffs made to Washington through some new channels. I thought it was just pre-election campaign money."

"That's what I thought when he first mentioned it, but what's going down is much bigger. Kevin said that over $9 billion in payoffs have been circulated through the group this past year."

"Nine fucking billion dollars!" He sputtered out his coffee.

"My reaction, too. But these payoffs aren't made in D.C. for obvious reasons, like campaign contributions. They're made to buy preferential treatment and to kill direct competition. Kevin called them 'fees.'"

"Fuck-over fees," Mickey nodded.

"Basically. Thing is, there's no hard evidence of where these fees are getting paid, and how or where the money is switching hands."

"Offshore, I'm guessing," he said, scratching his head.

"Exactly. Kevin thinks some major transfer is taking place in Belize. This Tuesday. Maybe a payoff, maybe something else, he wasn't sure. He gave me this." She peered over her shoulder to make sure no one was watching them, extracted Kevin's folder from between another two, and slid it across the table.

Mickey flipped through the pages of documents, searching for something specific. "Bingo!"

"What?" asked Sharon. "Tell me you see something I don't. Aside from the fact that ITA seems to have re-incorporated in Belize, which in itself doesn't mean much. I'm not sure what's so unusual."

"Take a look at this, kiddo. Silverman to ITA. One billion dollars! Stock and cash payment."

Sharon examined the piece of damning paper upside down as Mickey scanned through it. It looked like a legitimate contract. "This is bizarre. Silverman contracted to pay ITA for network access to other tech companies. It's a huge fee from a bank to a company, but—what are you seeing that I'm not?" she asked.

"You've gone rusty."

"Well, it's not entirely illegal, is it?" she ventured.

Mickey smirked at her from behind his espresso. He knew she'd get it shortly.

She continued, "I mean—if ITA was paying Silverman for competitor information, that's okay. But how does it relate to fees paid to some subversive government group that's dictating corporate behavior?"

"Who did Kevin say runs this enforcer ring?" he prodded.

"The vice president."

Mickey grinned ear to ear.

"Oh my God, that's it!"

"You had me worried there, kiddo."

"Silverman! He's had a special relationship with the vice president forever."

"The ties that fucking bind."

Sharon was on a roll. "Silverman is the front company. Different corporations gather bunches of these fees together each time a large pay-off gets made. ITA is the cover to make it look legit, in case anyone notices or asks questions."

Look beneath the surface.

"Something like that," said Mickey. "This document probably gets filed with background material for Silverman's next quarterly financial report to the SEC. Becomes part of public record. After the fact."

"And, no one will check whether these networks come to fruition. That's beyond the scope of anything the government would ever bother to do."

"Right. Meanwhile, someone pockets a cut of a billion dollars from tech companies wanting to buy protection from investigators, through a bogus network contract, which gets exercised on..."

They scanned the document for a date. And there it was. Plain as day. Tuesday, August 22. Sharon examined the document more closely. Its business jargon passed for a normal network deal. It appeared as if Silverman was simply financing ITA, on behalf of its clients, to expand or build new networks. For a billion dollars. Something else jumped out at her. "Wow, look at this," she pointed to a paragraph on how financing was contingent on Silverman receiving a full analysis of the financial status of all involved companies.

"Guess I didn't give that bastard enough credit," said Mickey. "Not only is Silverman scooping up hush money from these bozos, ITA is handing their financials to Sam Peterson on a silver fucking platter."

"Getting a leg up on future business. Good way to keep ahead of WorldWell Bank."

Mickey scratched his head with his pinky, releasing a dust of dandruff. "I don't get it. Sam is on ITA's board. Why bother concocting some intricate contract if he can just ask Ivan for whatever he wants over drinks?"

"Maybe this contract is a smoke screen for something else." Sharon examined the document once more. The contract called for fifty mini-networks, each "financed" at $20 million a pop. It was corporate pocket change; no one would ever notice the money moving around. Then it hit her.

"Fifty. The same number of companies in the trail document!" she exclaimed.

"I'm going with you," Mickey announced decisively.

"With me, where?"

"To Belize. I'm not letting you go down there alone. Interception is a dangerous game."

"Mickey, I'll be fine. I know people down there."

"You drive a hard bargain, kiddo, but no."

"No?" she repeated.

"No, meaning no. A transfer this big—even broken up into bits—won't happen without solid shooters around. Not gonna let you do it. Period. No fucking way!" Mickey opened his cell phone and hit a button. "Yeah," he said into the receiver. "Can you do me for Monday. Yeah, uh-huh. South. Mexico."

"Mexico?" Sharon mouthed the word quizzically. Then, she realized Mickey was a step ahead. Belize City's airport was tiny. So was the airport on Ambergris Cay, where most people stayed while on business in Belize, because it was far more pleasant. Anyone watching would know about an extra plane coming in to land. A fast boat from the southeastern coast of Mexico would reach Belize in a matter of hours.

Mickey was suddenly agitated. "What? When? I'll be damned. No, thanks. Thanks. Later." He shut his cell.

"What is it?" she asked.

"Sam's on his way to Washington," he told her.

"It's gotta have something to do with all this."

"Fair bet. He was supposed to ring the opening bell for the stock exchange today in..." Mickey checked his watch, "... an hour. Sam doesn't miss opportunities to look important."

"Kevin said that enforcers who've tried to talk have disappeared, for good."

"Who's watching his ass?" asked Mickey.

"Nobody. I said I'd get to D.C. today, after making an appearance here. He was on his way to Janet, his wife." She quickly extracted the back-up cell Kevin had given her. "Hang on," she punched in his number.

"What's wrong, kiddo?" asked Mickey.

No answer. She punched in his number once more. "There's no answer. This isn't right." She stood up. "Mickey, I need to get to Washington, forget about how it looks to Silverman."

"I'll have the copter get you to the airport ASAP." The Wall Street helipad was a three-minute walk from Starbucks, off Pier 23.

"Thanks." She gathered the contract and stuffed it back into the folder.

"You okay, kid? Talk to me. Sam plays for keeps—so does the vice president," he warned.

She took a deep breath and paused, almost unable to voice the words. She held up the back-up cell. "I can't reach Kevin. I *need* to find him, Mickey."

"Of course you do," he soothed, smoothing an errant strand of hair off her forehead. He sensed the tone of responsibility in her voice. She had given her word. Not much to some people, but he knew what it meant to her. He was worried, but didn't tell her for fear it would be more of a burden to her. He knew these people didn't mess around, and wouldn't hesitate to kill.

"Mickey..." She paused, her forehead lines crinkling into the blues of her battered eye. "I'm scared."

He patted her shoulder as they left Starbucks in solidarity. If anything happened to Sharon—she was like a daughter to him..."I'll be watching your back this time, Thomas. I promise."

"Thanks. For everything." But she wasn't sure if even Mickey's words were comforting. Whatever was unfolding appeared to have a wider reach than even Mickey's enormous arms would be able to contain.

CHAPTER 38

Sharon arrived at the landing strip of Dulles Airport two hours after she left the Wall Street Starbucks, courtesy of Mickey Mancuso's private jet. She made numerous attempts to reach Kevin before take-off. All unsuccessful. She even had Mickey use his contacts to locate Kevin's private home phone number and address. No answer when she called there either.

She didn't want to think about what this could mean. Kevin had already been running scared the night before. Then the brute appeared out of nowhere shooting at them. Meaning whoever hired him had linked her and Kevin. Now Kevin was unreachable.

Enforcers who've tried to talk before have disappeared.

One of the benefits to flying private was that cars could meet you as soon as your feet hit tarmac. Mickey had one waiting for her fifty yards from where the plane touched down. She got in and headed toward the Waters' home in Georgetown.

But she never made it to the house.

Both ends of Dumbarton between Thirty-second and Thirty-first Streets were closed off, barricaded by a set of orange cones and flashing red warning lights. Her stomach sank. She thanked the driver and asked him to wait for her as near as he could. Jumping out of the car, she began walking along the sidewalk that fed into Dumbarton Street. On watery legs, she approached, but was immediately stopped by a policeman.

"Sorry, miss, only residents allowed in."

"I am a resident," she responded quickly.

"Can I see some ID?"

"Uh, I'm from New York. It's my sister, Janet," improvised Sharon. "I'm staying with her a few days. My name's Sharon, Sharon Thomas. Here," she showed him her license.

The officer inspected both sides of the card. She waited, hands wringing, until he handed it back to her.

"I'm sorry, Miss Thomas. I can't let you in."

"Please, sir, I totally understand, but my sister, Janet, Janet Waters—I really need to see her." She shot him a look of desperation, eye-to-eye, hoping he would read it as genuine.

"Wait right here for a moment," he said and walked over to his partner with Sharon's license. The officers conferred for a moment. The second one, a big bulky guy, approached her.

"You say you're Janet's sister, is that right?"

"Yes, sir." Sharon's eyes darted to the ground.

"From New York? You just *happen* to be here for a visit?"

"Alright, look, I'm not her sister, I'm..." She trailed off. Who should she be? A reporter? A banker? Neither would be helpful. This was no time for an identity crisis.

"Look, lady, whoever you are, you've got to move along. I can't let you in here."

"Please, Officer Lewis," she said, reading his badge. "I'm..." She chose the lesser of two evils for a cop. "...a reporter. Here." She extracted her press pass from her purse.

She waited for the abrupt dismissal.

"Hey, no kidding, a reporter? My son wants to be a journalist. He's always going on about the news, spends hours glued to CNN, writing stuff up in his room."

"That's terrific—it's a great job. How old is he?" She had lucked out.

"Thirteen—no, actually just celebrated his fourteenth. I'm losing track of my own children. Or getting old."

She smiled at him. "You don't look old at all, officer. Here's my card. If your son ever wants any tips or anything, tell him to call or email me."

"Thanks, I will. It's amazing how you people have a nose for the news as it breaks. Is that what brings you here to this mess, then? I was wondering why no reporters had shown up yet."

Sharon wondered the same. Someone was definitely keeping the press away. Someone powerful and influential.

"Yeah, it's awful, you know, here I am in D.C. covering— the protests—and this happens, right on this, this fabulously beautiful and wealthy street."

"Yeah, go figure," he responded. "When the rich screw things up, they go big,"

"Unbelievable, isn't it? I mean, the Waters were so...so... well, you know?" She was fishing for anything.

"Guess so. I've been doing this a long time. In the end, no matter who you were, you all bleed the same."

"Yeah, I only met Kevin once—old story. He seemed so nice, so young for this to happen to him. Tragic."

"It's always the nice guys that shoot from the closest range, so they don't need a second shot to kill."

"Shoot? Kill?" she strained.

"I'm not in the inner circle, but looks like Waters is going away for a long time. Don't quote me on that."

Sharon had been preparing for the knowledge that Kevin was hurt, maybe dead. She would meet his wife, Janet; tell her that her husband died because of his integrity. All he ever wanted was to do the right thing and protect his family. Officer Lewis' words threw everything into a confusing new light.

"Do they know when he did it?"

"Not sure, maybe late last night—they got him around two a.m."

Sharon guiltily recalled what she had been doing at two a.m. Kevin definitely would have gotten home by then, even with the rain. Could he have lied to her, caught a fellow conspirator in his home? Did a fight break out? Was he capable of murder? If his family was threatened. She had thought once that she wasn't capable. After the brute, she was no longer sure.

"Officer, is it okay if I just make my way toward their house, check out the scene for my editor?" She inched forward.

"I don't think they're letting anyone near there," he answered.

She thought she had made headway. She was growing desperate and fought back a forming tear.

"Hey," he relented, studying her face, "just doing my job."

"Sure, I understand," said Sharon. As the officer walked over to answer a squad car page, she turned and ran to number 1245. *And, I'm just doing mine.* The driveway, sidewalk, and lawn were swarming with cops. Yellow and black crime scene banners marked the front door.

A policeman whose badge read "Officer O'Harris" stopped her by the Waters' front walkway. "Hey, what are you doing here?"

She decided disclosing her newly formed connections might complicate her chances of finding out more. "Just covering a story," she answered. *This isn't going to happen.*

"Cover it later," said O'Harris, brushing her aside. "You can do your work after we've done ours."

"Okay, thanks, officer," said Sharon, relenting.

Yes, less was better. Besides, there was something else plaguing her. The police scene itself. She shuddered with memories and clutched her ribs. She shrugged the demons away, tried to focus on the next task. She was sure the cops had done so, but she had to get to Janet, ask her some questions, tell her it was going to be okay, because, it was, wasn't it? She left the crime scene and hurried toward the car waiting for her, almost knocking over another officer in the process. They caught each other's eye briefly before she bolted off.

CHAPTER 39

It didn't matter if it was the right thing to do. It was done. Irrevocably done. Julian picked at the remaining dried blood from beneath his fingernails, saw the brick-colored water swirl down the drain. He had been engrossed in this cleansing ritual since dumping Simon Caldwell's body in the Potomac early the previous morning. For hours that stretched into a full day. Periodically, the enormity of his situation acted like an invisible hammer, beating at his head, whacking him to the floor of his bathroom. He didn't even know if he should stay in his apartment, but he didn't feel safe outside.

And yet, he felt oddly smug. He had gotten rid of a weak link. Surely, the vice president would be proud of him. Fuck, Simon. *He didn't understand the importance of lineage. Simon might have gone to Harvard. The vice president might have been his godfather. But Julian's mother was born a Peterson. That made him the nephew of one of the richest men in the world, the CEO of Silverman and Sons, Sam Peterson. Blood runs thicker than titles. So does money. Old blood always wins.* Simon got what he deserved.

Julian vaguely remembered the moment that the ear-splitting pop shattered the air. He remembered staring, first at the revolver in his hands, smoking in acrid mist. Then, at the gory mess that had been his unit manager, Simon Caldwell. He had killed many an animal before on hunting expeditions with his dad automatically pulling the trigger when, just as now, adrenaline had taken over, but their thick hides relinquished blood much more slowly than the human flesh that wrapped the more delicate human bodies.

When the roaring faded from his ears he had blinked, unsure for a moment where he was. Then reality had slammed him like a physical blow: There he was, standing in Kevin Waters' home. In Kevin's study. *Having just killed a man in cold blood.* And there were no witnesses. *Who would know?* He had been wracking his mind for any other possible options but couldn't come up with any.

I am not going down because of Simon fucking Caldwell. Let Kevin be the fall guy. One call to 911 was all it took.

* * *

"911 Dispatch, what's the trouble?"

"Uh, I think I heard some loud yelling...men's voices...a gunshot...I think, I'm not sure."

"Sir, where?" asked the operator.

"Middle of the road, Dumbarton...I'm not sure, a few minutes ago." *Or an hour ago.*

"We're sending a police car over now. Can I have your name, sir?"

"Sure, it's..." and Julian clicked the payphone receiver to end his call. Then, he headed back to his car, so he could attend to the bloodied corpse in the trunk. He did not realize that someone, far more important than he was, made a few additional calls after Julian hung up the payphone.

* * *

Now, Julian had to ensure that no one ever found out what had transpired last night at the Waters' home. Before he disposed of Simon's body, Julian had contemplated turning himself in. But only for a nanosecond. *It was self-defense.* He could always use the self-defense angle, if they found the body and linked it to him. Julian had it all worked out. *If* he got caught. He imagined the conversation with the police:

"What happened that night, Julian?"

"I was scared. I had worked with Kevin for over a year. I loved the guy. I was just a devoted junior employee, involved in every project Kevin worked on. When Kevin didn't come into the office that day, I decided to drop off some paperwork at his home, to help him out."

"Why?"

"The two of us had been working together on the WorldWell Bank case. It was about to break. I thought he'd want more material. I was just trying to help."

"Any more revelations you'd like to share with us?

"I was shocked to find Simon there. Like a common thief, rummaging through Kevin's study."

"So, what did you do then?"

"Well, before I could ask him what he was doing, Simon pulled out a gun on me. I panicked. I tried to reason with him, I approached him, told him to put the gun down, but he wouldn't. There was a struggle. The gun went off. It was an accident. I was so scared. I never meant to harm anyone. Ever."

"And afterward?"

"Well, I can't remember exactly."

" Why didn't you call the police? An ambulance?"

"I don't know. It was like I entered temporary insanity."

"What about the body?

"All I could think of was getting rid of Simon's body. I was in shock. I freaked. I reacted the only way I knew how, the way I'd been taught for years—to lie, cover it up, and deny everything. Politics as usual."

But this would only be necessary if he got caught. It would be *much better if he didn't.*

Okay, so what really took place?

Only one person knew I had the keys and combination to the Waters' home: the vice president, who I would not let down. He gave me my mission himself months ago.

"Keep a copy of Kevin's keys. You will be back-up in case something happens to Simon Caldwell," said the vice president. Why he even bothered with Simon was always a mystery to me, but my uncle always said that it was important to let the expendable people do as much of your job as possible. It saved time and energy.

The vice president's instructions were clear, "Go get her, Julian. There's too much at stake here for a turncoat like Kevin in our ranks of enforcers. We need to put pressure on him to come out of his hiding.

"Good luck, son," the vice president had said during that face-to-face meeting. "I'm counting on you."

That's all he was planning on doing, really. From the phone taps they knew that Kevin's daughter was away at a neighbor's house. If Kevin was not there, he was to re-assess the situation. Take his wife. Leave a note. Then, all he would have to do is wait until Kevin caved.

Janet didn't recognize him. Julian was positive about that. He was wearing dark glasses, a false beard and mustache, and a raven-haired wig. He hadn't even recognized himself. He looked much better as a clean-shaven, blue-eyed, dirty-blonde.

The struggle was minimal. Janet was thin and weak. She backed away from the door when he entered. He approached her at the base of the stairs. He had his own gun. He told her not to make a sound. Then he covered her mouth with an ether-coated handkerchief. She passed out within seconds. He carried her upstairs

I was there to kidnap Kevin's wife, get her out of the way until the vice president gave me the 'all's clear' command. After tying her up and getting ready to cart her off, I heard someone downstairs. I

thought it was Kevin, so I left Janet in the bathroom and went to find out. It was Simon Caldwell, rummaging through Kevin's PC and desk. I certainly surprised him.

"What the hell are you doing here, Julian?" asked Simon.

"I might ask the same thing," I said calmly.

"Look, this doesn't concern you," said Simon, removing his gun from his back pocket, raising and pointing it at Julian.

"Oh, it concerns me more than it does you," I answered, pointing my own gun at Simon, knowing I would be the quicker shot if it came down to that.

"Look, I don't have time for this," said Simon, "that bastard Kevin double-crossed me, after all I did for him —and I'm going to find out how."

"You idiot," I told him, "and your petty issues." Then I fired.

* * *

Simon was now lying at the bottom of the Potomac with half his head blown off. Julian shuddered, not from picturing Simon's body, but from what could await him. He felt confident the vice president would not get involved. Not before the election. He was safe—for now.

Then he thought of Janet Waters. Of his original intent for being in the house. He had been given a directive straight from the vice president. Kevin was acting shady. He could not be trusted. *He could not be found.* He had ditched his BMW at Dulles. The cops couldn't find it. Enforcer cars were untraceable. So, Kevin had rented another one by Union Station. A white Ford Taurus. Kevin was smart, the vice president had told him. He had removed and replaced the license plates. That, and the fact that the car was the most prevalent in the country, made tracking him down harder.

* * *

Not that he meant to kill Simon. Julian was not a killer. Of ducks and deer, maybe. He tried to calm his mind and remember the many hunting trips in central Texas on the grounds of his uncle's ranch. The vice president and Wall Street power broker, Sam Peterson, would let him in the helicopter to better spot game. He shot while they discussed business. Shooting animals was legal. Shooting a human was a totally different story.

It was Kevin's home. It was Kevin's gun, he reminded himself in order to steady his nerves and thought about the prior night again. He had fucked that up, too. His instructions were to kidnap Janet, but he chickened out at the idea of forcibly removing her from the house. *What if someone saw him?* Instead, he tied her up and locked her in the upstairs bathroom. That way, he could go through Kevin's study in peace, allow some time to go by during which the neighbors would all be asleep, and slip out into the night with her, undetected.

Why the hell did Simon have to show up? He cursed himself for not answering that page from Simon earlier in the night. Maybe it had been Simon telling him what he was planning.

NO! No! Simon never told him anything. It was Simon's own fault he showed up at the wrong time!

Julian checked his watch. 5:00 a.m. Three hours ago, he watched the cops escort Kevin from his home. Ten minutes later, Janet slumped into her SUV and turned right on Thirty-third Street, probably to the Patriot Hotel. Damn that bitch! She was more proof that he had failed in his objective to do what was asked of him. Two minutes after that a veritable department of cops descended on the Waters' home, blocking the site off. Beginning their investigation. That felt good. *They were building their case against Kevin. Because of my work.*

He had to tell the vice president what had happened. He'd be so impressed. And, the vice president would make sure that Kevin wouldn't stand trial for anything, either. That was too risky. Kevin might expose too much. So, he would be taken care of by a professional, as planned. *An unfortunate accident of some kind. Jail can be a harsh place.* In the meantime, someone would have to get to Janet. That part would be easier. She loved her little girl. Yes, he couldn't wait to tell the vice president what he had done. Julian continued scraping his hands as he considered Kevin's fate, and Simon's, and his own. The skin around his fingernails was reddened, chafed, and raw. His nails finally looked clean, but he kept going.

CHAPTER 40

Sharon instructed Mickey's driver to take her to the nearest hotel, the Georgetown Inn. As quickly as possible. *Unless Janet was staying with friends, she'd be staying at a nearby hotel.* The hunch was correct. Her choice of hotel wasn't. Same luck with the Four Seasons. It was the third hotel she tried that did the trick. At the front desk of the Patriot Hotel, she asked for Janet Waters' room. The clerk refused to provide her the number. Security risk.

"Please, sir, can you dial her for me then?" asked Sharon, flirting.

"That I can do, miss," he responded and dialed while smiling at her. Sharon leaned forward, showing some cleavage and watching his fingers. Eight-something-something, as far as she could see, without straining forward too obviously.

He let it ring for a long while. "Sorry, miss, there doesn't seem to be anyone in the room."

"No problem, thanks anyway. I'll just wait in the lobby until she returns."

"You'll certainly be adding to the décor," he smiled.

Sharon walked away, as if to take a seat on one of the lobby couches. She watched the reception desk until the clerk turned his attention to the next person checking in. She dashed to the elevators and pressed the eighth floor button.

The doors opened to a ruby paisley carpet and cherry-wood doors. The clerk had pressed the second digit twice. The room had to be 800, 811, 822, or 833.

Room 800 was opened by a chamber maid who didn't speak English. There was no answer to her knock at room 811. At room 822, more of the same. Sharon pressed her ear to the door, listening for any sounds. She thought she detected a low whimpering, muffled sobs. She knocked on the door more loudly, hoping she was right.

"Please, Janet, it's Sharon Thomas. I need to talk to you, I—I saw Kevin last night."

A slender blonde woman, her eyes puffy and red, opened the door. The two women embraced like long-lost sisters.

"Look, I can't even imagine what must be going through your head right now, Janet, but we need to help each other. To help Kevin," said Sharon.

"I don't know what's going on," Janet slurred.

Sharon tried to look reassuring, though she knew Janet had no reason to feel reassured.

"In the past forty-eight hours," Janet continued, seemingly bolstered by Sharon's presence, "my husband disappeared, then returned for ten minutes to tell me we were in danger, then I got drugged and bound on my bathroom floor, and then someone was shot in my study. Kevin's been carted away for murder, probably stuck in some shitty prison cell as we speak. It's too bizarre!"

Sharon detected the alcohol coating Janet's breath. "I know. I was with Kevin." She took a couple steps into the room. She could smell alcohol emanating throughout. Glancing over at the mini bar, she spotted a collection of tiny empty bottles strewn on the floor beside it.

"What? You were with my husband?" Sharon saw the color drain from Janet's cheeks as she processed that information before erupting, "Get out of here!" screamed Janet. "Just get the hell out! I don't need your...help!"

"Look, Janet," Sharon tried to soothe, "I'm so sorry about what's happening, but there are reasons. Please, we need to get your husband out of jail, where he'll be safer, and piece things together."

"How do you know my husband?" Janet asked, instantly calmer, more resigned.

"I met him last night. He came to me with some information about his job, thought I could help uncover some things. That's why he left you my name, he said in case..."

Janet collapsed to the floor in wrenching sobs. "And now he's sitting in prison, for having murdered his best friend."

"Do you have any idea who gagged you?" asked Sharon, who was having difficulty connecting Kevin's description of Simon with the fact he was now dead. It didn't seem to her that Simon was someone who'd be a whistleblower, unlike the other enforcers who had been murdered.

"I don't know." Janet shivered, reaching for a Kleenex. "It happened so fast—I thought it was Kevin returning. I never should have opened the door, I never..."

"Hey, you couldn't have known," comforted Sharon. She'd been through her own agonizing *I never should have's. I never should have walked down that block. I never should have let that child die.* "Did you notice anything at all about this man?"

Janet shook her head. "No, he was young, nervous. He had white gloves on. A red beard that the cops found outside. I can't remember anything else." She burst out crying.

At that moment, there was a loud knock at the door. "Police."

"Oh God, I can't take any more questions," cried Janet. "Make them go away."

Sharon opened the door. Standing in front of her was the same officer she had exchanged looks with outside the Waters' home. "Ma'am, I'm Officer O'Harris. Just checking to make sure she was okay." He pointed to Janet.

"Okay is relative," replied Sharon, slightly hostile. This seemed a bit beyond regular police procedure as she knew it.

He peered around Sharon. "Mrs. Waters? How are you holding up?"

"Fine. I don't know. When can I see my husband?" she asked.

"I'll make sure you see him this afternoon," said Officer O'Harris. He was being nicer to her than he had been when he barged into her home to cart Kevin away. "I know this is really hard for you. I'll take you there myself, and maybe we can ask you some more questions then."

She nodded, rubbing her eyes with a Kleenex.

"Are you okay with *her*?" he pointed to Sharon, recognizing her as having busted into the crime scene earlier.

"Yeah, fine, she's a good friend of mine," said Janet, earnest enough to convince him.

"Great, you shouldn't be alone. Well, I'll be back later. Goodbye for now."

"Goodbye, officer."

Sharon shut the door as he left. Janet had been digging for something in her purse while he was there.

"There's something else," Janet said. "Kevin left this next to the file with your name on it." She held up a miniature cassette. "I haven't listened to it yet."

Sharon took it from Janet's fingers. "Let's listen to it together."

"Sure." Janet half-smiled, and Sharon inserted the cassette into her microcassette recorder.

"Ivan, we've got to discuss these books," said a cultured woman's voice.

Sharon's blood curdled at the mention of the person who could only be Ivan Stark, CEO of ITA.

"What's to discuss?" he replied. "Your figures are impeccably constructed, and once this IPO happens, my darling, you and I will be rich beyond our wildest dreams."

Janet looked at Sharon, confused. Sharon knew she couldn't explain what she was hearing. At least not yet. She placed a hand on Janet's knee—all the comfort she could muster as her mind spun—and returned her attention to the tape.

"But the numbers are fake—you know that," said the woman's voice.

"I know that the numbers are a realistic depiction of where this market can go," he countered.

"And fake. Look Ivan, for one, maybe two, maybe even twenty acquisitions, you could argue revenues will skyrocket once they are a part of ITA—but all of them?"

"Do you have any idea how many banks are desperate to get this IPO business? To get a piece of the biggest fucking rocket to shoot out of Wall Street in years?"

"I do, Ivan, that's exactly why I'm warning you to be careful. Once you go public, it's a whole new ballgame, everyone will get to take a look and—"

He stopped her mid-sentence. "Everyone will see a huge fucking success. The books scream money."

"Yes, that's my point, they scream money being fabricated, and I—"

"You what?" he yelled back. "You will not ruin this once-in-a-lifetime shot at everything!"

"You're playing with fire here, Ivan, I ran the comparison reports today. The Wall Street report is higher by two billion in revenue. ITA only makes 2.6 billion to begin with. It's totally out of whack."

"So the fuck what? The acquired companies don't exist anymore, who's to say they weren't going to make more money when I bought them? Maybe," he seethed, *"maybe that's why I fucking bought them!"*

"Ivan, all I'm saying is that once you are public, the SEC gets to see these books, so do the analysts, the reporters...Someone is going to notice they don't match reality and..."

"You're giving me a fucking headache. That's why you are keeping two sets of books, right? The SEC gets one, and the Street gets one. As far as reporters, I don't give a fuck. It's simple. A child could do it."

"Exactly, a child could do the comparison and see the wide gap between the two."

"No, because a child is not going to rip apart consolidated reports that now represent like eighty smaller acquired companies and figure anything out. And, if anyone does even ask a vaguely related question, we will adjust our figures accordingly for the next quarterly earnings we give out. It's really simple."

"Ivan, it's fraud!" the woman screeched. *"It's a felony! You're borrowing billions of dollars on the back of non-existent revenues, and your IPO is going to shed light on all of them."*

He took a deep breath. *"Sweetie,"* he said quietly, *"I hate to see you this worked up. I know you are concerned, but trust me, things will be fine. Once we really start pumping profits in, no one will even bother to figure out how. Please, stay with me on this."*

"I just...this is getting too dangerous. Aside from regulators, if Damon, or any good reporter, even gets a whiff that I..."

Sharon choked back a cough at the mention of Damon's name. Her breathing quickened.

"Fuck Damon, okay, just fuck him!" Ivan pounded the desk. *"Mr. Brain Surgeon won't figure out a goddamn thing!"* At the sound of the pounding, Janet's body jerked. Her eyes sought Sharon's for some explanation.

"But you have to think about the consolidated books. At least think about decreasing the most obvious exaggerations." The woman's voice was strained.

He inhaled a deep breath. *"Marsha, who—besides you—knows all the details of both sets of books?"*

Sharon's throat grew dry. "Oh my God!" she whispered, covering her mouth with her hand. "He's talking about Damon's wife. Marsha."

She hit the rewind button to make sure she was hearing everything correctly, even though she knew she was. Then she hit play and paced the room while listening to the rest.

"No one," Marsha answered, quietly.

"Good," he said authoritatively, *"let's keep it that way."* The tape stopped with a sharp click.

Sharon turned slowly to Janet. "This woman, Marsha, was murdered a year ago." She swallowed twice to wet her throat and steady her breathing. "How did Kevin get this tape?"

Janet shook her head, her lips pursed. "I have absolutely no idea."

CHAPTER 41

An hour later, Sharon managed to talk herself into fifteen minutes with Kevin. It was easier than she expected to pose as his attorney. A prison guard escorted Kevin from his cell. His hands were cuffed. He was wearing a bright orange uniform. Gaunt didn't begin to describe his tightened face.

The two sat opposite each other, a layer of bulletproof glass between them. They reached simultaneously to pick up their receivers. "Hi," said Kevin, eyes on her, ear against his receiver, "this wasn't in the plan."

"You didn't mention the tape," said Sharon. No time to inquire about how he was feeling; that was pretty obvious from the dark circles under his eyes. "Where did you get it? How do you know Marsha? Why didn't you tell me this before?" Her fingers flexed to accentuate the many question marks.

"Marsha Stark is Ivan Stark's sister. Well, half-sister," he answered. "I couldn't tell you—you would have told Damon, and I had to keep our hunt as quiet as possible."

Thanks for the vote of trust, Kevin, she thought. Then she relented. This was bigger than her ego. Still, she couldn't believe she never had known that Marsha and Ivan were related. And what about Damon? He couldn't have known either because surely he'd have said something to her once they started their investigation of ITA? On the other hand, she'd always felt he was hiding something from her. But why? Her eyes sought more answers from Kevin. She pressed toward the glass.

"So, how do you know her?" she said. *Ask the same question again, get a better response.*

"Through her art. My first job in Washington was representing insurance companies. A bunch of firms had reported artwork stolen. We needed an appraiser. I met Marsha for the first time, over four years ago, at the National Art Gallery. We stayed in contact."

"Why was she in Washington?" said Sharon, thinking it had something to do with ITA's first incarnation.

"I don't know. It didn't seem relevant at the time," said Kevin.

"When was the last time you spoke with her?"

"About a year ago." He scratched his head. "I was working as an enforcer. I think she knew about us, somehow. But I didn't let on about the unit. I was loyal—it was a secret. She was scared. We met out in Arlington. She said that Ivan's company was built on sand. That it was fronting something bigger."

"She was right," said Sharon. "ITA was on a shopping spree. Buying up everything it could."

"It was Marsha's job to consolidate the books after every acquisition. But the numbers behind the books became increasingly complex. The network revenues she added to the ITA bottom line, as each new company became part of the ITA empire—they were complete lies."

"I knew it! I was working at Silverman, just before they took ITA public. I didn't understand any of the numbers. They were worse than any number-dodging scheme even I created for Ivan's first company. I told Sam and Katrina that we were asking for it if we stood behind ITA."

"You and Marsha must have been scared of the same thing. She just stuck around longer, and you..."

Sharon shook her head at her past. "I quit. I had to get out. Ivan was going to do it all again. Just bigger. I couldn't live with myself after the first time—Melvin's suicide, his daughter, so fragile and trusting. They told me not to say anything."

"What did you do?"

"I said that I couldn't promise. Then, I quit. A month later, I..." Her lips quivered, her heart jumped around her chest, "I thought it was an accident at the time. I never thought they would—stoop that low."

Kevin nodded. "There's no depth low enough."

"I know that, now," whispered Sharon, her breath shallow. The pieces started falling into place. "Marsha was murdered a year ago."

"I know." Kevin lowered his head. "It was two days after she met with me. I had my suspicions about the Enforcer Unit, but I couldn't imagine how bad it was. It was her murder that made me start digging into it. Now I understand; now I know I could be next. I knew it couldn't be as random as the media made it sound. Just an affair gone wrong."

"Why didn't you tell Damon when it happened?"

"I didn't have anything to go on. Besides, I'd never met the man, although I felt for him—I did. I just had nothing. I was at a dead end—until last week. That's when I came across the contract; an old one, with Ivan's name on it, and Marsha's, and yours, from when you were at Silverman. I knew you would help."

The prison guard sitting in the corner rose to tell them they only had five more minutes. "I thought ITA was a sham; I tried to get that out before their IPO," said Sharon.

"Your concerns were hers, you see..." said Kevin, trying to remain calm for both of them. He needed to get this out before time was up.

Sharon stopped him as another piece fell into place. "You don't understand—Ivan tried to kill me for those concerns. Just like Marsha."

Kevin's eyes widened. This attempt on Sharon's life was beyond the information he had. "I'm sorry, very sorry. Marsha knew how fraudulent the numbers were, because she made them happen. She was in as deep as Ivan. And it wasn't just an adjustment made for one or two companies. ITA was closing a buy-out a month. Each company had their books altered on its way to being consolidated into ITA."

"Each company," Sharon repeated to herself. *Were these companies the ones on the trail document—the ones that now belonged to ITA? No. That was impossible. They all existed as independent entities. On paper anyway.* Her head was spinning. She had to get herself in front of the trail again. She had to shut down Ivan and ITA before they shut anyone else down.

Kevin became more animated. "Eventually Marsha had no choice but to take the matter up with Ivan—before things got too out of control. To warn him to show restraint on the earnings figures; she knew the Wall Street analysts would realize the lies eventually."

"And the media," added Sharon, thinking of all the corporate puff stories that saturated the press. "Because if someone looked beneath the surface, they'd realize that ITA was nothing but a pack of lies."

Look beneath the surface. It was so obvious to Sharon now.

"Marsha knew she was responsible. If a full investigation was launched, Ivan would go to jail for life. She'd be implicated, too, maybe used by prosecutors against him," he said softly. "She wanted out."

The guard tapped her shoulder that time was up. "Yeah,

we both got in deeper than we expected. We both wanted out," said Sharon, dotting a tissue to her eyes, "just not permanently."

CHAPTER 42

Sharon was back at the Wall Street heliport by seven o'clock that night. Her hours in Washington had her head spinning. Kevin was in jail for the murder of one of his closest friends. Damon's murdered wife was Ivan Stark's half-sister and former business partner. And it seemed more and more likely that Ivan was responsible for Marsha's death and the attempt on her own life.

She tried to piece together the possible timeline of Simon's murder. The brute and whoever hired him was after both her and Kevin. Then he crashed his car into a FedEx truck. But she and Kevin were only in the coffee shop for twenty minutes before Kevin drove back to D.C. Sharon couldn't figure out how he would have been able to untangle himself from the wreck and reach Kevin's Washington home to kill anyone.

Idiot, she mumbled to herself on her walk back to Silverman. Simon was killed in Kevin's home the night before. *Which meant Simon was killed before she met with Kevin in New York, while Janet was tied up.* For a day. *But by whom?* Janet said the man was slight and nervous, not exactly the brute. Then who?

And what about the other enforcers? The ones that Kevin said had turned and then disappeared? Who murdered them? Kevin seemed sure that the Capitol yuppie murderer was responsible for the enforcer murder trail—which now included her friend Roger. The fifty contracts in Kevin's list and the fifty companies in the trail document all connected to ITA—

so Ivan had to be connected to the Enforcer Unit somehow. Maybe ITA provided its network? Maybe the brute was the enforcer killer?

It had been half an hour since she last checked her voice mail. She had missed five calls, two from Katrina Sullivan, two from Mickey, and one from Damon.

* * *

"Where the hell were you?" said an irate Katrina, as Sharon walked into her office. "How could you miss this?" Katrina held up a scathing print-out of a web piece the *Times* broke at noon, centered on a tip from some anonymous employee at WorldWell Bank.

"Sorry. I was following a lead," Sharon answered, knowing that sounded impossibly lame.

"WorldWell Bank attacks us on page one of the *Wall Street Tribune* with unfounded nonsense, and you're following a lead. Look, if you can't handle working here and uncovering what we need, then…"

"Katrina, I can handle it. I'll be at my desk," Sharon responded, already in the doorway of Katrina's office. She turned to leave and bumped straight into Damon.

"Hey," he said.

Sharon looked at Damon, then Katrina, and then Damon again. "Damon," she said, tightly, "I didn't expect you to be here. What a crazy coincidence."

Damon dug his hands into his pockets and looked away from Sharon.

"Sharon, I thought you were going back to your desk," said Katrina curtly.

"Yeah," she replied, swallowing deeply. "That's where I'll be."

When Sharon slipped into her office, she slammed the door shut. Something about Damon's appearance at this particular moment unearthed her. All of a sudden, she had no interest in speaking to him. She would have to tell Damon what she found out about Marsha and Ivan, but she had no idea how or when. Sharon set her elbows on her desk and lowered her head into her hands to gather her thoughts.

When that did nothing, she called Mickey. There was no answer on his cell phone. His secretary informed her that he had left for a meeting early that afternoon and hadn't returned. Then she prepared herself to leave a message on Damon's voice mail. She picked up the phone several times. Each time, she stopped herself. She didn't know what to say; she didn't know where to begin. First, she had to get some more work done on the trail. And she had to shove aside mental snapshots of her passionate night with him.

She sunk into the Silverman database.

An hour later, she was completely engrossed in one of her favorite occupations: financial detective work. She had examined in detail each deal contract and financial statements for twenty-seven of the fifty companies. Of those, eight were under SEC investigation for accounting fraud, and six for securities violations; four of their CEOs were being investigated for insider trading of shares in other companies in the list. The tech market was a small club. Everyone sat on everyone else's board. Everyone had insider information about everyone else.

But she couldn't detect any money that might be disappearing to the Enforcer Unit from any of these figures. Mickey's phrase flashed into her mind. *Where was the fuck over your competitor money?* The companies all had offshore operations in tax havens around the world. Cayman Islands, Bermuda, the Seychelles, Guernsey. All of those documents were harder to decipher. Had more layers. Only one company besides ITA had an operation set up in Belize. PlanetPort. She isolated that one, putting its financial report papers to one side of the desk.

She took a swig from the liter bottle of Diet Coke on her desk. She was exhausted, but felt unable to stop. She continued going through numbers frenetically. She inspected the contracts and SEC-filed financials from company number twenty-eight, looking for any large revenue amendments made in between the official filing of each quarterly report, and whether it amended its figures the following quarter.

Her eyes stung from concentration, but she knew this was the best way to uncover missing money. Consistent revenues might be padded, but usually didn't signify a larger fraud. She kept digging. Flicking up windows for each company, each quarter's financials, looking for deviations. She wasn't even sure exactly what would alert her to a company she could use to rip apart the trail fees, to use as a lever to get inside next Tuesday. But she sensed she'd know when she found it. After all, she had faked enough of these contracts in her own past.

She took another swig of soda and glanced out the window into the pitch-black night. It was 10:30, and she was only up to company thirty-one. Even most investment bankers had gone home. Her heart jumped when she heard a sharp knock at her office door. "Yes?" she called out, nervously walking toward it. She turned the knob.

"Evening, miss. Should I vacuum in here?"

Sharon breathed a sigh of relief. She recognized Alice from her prior time at Silverman. "No, that's okay, thank you."

"But I need to do each office," Alice said, then added, "so I can get home tonight."

"It's okay," said Sharon. "Pretend you did. Have a good night."

Alice smiled, thanked her, and departed for the next office.

Sharon returned to her numbers. The thirty-second company. The thirty-third. She couldn't stop yawning. Part of her wanted to go home, crawl into bed, and deal with this in the morning. The other part of her needed the puzzle pieces to fit in place. And she was eager to avoid the bed she had shared with Damon just last night. She willed herself to keep going.

By company thirty-four, she settled into a steady pace. Company thirty-five was placed in the side pile for further inspection, having a Belize subsidiary. At company thirty-six, her rhythm was abruptly broken by the phone. Her heart leapt at the disquieting ring.

"Hello, Sharon Thomas," she answered.

"Hard at work, Sharon?"

She stiffened. "Damnit, come on, who is this?" She tried to hide the quivering in her voice.

"Look beneath the surface."

"Yeah, so you've mentioned," she said, opting for a false bravado.

"Why aren't you doing it?"

"What do you mean?" she asked defensively. "I am, I'm going through all the..."

The phone clicked off. Sharon immediately rose from her desk to inspect the hallway. Alice had already moved on to another part of the floor. There was no one around. Just the glimmering fluorescent ceiling lights illuminating the grey carpet that lined the dark offices.

She seemed to be the only one working on this part of the floor. She returned to her desk and left another nervous message on Mickey's voice mail. Elbows on the pile of company contracts, she dropped her head in her hands. She was struggling to figure out who this man was and how he knew her movements.

The phone rang again. She cursed herself for leaving her recorder at home. Steadying her hand, she answered. "Hello?"

"Look beneath the surface."

Her anguish and frustration boiled over. "I am looking beneath the fucking surface! Who are you? What do you want!"

"No, you are not."

"Tell me what you mean. Look, I don't know who you are, but you're really annoying me, and your being a goddamn coward in the process..."

"Follow the money. The trail."

"I am following the fucking money!" she lashed out.

"Thirty-seven companies."

She stiffened. She realized that the voice could see more than her physical movements. He could see her electronic ones. There was only one man, besides Trevor, who could be that good at intruding on her e-behavior, the man who controlled flow over the Net.

"Ivan?" she ventured.

The voice erupted into a hideous cackle. *"Look beneath the surface,"* it droned, emphasizing "beneath."

"Tell me what you mean!"

"What is money?" the voice quizzed.

"What?"

"What is money?"

"I—I don't know what you're talking about, I..." Sharon was thoroughly confused. She had been thinking for three days straight, had faced two life-threatening attacks, and had slept with her editor. She drew a blank.

"Time." The voice ended the call with a click.

CHAPTER 43

As soon as she replaced the receiver, the phone rang again. Sharon let it ring. This game was becoming more than she could take. She was sick of piecing everything together. The clues, the documents, the murders, her own life. Why had Ivan called while she was searching for that information? At that moment? She shook her head to clear her brain. It *had* to be Ivan Stark, right? *Right?* And if so, what the hell was he playing at? Was he trying to point her to something that could take down Silverman? WorldWell Bank? Parts of the government?

And where was Katrina in all this? According to Mickey, she was pulling a bunch of strings of her own. And what about Sam? He seemed clueless, but was he? All the players in this high stakes, homicidal game wanted to take each other down as much as they wanted to pump themselves up. A few numbers in the hands of the right people, and any one of them stood to make billions.

But, except for the violence, wasn't she trying to do the same thing? Why was she back at Silverman, really? Was it to find evidence against WorldWell Bank? ITA? Scoop an epic story? Or was it to see Sam go down? Nothing more than retribution. The thought made her numb with loathing and that all too familiar guilt. If she hadn't been so greedy herself, Ivan's former CFO wouldn't have gassed himself and his young daughter. All because of her financial wizardry, her ego gone deadly.

"What is money?" the voice had stated. *"Time."*

Time is money. The oldest cliché in the business handbook. She rolled the concept around her aching head. *Time.* She rubbed her eyes viciously, hoping for focus, hoping to alleviate the stabbing pain around her wound. All she knew for sure about time was that it was running out.

She returned to the computer screen. To company thirty-eight. She attempted to bring up the usual deal details. A dialogue box flashed across her screen. *Access Denied.* She hit the enter key. Then the space bar. Control Alt Delete. All were equally useless. She smacked both hands on the keyboard and grunted.

Damn it. Sharon jotted down "Company 38" on a yellow sticky, ripped it from its pad, and stuck it on top of the other two companies she had piled separately. Then she rebooted the computer.

Time. Sharon got up and swigged the rest of her Diet Coke. She had just begun to pace her office when another voice interrupted.

"We have got to do something about your hours, kiddo."

Sharon jumped back at the sound of Mickey standing in the doorway, Dunkin Donuts and coffee in hand.

"Mickey!" she exclaimed. "I love you!"

"Here—whatever you're doing, this will help," he said, offering her a powdered raspberry jelly donut.

"I see Dunkin Donuts is still the way to go," said Sharon. She took his offering, trying to ignore the knots in her stomach.

"Kiddo, I'm loyal. None of that mini Krispy Kreme bullshit," he said, taking the seat in front of her desk. His eyes scanning her printout piles.

"Mickey, if I asked you, 'what is money?'—what would you say?" Sharon pounced.

"Power," he declared, without missing a beat.

"Wrong. What else?"

"Time?"

"Yes, that's what the voice said."

"What voice?"

"Okay, long story short. Since Monday night and the whole brute visit and my glorious rebirth at Silverman, I've been getting these calls, mostly at home, but also on my cell, and tonight, here. It's concise, eerie shit. I think it must be Ivan, or someone he's hired, but I haven't been able to figure it out."

Mickey shook his head. "Jesus, you've got a few worlds of crap colliding around you."

"Yeah, well, tonight the voice added a new concept. Time. As in 'What is money? Time.'"

Time. Mickey mouthed the word silently. "Okay, let's think: what else is time?"

"I don't know, time and space. Time and tide. Maybe something to do with Belize. The ocean? A boat transfer?"

"Maybe." His brow crinkled. "But we already narrowed the Belize transfer time. Maybe the timing has to do with tides, but, I dunno; I think there's something else."

"Um, time and...Time and...What *is* time? A dimension? Damn, I don't know!" She threw up her arms.

"Hey, kiddo," soothed Mickey. "What did I teach you?"

"Never lose your cool? You're right, I'm sorry. This is all just so—fucked up!"

"What else did this mystery voice say that might be relevant to time?" guided Mickey.

"In every call, it talked about looking beneath the surface. Maybe it is time and tide. Beneath the surface. The ocean. Really offshore."

"I dunno, maybe," said Mickey, unconvinced. "What's the tie between time and going beneath the surface, though? There's gotta be some line that connects those dots."

"That's it!" Sharon exclaimed. "Mickey, you're the best!"

"I try," he replied, looking confused.

"A time *line*. Beneath the surface. That's it."

"What's it?"

"I've been looking at the current deals of the companies listed on this 8-K, which also happen to be the companies in Kevin's documents. And so far I've come up with nothing—God, why didn't I think of it sooner?"

"Think of what?"

"Of what I did every single time I did diligence, every time I did a background check on a corporate deal. God, what an idiot!" she reprimanded herself.

"Careful, that's my star trader you're talking about."

"Look at the time line. Not the financial reports and how their numbers change over time. But the time line of the company itself. Was it taken over, or acquired? Did it undergo a name change?"

"Gotcha, kiddo—I see where you're going. Companies hide all sorts of things when they change their names and combine their balance sheets."

"Exactly. Numbers are easily hidden when balance sheets get combined. Especially when companies buy other companies. This trail isn't about the fifty companies dealing with ITA. Or maybe that's part of it. But the other part has got to be what's stacked under ITA itself. The companies that ITA acquired."

"Good sleuthing, kiddo. You gotta look at what ITA used to be."

"Yes! Yes! Yes!" She high-fived him. "You're right! That I can do, but not here. At home. I've got reams of ITA history there. Mickey?"

"Yes, kiddo."

"I'm calling it a night." She gathered the documents stacked on her desk, including the ones from Kevin's folder and the 8-K. "Come on, let's blow this place!"

"I'm with ya," said Mickey. "But wait, we haven't even discussed what you found in Washington."

"Washington's a mess. Kevin's in jail. He's being framed for murdering some manager enforcer, who was also his best friend. Kevin's wife is beside herself, staying in a hotel near their home." They were standing in front of the bank of elevators.

"That's not all that's going down in D.C.," he said softly.

She looked at him, afraid to ask what else was going wrong.

"Okay, brace yourself," said Mickey, "there's another bomb."

"What is it?" Sharon knew it couldn't be good.

"After Sam flew to D.C., I spent the day calling in every favor I could, digging into this crazy Enforcer Unit, and..." He stopped, his lips pursed tight as he loudly inhaled.

"And? Come on Mickey, spill it. I can take it."

"The Enforcer Unit is being disbanded this weekend. Come Sunday, it'll have no computers, no networks, no offices, and no people. It'll never have existed."

"Before the Belize transfer," she said, her face draining to white.

"Yup."

Sharon agreed to let Mickey drop her off at her apartment. She didn't want to walk to the subway alone. With the Enforcer Unit destroyed, it would be impossible to prove the trail of fees to Washington. And even harder to figure out who was framing Kevin for the death of his boss. And who was killing enforcers. She needed to go back to D.C.

Mickey seemed to sense her brain spinning and didn't disturb her. Sharon tried to remember the name of the sergeant in charge of Kevin's homicide investigation. He had seemed like a good person. She tried to conjure the image of his badge in her mind. He was tall, darkish skin, warm chocolate eyes. Stubble like he hadn't shaved for days. Jose. Jose something. Jose...Jose Rodgers. No, that wasn't it; it was her mind centering on her SEC friend. No, Jose...Jose Rodriquez. That was it. She'd pay him a personal visit on Saturday and try to talk to Kevin again. Before there was nothing left at the SEC unit to investigate.

First, she had to dig further into ITA's past. Now she was no longer sure that the voice was Ivan's. The only other person connected enough to know her movement, especially on the closed networks of Silverman & Sons, was Sam Peterson. Equally evil, maybe more so. Katrina was another possibility. But that made less sense. Katrina had bigger male fish to fry. Maybe Sam was trying to throw her off Silverman's criminal activity by pinning it all on Ivan. Maybe the ITA board that the two men sat on wasn't such a cozy, buddy-buddy place after all.

As Mickey's car approached Fourth Street, they were confronted by flashing red and white lights. And shrill sirens. And fire engines. Crowds of onlookers lining the sidewalks, craning their necks toward the sky.

"Oh my God!" screamed Sharon. The trucks were concentrated in front of her building. "No!"

She leapt out of the car as it slowed down, leaving the door ajar behind her. She ran to a fireman who was screwing a hose into the nearby fire hydrant.

"What's going on here?" she demanded, legs wobbly beneath her. The man ignored her.

Sharon counted up to the floor the smoke was streaming from. A team of firemen were hacking open the building's front door. She slumped to the ground, clutching her stomach.

As Mickey walked toward her, she burst into tears.

"My apartment is going up in flames!"

CHAPTER 44

The chief fireman introduced himself to Sharon in the hallway as Sheldon. The blaze in the apartment, he explained, had mostly been contained to the living room. It started, apparently, because of a short in her laptop, the one that had remained when the brute stole her hard drive earlier in the week. But he told Sharon that the department considered the fire suspicious.

The fire raged through Sharon's Indian cabinet like it was a matchstick. The fire destroyed all her paper files and folders inside it, as well as the ones strewn on her coffee table.

Mickey stood by her side as she surveyed the watery, smoldering wreck that had once been her home. She entered her bedroom. It was intact, but reeked of smoke. At least she still had clothes and the personal effects and documents she kept in her bedroom closet.

Chief Fireman Sheldon hovered in the doorway. "Are you insured?" he asked her.

"Insured?" She had to think about that for a moment. Her clarity had been shattered by the state of her apartment.

"Yeah, do you have home damage or fire insurance? We can help you fill out the report."

She studied his face. "Report...?"

"When you're ready, of course," he added.

"Yes, thank you," she responded, unblinking. She jerked her head back toward him. "Was anyone else in the building—?"

"No, ma'am, the fire was contained."

"Of course it was," she said, her shoulders hunching forward. Then she turned to Mickey, "Good thing I've got my beach house, huh?" she asked with tears in her eyes.

He smiled at her weak attempt at humor. "You can stay with me tonight. I've got more than enough room."

She returned his smile and added a hug. "Thank you, Mickey. I don't know what I'd do without you."

"Without me, you might never have become a banker and had a bunch of corporate crooks up your ass."

"Somehow, I think it's the fact that I became a reporter that has them all up my ass."

"Are you sure about that?"

"Of course, I'm sure. I think."

"Okay, kiddo, you should get some rest. Save some energy for tomorrow. To get those bastards."

"I can't, not yet. I need to finish what I haven't even started yet tonight: digging into ITA's past."

Time beneath the surface.

She ran her fingers through her hair to shove it behind her ears, realizing again the enormity of the fire. "Oh, Mickey, half the research I accumulated is gone. I should have stayed in Belize when I had the chance. I could have become a diving instructor. I could have had a simple, happy life."

"You'll be fine, Sharon. You're a fighter. This is what you do."

She spotted the caller ID as her cell rang and smiled. "Trevor!" she answered. "I'm so happy it's you!"

"Gee, Share. Love you, too. Listen, just calling to remind you that you left your laptop at my place this morning and...."

"Oh Trev! You're amazing! I mean...I left my...thing...at your place this morning, didn't I?"

"Yeah. Uh, I just said that. It was getting late and I figured you might want to stop by and pick it up."

"You figured right. Wow! That's so...great! I totally forgot, and it contains—"

Mickey, motioned her to stop talking, making a little bug flying motion with his hand.

"Never mind, Trev. Talk to you later." She shut her cell.

She turned to Mickey. "Thanks. That laptop has all the scanned documents I ever had. At least, I think all of them. But whatever's in there, it's better than the ashes of the originals." Surveying what was left of her apartment, she said, "I can't deal with this right now. I'll take care of it...whenever."

"Do what you need to do," said Mickey.

"Thanks, I just need to grab a few things. Would you mind if I turned down your amazing offer? I got to get to my laptop."

He nodded. "You got it, kiddo, but at least let me drop you off." It was only a few blocks, but she thanked him for the ride. She knew that she would need Mickey for much bigger favors soon. She would need his plane again, this weekend, to go back to D.C.

* * *

One look at her and Trevor exclaimed, "Jesus, Share, you look like shit. What's going on?"

"Thanks, Trev. My place got torched. Everything in the office—gone."

"What? Let me guess: it wasn't an accident."

"Yeah."

"If you don't mind my saying so, your life has become a horror flick the past few days. You got to get the hell out of whatever you're into."

"How? I can't just walk away. I didn't ask for any of this. I didn't choose to get a black eye, or dive back into that shark-infested purgatory or have people I barely know get arrested for murder or..." Suddenly, Sharon was sobbing.

"Whoa, sorry, sorry. I'm just worried about you," he said, wrapping his arms around her. "I know you'll stick this out."

"I'll be fine," she said, hoping that saying it would make it so. "I just need to get my laptop."

"Sure, no problem; I'll get it. Meanwhile," he said, offering her a joint, "take a load off."

She stared at him as if he had just offered a surgeon a shot of tequila before surgery.

"Trust me, Share, this one you need. It's high class shit—take a puff."

She wavered. "Okay, but just one. I need focus."

Over the next hour, Sharon and Trevor extracted and examined every bit of ITA's publicly accessible history. Sharon re-familiarized herself with Ivan's ascent. His personal and corporate trajectories. The companies ITA ate up along the way. The company ITA had once been, before tech IPO's were fashionable, then unfashionable, then back again.

The initial private firm that Ivan created had no remaining financial records of its own. It was a tiny, failed start-up. *WorldWideCom*. She shivered at the awful memories. She had created their initial network contracts, their offshore subsidiaries in Bermuda. She helped dissolve it before the SEC got there, but that was too late to save little Katie.

Her cell rang. It was Damon. "Yes?" she answered, realizing she hadn't thought about him for hours.

"Sharon, I've got to talk to you. I feel like a jerk for running out on you, but I swear, I had my reasons."

"It's late, Damon. I'll talk to you in the morning," she said coldly. She didn't have the time or inclination to deal with emotional distractions.

"Sharon, look, I've been reliving Monday night a million times in my head."

"You mean when I got knocked out?"

"Yes. But you weren't the only one who had a visitor that night."

"What do you mean?"

"Sharon, we need to talk face-to-face." His voice faltered as he realized that he was still confused. Was it time to tell Sharon the full story? Trust or not? Danger or not?

"Damon, this really isn't a good time." She, too, had contemplated coming clean with him about the trail, Kevin, the Silverman-ITA contract, and how she thought it was a front for more insidious crimes. But too much was happening at once. She could only trust a few people right now. Mickey and Trevor. She had instinctively turned to them. Plus, she had her own regret over whether she ever should have slept with Damon. It only complicated matters more.

"Please, Sharon, just listen to me."

"Damon, I can't talk right now, really. My apartment's burned down. I'm at a friend's—"

"Oh my God! When?"

"Sometime this evening. Damon, it's been a long day. I'll give you a call tomorrow."

"Wait, Sharon. It's…it's my fault. I…I haven't been straight with you. I need to tell you something, about that Monday night before I came over, before you got hurt…"

She knew he had been hiding something. Whatever it was, discussing it over a cell phone was probably a bad idea. "Fine. Then come over. Let's talk in person." She gave him Trevor's address and hung up.

When Damon arrived twenty minutes later, Trevor glared at him. "I'll be back, soon," was all Trevor would say. Sharon thought she heard him mutter "asshole" under his breath as he grabbed his denim jacket and left.

Sharon had changed out of her suffocating business suit and into Trevor's clothes, a pair of gray sweats and a vintage Grateful Dead T-shirt. "Hey," she greeted Damon with an abbreviated hand-wave.

"Sharon," Damon said, leaning in to hug her.

She backed away. "Let's sit down, over there." She motioned to some African throw pillows that marked Trevor's sitting area. "So what happened on Monday?"

"Before you were attacked, I had a visitor at my place in Easton. A young woman. Short blonde hair. She appeared out of nowhere in my house, made me call you about—"

"A filing for ITA," she finished, studying his face. She had the gnawing sensation that as much as his words were revealing, his face was holding something back. She couldn't place what it was. Maybe it was because she was a little high. Maybe it was because their lovemaking the night before meant something. Maybe it was both. She tried to focus back on their conversation.

"Kind of, yeah," he was saying. "I'm so sorry."

"What did she do?"

"She made me dial you. That conversation we had, about ITA, she told me what to say. Very specifically. At gunpoint. She was much calmer than I was, I'm afraid."

Sharon shuddered, crossing her arms. "She needed you to make sure I had the ITA documents, before the brute busted in. They must have been working together. Working us. She wanted us both involved."

"It seems so, but the brute could have just busted in and gotten the documents himself, without my calling to verify they were at your place."

"That's too coincidental, Damon. Now, what did she say?"

"I don't remember," he said, tugging at his chin.

"Think. What were her exact words?" She was annoyed that he had kept this information from her. She wondered what else he was hiding.

"I can't. I don't know." He scratched his head.

"Okay, it'll come back to you," she acquiesced. "But we know that she wanted you to link ITA and me."

He nodded. "Yes. Plus whatever is going on with ITA now."

"Makes sense. I'll check into it."

"How?" he asked.

"By letting the numbers talk."

"So you have enough left, after the fire, to work from?"

She was about to answer when Trevor returned. "You still here?" he asked Damon.

Damon checked his watch. He couldn't believe they'd been sitting there for almost an hour. "I guess it's time for me to go."

"You guessed right, buddy," agreed Trevor, motioning him toward the door.

"It probably is a good idea," said Sharon. "I need to sleep. Thanks for coming over."

The two embraced in an awkward hug. "About last night," he said under his breath.

She turned to look for Trevor, who was standing discretely on the other side of the room. "Let's not talk about it," she said, her voice a whisper. "It happened. It was...amazing. But, let's leave it for now. Good night."

"Good night."

As soon as she shut the door behind Damon, Trevor remarked, "That guy's hiding something."

"Maybe," she replied flatly, biting her thumbnail. "One more piece of the puzzle to figure out."

"You didn't tell him about the trail, did you?"

"No, and I also didn't mention that I knew his dead wife worked for Ivan Stark."

"Way to go!" Trevor exclaimed. "Did he say anything useful at all?"

"Maybe. At any rate, I think I got my timeline. Marsha spent three years with Ivan. At least. She must have seen or done quite a bit. Now, I just need to dig more into the ghosts of ITA's past." She yawned. "In the morning."

She fell asleep almost immediately in the sleeping bag that Trevor laid out for her.

CHAPTER 45

After a short, troubled sleep, Sharon awoke the next morning determined. She had a plan. Nudging the crumpled heap on the futon that was Trevor, she informed him of their plans. "Hey, Trev, I need a big favor. What do you think about accompanying me to Washington tonight?"

"I'm almost afraid to ask, but why?"

"To get into the SEC building and hack into its computer system."

"That's a government network, Share. Have you lost it? We'll be shot as spies by Homeland Security. Or we'll get taken to Guantanamo awaiting trial for treason, and then get the chair."

"We have to get in there before it's too late. If Mickey's right and the Enforcer Unit is being dismantled, all retrievable fee records will be lost forever. I can't let that happen."

"So, you just want to go there and randomly start hacking?"

"Trev, I don't do random. We're going to bust into Simon Caldwell's computer." She was being at her most methodical. All night her dreams were about the Enforcer Unit. They had mercifully distracted her from the state of her apartment and the attempts on her life. Now she had to act.

"Who's Simon Caldwell?"

"One of the dead guys."

"Uh-huh, well, that's different then."

"He was the manager of the Enforcer Unit; his PC has to have the best information. That's where you come in." Simon was dead. His computer, hopefully, was not.

"Okay. You're crazy, but I'm there, Share. If I get busted, you're posting my bail."

"Deal. Before that, I've got Silverman, and four years of ITA's history to sort out."

CHAPTER 46

That night, Sharon and Trevor checked into the Intercontinental Hotel, near the SEC. In the political heart of the country. She had reserved the room under his name to throw off anyone looking for her. The unlikely pair, she looking every bit the banker, he the rock star, entered the speckled marble-floored lobby and approached the reception desk.

"Mr. Wood?" the reservations clerk inquired skeptically, as he took in Trevor's tattoos and casual attire—formal for him—black jeans with no holes in them and a black Rolling Stones T-shirt.

"That's right. I'm in a rush, so if you could give us the room key, that'd be great," he said grandly.

Sharon batted her eyelashes at the clerk, as if to say, what can you do about these loveable creative types? She was dressed in typical Washington professional garb, navy blue suit, cream blouse, nude stockings, and low-heeled navy pumps. In a small traveler's suitcase, she carried a change of more comfortable clothes, her two cell phones, laptop, and Kevin's folder.

Trevor was carrying a briefcase that contained his own laptop with necessary spy-ware. It also contained a toolset with an assortment of tiny screwdrivers and various microchips. He was prepared to hack.

Sharon knew the SEC building well from interviews she'd done there for *Riche$*. It had cameras everywhere. Fortunately, one of Mickey's unnamed contacts was able to obtain two sets of janitorial clothing and badges. It wouldn't make getting into the building any easier, but it would alleviate suspicion once they did enter. Sharon felt like they were in a bad action movie.

Kevin had told Sharon that the Enforcer Unit entrance required a retina scan. Accessing offices needed a thumbprint. That part was simple. Kevin's prints were all over the folder he had given to Sharon. Trevor had brought along a micro-scanner that could re-configure Kevin's actual thumbprint into an electronic computer image. He could stream that image to the scanner to unlock his computer.

The retina scan would be more complicated. For that, he had to use an imprint of a contact lens that Kevin would have to insert into his eye to capture a reading, then remove and invert. Another high resolution scanner would create a file image of the electronic picture of his eye. Trevor had been practicing on himself all day, transferring a picture of his own eye onto a lens and then creating a computer image at the same resolution.

What they didn't have was Simon's thumbprint. They could only hope there was an intact print somewhere on Simon's door handle, or on whatever device he used to access his office. If that were the case, Trevor could read it into his image scanner and stream it to the access device.

While Trevor tested his equipment in the hotel room, Sharon made a visit to the Fifth Precinct. She had called ahead to Sergeant Rodriquez and told him she had some important matters to discuss regarding the Kevin Waters case.

At the precinct, Rodriquez greeted her. "Good to see you again, Ms. Thomas. Would you like a cup of coffee? Tastes like hell, but does the trick."

He was very warm, Sharon thought. "Sergeant, I never turn down caffeine."

"Call me Jose," he said, pouring her a cup from the pot brewing in the kitchen galley.

"Thanks, Jose."

Officer O'Harris appeared at the doorway. "You again?"

"I see you've met my partner?" Rodriquez said to Sharon.

"Kind of. First at the Waters' home, and later on at the Patriot Hotel."

Officer O'Harris elaborated for his boss. "I went over to check on Janet. The girl's gone through a lot, just wanted to make sure she was holding up."

"Oh," Rodriquez said, and then to Sharon, "please, come to my desk and sit down. Let's talk."

Sharon followed him. O'Harris returned to his own desk, but kept an eye on Sharon.

"Sergeant, I mean, Jose," she began, taking a sip of the steaming black coffee, "Kevin didn't kill Simon."

"I know."

"You know?"

"Kevin's right-handed. The trajectory of the two shots into Simon clearly came from a lefty."

"Then why are you still holding him?"

"Whoever did shoot Simon is still out there. As long as the killer thinks Kevin's taking the hit, he's more likely to let his guard down, make a mistake. Help us catch him."

"Or her."

"Her?" His voice perked up like it was honing in on some crucial piece of new evidence.

"I just meant that, well, equal opportunity and all," she said. Sharon thought of Damon's recent female visitor. Maybe, despite the fact that Washington was a town drenched in testosterone, she was the killer.

"The body was dragged to the shores of the Potomac. We found the blood trail. Simon weighed about 165. It's more likely the killer was male."

"Sergeant, you don't think Simon's death was, well, an isolated incident, do you?"

"No. Unfortunately, no. But his killer got sloppy with the shooting this time. The other two got clean shots to the eye and the hand. Simon fit the type of the boys we found earlier this year."

"The Capitol yuppie murders?" Sharon asked, already knowing the answer.

"Yeah, but we never got ID's on the other floaters—this time we do."

"Floaters?" Sharon shuddered.

"Yeah, our pet name for folks who get dumped in the river. Puff up like blowfish. Ain't a pretty sight."

Enforcers who've tried to talk before have disappeared.

"Do you have any leads, then?" she asked.

"Ms. Thomas—"

"Call me Sharon."

"Sharon, as far as I can tell, you've been asking most of the questions. Do you have information for me?"

O'Harris walked passed them, headed to the copier.

"Sharon?" Rodriquez repeated, trying to regain her attention.

Sharon leaned closer and whispered, "Simon's death and the two others were related. They all worked at this...this unit of the SEC, called the enforcers."

He followed her in closer, very interested. "They were federal employees?"

Though she was wary of spilling anything to cops, she felt she could trust Rodriquez. Plus, time was of the essence. "Simon was. So was Roger Francis, he was—a friend of mine. The others were private employees, not on the SEC's payroll, I don't think. Kevin should be able to fill you in with more detail."

"Kevin was part of this unit?"

"Yes, but it's being disbanded this weekend. It existed to move money around, from corporations to the government. As of Sunday, all those records will be gone."

"How do you know all this?" Rodriquez inquired, his eyes crinkling. This was the kind of story he joined the force for. This reporter was reminding him why he became a cop.

She knew she couldn't answer that question. She rose to leave, nervous she had said too much already. "Please keep an eye on Kevin. Keep him safe. And his wife."

"You have my word on that," said Rodriquez.

"Uh, can I just see him for a few minutes?" She needed his prints and eye image to enter the Enforcer Unit.

"Technically, it is after visiting hours."

"Please, Sergeant."

The Sergeant made a phone call. "Okay, I'll have the warden waiting for you. Deputy Officer Reardon will escort you." He gestured to a rookie female cop by the front desk. "Five minutes, that's all."

O'Harris walked passed them again, headed for the water machine.

"Thank you, Jose. Here's my card if you want to ask me anything else tomorrow."

He pocketed the card and walked her to the precinct exit. He watched as Sharon and Reardon slid into her cop car. Then he turned and walked over to O'Harris' desk. "Put an extra officer outside Kevin's cell. And let's tail Sharon. She may need us."

O'Harris asked, "You sure?"

"Yeah, I'm sick of the Feds taking everything over. Something big is going down and we're going to be on it. I believe that girl, Sharon. She's got a death on her conscience—I see it in her eyes. She's legit."

* * *

It only took Sharon a few minutes to take a lens imprint to make into a high resolution image of Kevin's eye, as per Trevor's instructions. He seemed in good spirits when she told him the cops were looking for the real killer, but was still nervous about his family. Someone was obviously after him, and with the murderer out there running around loose, his wife and daughter were clearly in danger. She tried to reassure him that everything was under control. But the only thing she could truly vouch for was the fact that she was intent on exposing the Enforcer Unit and their links to the vice president. She thanked him, and with a guard shooing her out of the visiting room, promised she'd complete the task at hand.

A few hours later, just before one a.m., Sharon and Trevor stood in the janitor uniforms at the entrance to the SEC building. They had Kevin's instructions and Trevor's abundance of imprints, gadgets, and scanner software. At the front door, Trevor entered Kevin's security access code. He dodged the camera as it scanned his presence, betting on the code being what activated access, not the picture of Kevin.

There was an uncomfortable pause. Trevor and Sharon exchanged looks. Finally, the automated voice greeted him. "Good evening, Mr. Waters." Sharon crouched behind Trevor.

"See," said Trevor with exaggerated assurance, "technology is never as good as its electronic chatter."

Sharon breathed a sigh of relief as the two moved inside. Just as Kevin had described, there was a night watchman sitting at the end of the first hallway. They approached the guard in their pale grey outfits. Trevor made small talk, complimenting the man on the hip-hop techno beat coming from his desk radio, and complaining about working the night shift. Soon, they were in and onto the next obstacle.

Following Kevin's instructions, they rode the elevator to the third floor, a second elevator to the sixth floor, and then took the stairs back down to the fifth floor. "Are they kidding me?" Sharon giggled.

Trevor smiled in agreement. "Good to know they keep things safely hidden."

On the fifth floor, Trevor punched in the second security code. With tiny pliers, he held the image of Kevin's eye up to the retina scan. The wait seemed interminable. Finally, as Sharon and Trevor exchanged nervous glances, the scanner whirred and clicked, and the door unlocked. They were in.

They crept down the dark hallway of offices, scanning the engraved gold-plated plaques beside each door. It didn't take long to find what they were looking for. Just as Kevin had said: down the long hallway, the last door on the left. *Simon Caldwell*. But there was still the problem of Simon's fingerprint.

While Trevor scanned the door with an electronic duster, hoping for a clean print, Sharon inspected their surroundings. The floor was creepy in its sterile brightness. At first, she thought there were no windows at the end of the hall. Then, she realized that there were a few, but they were hidden behind black glass. There was no way to see anything external. The halogen bulbs hanging from the ceiling shone like giant headlights. The atmosphere buzzed with the faint whirring of computers in sleep mode.

"Shit!" whispered Trevor, struggling with the door handle.

"What is it?"

"I can't get a clean print, damnit!"

"Relax. Keep trying. I know you'll get one."

For fifteen agonizingly long minutes, he tampered with the handle. Finally, he pieced together a print from two half images and pressed it to the access pad. The door sprung open.

"The techno-gods are with us!"

"Let's get into his computer, quick. This place gives me the creeps," said Sharon.

The same manufactured thumbprint accessed Simon's files on the computer.

"Bingo!" said Trevor.

"Excellent! Now for some sleuthing," said Sharon, taking over the command control spot, Simon's red leather chair. Her fingers zoomed over the keyboard, dancing between it and the mouse. She was searching for the trail, for the fees, old emails. Anything that could provide clear evidence about the Belize transfers.

"Oh my God!" she squealed after a few minutes.

Trevor, who had been keeping watch by Simon's office door, rushed over. "What have you got?"

"This!"

They stared at an indicting email from the "new" folder of Simon's mailbox:

To: scaldwell@sec.en.gov

From:graceson105@aol.com

CC: sampeterson@silverman.com

Date: Tuesday, August 17, 2006

Time: 8:40:06 PM

All systems for Belize are go. See attached list for full instructions.

Route the amount we discussed to my account.

AG

"AG," said Sharon, processing, "Arthur Graceson—the vice president!"

"Wow," said Trevor. "And this Simon dude never got the email."

"No, he must have been dead by then. Let's print this and the attachment out and get out of here."

"Sharon," he beamed, "you're awesome!"

As the printer spat out the evidence that would blow the ring apart, the sound of a click filled the air.

"Hold it right there."

Lurking in the doorway, gun in hand, was a young blonde man.

"Who are you?" she asked.

"Shut up!" he commanded as he stepped in front of the desk, his blue-grey eyes flashing colder than his years. "Hands on your head."

Sharon could hear the buzz of the printer in the background as she complied. The sound was suddenly deafening. "Wait, you know Simon, don't you?"

"So?" he said with a scowl as he turned to Trevor.

"Now, you," he gestured with his gun, "hand me those papers."

Trevor sauntered to the HP LaserJet and casually lifted the freshly-inked document from the paper tray. He sauntered back. "These?" he goaded. "You want these, do you?"

The gunman cocked the trigger in response.

"Trevor." Sharon warned. This guy was more nervous then they were, and she knew that couldn't be good. "Just give him the documents."

"You little shit," said Trevor insolently, holding the pages out, and then retracting them to his chest. There weren't a lot of people Trevor normally thought he could take on, especially when they were waving a gun at him, but this little yuppie dick seemed to be more bark than bite. "Tell us who you are, first."

"Whatever," he said, "The name's Julian, okay? And, maybe I didn't make myself clear," said Julian. He leaned forward, grabbed Sharon's upper arm, and turned her so that her back was pressed against his chest. He poked the barrel of the gun into the side of her throat. "Give me those documents or she gets the same treatment as Simon."

"Simon?" gulped Sharon. "You killed Simon?" He didn't seem capable of murder. He seemed...too well-bred, too much of a WASP.

"He was in my way, okay," Julian said. "It was an accident. But it will all work out well. Kevin Waters will take the rap and no one will ever know I shot Simon."

Sharon was armed with her own weapon, her pocket Sony ICD-BP150 recorder, quietly set to tape. "But why?" she asked, curving her neck away from the gun and toward his eyes to ask the question. This kid seemed proud of his feat. As if he didn't understand the real consequence—not the possibility of getting caught, but of having killed another human being. She knew he would want to talk.

"Because he fucked up. Because he was a bad manager. He let Kevin get away for too long, with too much information. Because, it was...it was...an accident!" Julian seemed about to sob.

Sharon sensed an escape opportunity. She had studied this in Aikido. Wedging the side of one hand into Julian's elbow she forced his arm upward with her other hand. A stray shot fired into the office ceiling, unleashing a powdery cascade of asbestos.

Using the sound of the pop as distraction, she then forced his elbow to the ground, pressing against its natural curve. Natural instinct was to protect the joint and let the fingers splay open. Julian moaned as the gun fell from his outstretched fingers. Trevor was reaching to pick it up, still holding the printout, when the cops appeared at the office doorway.

"Freeze, police!"

Sergeant Rodriquez and Officer O'Harris rushed Julian. As Julian was pushed to the floor, Trevor quietly slipped the pages from the printer into his pocket.

Sharon caught the sergeant's eye. "How did you know to come here?"

Rodriquez winked. "Been doing this a long time. You learn to read people, probably as much as when you're a reporter. I read you. I had your back. Thought a little tail might come in handy."

"Well, you read me right. I don't know how to thank you."

"Just stay out of trouble next time," he replied.

"I don't seem to be very good at that, Sergeant. Besides, what's the fun in that?"

* * *

Hours later, a frustrated Rodriquez called his partner to his desk. "This doesn't end here," he said sternly, the Capitol yuppie murder case file notes spread before him, "this just doesn't add up."

Officer O'Harris looked confused as he walked over. "Boss?"

"Julian had nothing to do with those other floaters. They were shot by a pro. There's still a killer loose out there. We got more work to do." He sighed. "Something tells me it ain't gonna be easy. I just hope it's in time."

CHAPTER 47

Sharon was sitting on the floor of Trevor's apartment, which was covered with a mess of multi-colored pieces of sticky paper, each one tagged with a code from the trail document, a calendar of ocean scenes opened to August, with a bright red circle around Tuesday, the twenty-fourth, and a set of plane tickets to Belize. Her cell phone summoned her away from the jumble of numbers and codes. It was the sergeant's number. She felt a pang of guilt. Much as she wanted to aid the investigation for the Capitol killer, the clock was ticking on the big day, looming.

"Yes, Sharon here," she answered, taking a swig of Diet Coke

"Hi Sharon, it's Sergeant Rodriquez."

"Hey, Sergeant, any luck over there?" she asked hopefully.

She heard a deep sigh pervade the wires.

"Sergeant?"

"Nothing. Nada. Two days I been navigating this crap Washington red tape bullshit before I even get the Feds to respond to this enforcer thing. I called in every favor I could think of. Turns out, I don't have enough favors to call in."

"So did you find anything left behind at all?" *Reporter's instinct. Ask the question. Know the answer. Hope you're wrong.*

"Nope. Finally, on Monday morning, I got clearance to send my SWAT team down to the area there, that mysterious floor of the SEC building. But all they found was a crowded, dusty storage area. Old boxes, bubble wrap, stacks of yellowing documents, IBM Selectrics, frayed wires, stink of mold and mildew."

"Anything else?" *There goes my story. No glorious high-tech operation that had been funneling money to a bunch of elite assholes who would collect it all so they could become even richer.*

"Nothing, sorry."

Nothing but a dead end. Someone was pulling strings out there. Someone powerful. Someone who might not want to get caught, but might want to have someone else take the fall.

"What about any other leads on the killer?" she asked.

"How do you know that we didn't think it all fell on that little Yuppie twerp?"

"Just a hunch, Sergeant, just a hunch."

"Well, same hunch I had," he said with respect before adopting a serious tone, "which means..."

"Yes?"

"Means you gotta watch your back, honey. I might not be around to help you out next time."

"I'll be careful, Sergeant," said Sharon. "Thanks for everything."

"You got it," said Sergeant Rodriquez.

As soon as she got off the phone with him, Sharon placed another call. She was treading on dangerous, deadly territory, but she was pretty sure she knew how to get one of the big crooks, the one hiring the killer, the one with the greatest ego and the least lineage. Ivan Stark. She was disappointed because she had hoped for a bigger fish, but this would have to do in the meantime. And there wasn't time to waste. She placed another call. *I have to be right about this.* And with that, she unleashed the power of the media.

BREAKING NEWS:
"Trail Gone Cold: Back to Normal on the Hill"

She smiled when she was done, pleased with herself. *That should do the trick.*

CHAPTER 48

Ivan Stark stood on the bow of his yacht, a worry line imprinted across his forehead. His captain, Steve, waved as he came down from the cockpit above to meet his boss, "Mr. Stark, sir. How are you this fine day?"

Ivan didn't reply. He had read the headline. He was covered.

Steve continued, "Two o'clock on Tuesday afternoon and the sun's shining brightly overhead."

Turning to Steve, Ivan said curtly, "Yes." *Please shut up.*

"Look at those pristine turquoise waters sparkling above the world's second largest barrier reef."

Ivan stared blankly at the horizon, and then his eyes traveled the length of his yacht. The *Ides of March* was a $120 million state-of-the-art mansion on water designed by the world's best craftsmen. Aside from the most luxurious mahogany finishing, there was an art collection that included an original Rembrandt and Pollock, and a 140-foot mast. "How far are we offshore?' he asked.

"About ten miles off the southern coast," the captain answered.

"Good," said Ivan. *Almost out of U.S. Coast Guard jurisdiction.* "I'll be down in the control room," he told the captain. *Just focus on your job.*

* * *

The control room was kitted with a closed network that monitored all money transfers from the unmarked bank accounts in Belize City. Katrina Sullivan was pacing, oblivious to the panoramic views of the ocean. Her hair was clasped by a diamond-studded ponytail holder. She was wearing bone-colored silk pants and a strapless milky-white top.

"So explain this to me again," she commanded.

"Just let me do what I need to do," retorted Ivan. *I can't wait to never see you again.*

"While you explain it."

"Fine," he huffed. "Right now, I'm going to execute the program that will initiate each of the fifty transfers."

"Fifty transfers of $20 million each—all $1 billion of it at once—is that smart?"

"Yes," he answered. *Great. She can fucking calculate and be a bitch at the same time.* "Simultaneously."

"Now what's going on?" Katrina leaned over the back of Ivan's chair.

"Money in the form of bank codes is being extracted from the balance sheets of fifty tech companies to fifty different undisclosed offshore accounts. Then, to another fifty. Then, to a third set."

"Three to lose the trail?" she asked.

"Yes, that and the fact that these are a high-tech cluster of secret networks that should shade the transfers to begin with, making them virtually untraceable," said Ivan, proud of his technical prowess.

"Why those specific fifty?" she asked, peering into the screen.

"Because," he answered. *Nosy bitch.*

"Because why, Ivan? Stop being such an asshole. We're in this thing together."

"It's complicated."

"Try me."

"Okay, each transfer belongs to a corporation from this government report, kind of a trail linking these specific companies and these specific bank codes. That's all you need to know."

"Is that all? When do we recollect everything?" she asked, with a sudden lilt in her voice.

"Almost all," he said, "after the third offshore account, the money is recollected and consolidated into one new account at a fourth location."

"And you're sure there's no trace of that either, genius?" she asked, back in stern mode.

"Yes." He sighed at her tone. "There's an entirely other secret network, on a separate fiber-optic system with a separate set of undersea cables, that leads..." he trailed off, savoring his brilliance, this moment where Katrina would know who she was dealing with. His brain.

"That leads where?' she sneered.

"That leads, my dear, right back to where it started from."

"Where. Is. That?"

"Right here.The *Ides of March* herself. This trail of transfers starts and ends at the same exact location. But, electronically, there is absolutely no connection between those starting and ending points. Brilliant, huh?"

"No connection, not even through the networks of the Belize Coast Guard?" she asked.

He raised his voice. *This bitch will never give me credit for anything.* "The Belize Coast Guard is funded by a corrupt government that takes its own cut for offshore banking business. Belize's government offers their offshore services to the smartest financiers from around the world, like me!"

"Fine, you're brilliant," she said dully, "and you're sure they wouldn't double-cross you? Set you up? Are you sure?"

"OF COURSE I'M SURE!" he yelled. "None of the officials running Belize have any interest in catching Ivan Stark, the tech king, in the act of laundering. It would cost them too much. They are, therefore, under instructions to draw as little attention as possible to the incident, OKAY?!"

"Okay," she said quietly.

"Now, let me finish what I have to do." He returned his gaze to his computer screen.

"Fine."

"Oh NO!" He typed something furiously. "NO! NO! NO! FUCK!"

"What?" she asked. "WHAT. HAVE. YOU. DONE?"

"FUCK! FUCK! FUCK!! The money is gone!" He rose and threw the keyboard across the room.

Katrina went to pick it up. "What do you mean, the money's gone?" she demanded.

"I mean, this program was supposed to transfer the money to the end account. The other program was supposed to confirm it hit the account," replied Ivan, pointing to two different screens and beginning to sweat profusely.

"What's the problem, exactly?" she seethed, hands on hips.

"Take a look for yourself, darling," he snarled back.

He turned the flat screen toward Katrina. Together they stared at the ominous monitor, line after line screaming the same message:

Transfer unconfirmed.
Transfer unconfirmed.
Transfer unconfirmed.
Transfer unconfirmed.

"Fuck!" bellowed Ivan, whacking the screen with the back of his hand. "I don't get it! This was supposed to be the grand finale! The money, the networks! Where the—fuck?" He whacked his hand against the monitor again.

CHAPTER 49

The U.S. Coast Guard had been instructed by a very important directive to capture this particular white-collar criminal. The directive came straight from the White House, from the vice president of the United States. They were to catch Ivan right after the electronic transfer was made.

Sharon accompanied them. She had questions to ask. It was unlikely *Riche$* would let her run a piece about the vice president's Enforcer Unit, with only one witness and zero evidence. But an article on ITA and Silverman creating faux network contracts to extort money and laundering it to undisclosed locations—that would be a cover story, indeed. And she was glad that her editor saw fit to accompany her to this scoop, awkwardness between them aside.

As the might of the U.S. government stood set to unleash its power on Ivan Stark and board his yacht, Sharon turned to Damon. "It's show time."

The look he returned her didn't seem to capture the same degree of glee. In fact, Sharon noted a look of panic in his eyes. Then, she heard the sound of Ivan's voice puncture the otherwise perfect tranquility of the ocean setting. It was a fantastic sound.

"FUCK!!!"

At which point, two federal agents raided the control room, backed up by several members of the Coast Guard. Sharon Thomas followed them in.

"Ivan Stark, you're under federal investigation for securities fraud. We'll be escorting you back to U.S. waters," said Captain Andrews.

"What? What the hell are you talking about?" Ivan demanded, smoothing his smarting hand over the top of his balding head. With his other hand, he hit a button on the tiny remote next to him. The control room's computer screens began retracting into their polished wood grooves. He was more concerned about the billion dollars that had just gone missing than the officials in front of him. As far as he was concerned, even with the Coast Guard and federal agents flashing their credentials, he hadn't done anything illegal.

Katrina grabbed the remote and stopped the screen's downward movement. It didn't make sense to provide more grounds for suspicion. *You ass,* her eyes said to Ivan. She always knew she was the smarter of the two of them. She knew something else. *They were set up. And she knew by whom.*

"And what the hell is she doing here?" Ivan sneered, eyes falling on Sharon.

"Great to see you, too," said Sharon, smiling ear to ear.

Katrina was concentrating on Damon Matthews, who was coming down the steps to the control room. He was escorted by a third federal agent. *Never let them see you sweat.* "Damon, thank God you're here." Her blue eyes bore into his, a mixture of trying to take control of a situation beyond control, and pleading.

He grinned at her. "I wouldn't miss this for the world. Or for all the story lines you've been feeding me on WorldWell Bank, trying to throw me off the real story." He felt like he was coming back to life. Then, he looked at Sharon, whose smile suddenly disappeared.

Her eyes narrowed. That's why he had a look of panic before. *Oh, Damon. NO!* "The source?" she whispered to him, a hesitant finger pointing in Katrina's direction.

He nodded before looking away, sheepishly.

"WorldWell Bank did make false loans," said Katrina, to Sharon not Damon, by way of defense and explanation. Sharon saw a look in the woman that she had never detected before. Like a cornered animal. There was no way for Katrina to get out of this predicament.

"Maybe so," said Sharon, momentarily ignoring the terrible churning in her heart, focusing on the scoop, "but the real story is how you two were set to bag a truckload of cash using Silverman and ITA as cover. That's grand larceny and conspiracy, Katrina."

The agents bristled at Sharon's accusation. The more junior agent stepped forward, about to say something. His superior shushed him with a finger to the lips and pulled a copy of the ITA-Silverman contract from his breast pocket. It was opened to the last page. Sharon had given it to them in exchange for letting her and Damon on the Coast Guard boat.

"Recognize this, Ms. Sullivan?" He showed it to Katrina. Her eyes widened at the sight of her signature on the bottom of the document.

"That double-crossing son of a bitch," she murmured.

"I could have told you that," said Sharon.

"There's nothing wrong with that contract," said Ivan, not looking at it. "I'll have my lawyers swarming over you in five minutes. Transferring finances for network construction is not a crime."

Katrina shot him a glare. Ivan was talking too much. *Trust a man to lose it when conditions got sticky.*

"Ivan Stark and Katrina Sullivan," said the senior agent, "we'll be taking you in for questioning regarding SEC fraud allegations and obstruction of justice."

CHAPTER 50

W ait a minute," said Ivan, his pitch rising. "Again, I must say that the contract you have there is perfectly legal. My friend Vice President Arthur Graceson will explain. I don't think you know who I am. I'm the CEO of Intact Technology Association. We're on an expansion program to combine networks around the globe for faster information movement. Those companies are my partners."

Sharon burst in, "I think you're forgetting a minor detail, Mr. Stark."

"And what might that be?"

"You never officially filed this document with the SEC. The unit that you filed with was never recognized by the SEC. That means you knowingly hid a revenue transfer of a billion dollars from federal regulators and the public shareholders. That's called securities fraud."

Ivan's face turned beet red.

"Oh, and another thing," said Sharon, "I wouldn't be too sure about the vice president being your friend. I'm just saying."

Katrina gritted her teeth. Her concern wasn't the vice president. That was Ivan's problem. She couldn't believe Sam had screwed her over this way. Her name was all over this. And, ironically, she was never even after the money. She just wanted the power behind the deception; the feeling of control. Now it would take teams of lawyers to get her off. She shuddered. She would be buried in this crap for years. She wasn't sure who she hated more at that moment: Ivan, Sam, or Sharon. She did the only thing she could. The only person she still had power over was Damon; he had to go down with her.

"I honestly thought we had something, together, darling." She turned to him, trying to conjure up tears. "Everything I gave you, every detail about WorldWell Bank was true."

"We never had anything, Kat," Damon said, almost reluctantly. "We used each other. I'm profoundly sorry...for all of it." He could feel Sharon's judgment smothering him. He couldn't look at her.

Katrina didn't reply. She was twisting one diamond earring in her fingertips. Damon stared at the jewel as it reflected the equatorial sun. Sharon's eyes followed his to the side of her head.

As the guards escorted Ivan and Katrina to their boat, Damon stopped them. "Before you go anywhere, Ivan, maybe its time you confess to what you did to my wife, Marsha."

Ivan faced Damon, his stance solid. "I loved Marsha, you idiot."

"You lying bastard!" Damon yelled, fists clenched, moving to strike before an agent stepped between them.

"It's the truth," Ivan scowled. "Marsha was an amazing woman. You were the one that used her—when you started sleeping with Katrina. Great cover story, Damon. Or undercover, I should say. So how was she? I always found her to be quite the animal in bed."

"You contemptuous piece of slime," retorted Katrina, her own fists clenched. "You make me sick."

Damon struggled against the guard to get to Ivan. "You're the animal!"

Ivan cackled. "Oh shut up. You were along for all of this, Damon, stud-reporter, as long as you got your story. She fed you everything and you accepted it. We're no different, you and I."

"But why, why did you have to kill her?" His fists beat the air.

"I didn't kill Marsha, you moron," said Ivan.

Sharon swore that she saw a tear forming in the corner of his eye. *Nice acting job,* she thought. Then she considered that maybe he wasn't lying. *And if he wasn't, who did kill Marsha?*

"I don't believe you," Sharon said, facing Ivan, testing him. "I heard the tapes."

Ivan's brow crinkled. "What tapes?"

"The ones of you and Marsha. Talking about the books you doctored. Nice way to treat your family."

"I have no idea what you're yapping about," said Ivan.

"You took her down with you, got her in too deep, and when she wanted out, you obliged. You got her out, alright. For good. How could you do that to your own flesh and blood?"

Damon covered his mouth and gasped. "What?"

"Sorry, Damon," said Sharon, "this is a really bad time to tell you, but Ivan and Marsha were siblings. Well, half-siblings. They grew up together."

Damon seemed to sag in front of her eyes. This was a worse betrayal than her affair. He suddenly hated his wife. "She never told me." *One more thing she never told me,* he thought.

"The more important point is that Marsha had tried to fix things," said Sharon. "She even confronted Ivan. She wanted him to reverse the bad numbers before the company went public. I tried the same thing at Silverman. But I discovered it wasn't possible." Sharon cocked her head at Katrina.

Katrina's eyes turned from Sharon's accusations. "So I

quit," continued Sharon. "That's when they tried to kill me—the day of the ITA IPO."

"Oh my God, Sharon," gasped Damon.

"Marsha stuck it out for another year, until..."

Damon's eyes welled. "Until she was murdered." The agent in front of him had moved toward Sharon. It gave him an opening into which he stepped forward and clocked Ivan with a sharp right fist to the stomach.

Ivan dropped back, winded. "I never laid a finger on her," he managed to sputter, "I wouldn't."

"I don't believe you" Damon lunged at him again.

"Then you'll never find out the truth." Ivan stumbled back as the agent reinserted himself between the two men. Ivan turned to address Damon, and then Sharon: "And isn't that your job—the truth?"

Damon shot a pained look at Sharon.

"Alright, that's enough," the agent interrupted. "Ms. Sullivan. Mr. Stark. It's time to go."

CHAPTER 51

Following a phone call from the ever-connected Mickey Mancuso, another couple of officers from the U.S. Coast Guard agreed to escort Sharon and Damon to the Belize City airport. Damon was due to board a flight back to LaGuardia, by way of Houston. Sharon insisted on staying behind to do some more sleuthing. She would fly back on Mickey's private jet the next day. It stood parked in the private hold behind the airport, with the other airplanes of the wealthy that used the country as their personal tax haven.

Damon headed for the airport bar, manned by a dark-skinned midget who offered travelers what he touted as the best rum punch in the world. "Ninety-five percent rum," the man bragged. Damon needed that toxicity to dull the self-loathing that churned through him. Tipping the man his remaining Belizean dollars, Damon took two specials to the waiting lounge. Sharon was watching the planes land and take off. She grabbed the plastic cup and took a swig. Damon sat beside her and placed his hand over hers, intertwining their fingers.

"You're something, you know," he said.

"I'm just doing my job," she said, gently removing her hand from his grasp.

"We still haven't discussed what happened between us the other night," he said.

"Here's the thing," she sighed deeply. She wanted to be diplomatic—he was her boss, and a bit of a broken man. "You're a sweet, if truly fucked-up person..."

"There's a hanging 'but' at the end of that sentence," he said, knowing how bad he must look to her. He felt the same way about himself.

"I'm sorry. Look, I just can't trust you right now. You lied to me about Katrina. You got in bed with her, in more ways than one." She turned to look out the windows. Puffs of clouds marked the sky as far as the eye could see.

Sharon watched the individual clouds move past each other, then slowly merge together, attracting and then repelling, slipping by each other than attracting again—like human beings. She realized that despite her disappointment in his methods, in his infidelity, she felt it was a thousand times worse that Marsha had cheated on him. Sharon knew she was in no position to judge. He did what he did to further his career. She'd be the world's biggest hypocrite if she didn't understand that much. Maybe, if she could learn to forgive herself, she could learn, eventually, to forgive him.

Damon sensed Sharon's body relaxing in the chair next to him. He knew that he had done everything wrong to get his WorldWell scoop. But he had also hired Sharon. He had done one thing right. "Hey, it's okay. We've been through a lot this week. This year. We both have."

"I guess so." She turned to face him, placing a tender hand on his forearm. She had made her own mistakes. Maybe they had even been necessary in order for her to move forward as a person. Or at least that's something her therapist would say.

"And I think it's time for me to come to terms with Marsha's death, and her life," said Damon.

"I can't even imagine what you must be going through. Not knowing what really happened."

"Well, at least I know that she was involved with Ivan's schemes for years. You discovered that before I did."

"Because of Kevin Waters. Because he decided not to just sit quietly and cash his checks."

"Yeah. The key to uncovering this whole mess," said Damon.

"He'll be an important witness for federal prosecutors. I spoke with Sergeant Rodriquez. He said he'd put Kevin and his family into a witness protection program," she said, leaning away from him once again.

Damon tugged at his chin. "What else?"

She raked her fingers through her hair twice before she spoke. "From what I understand, Ivan's scheme went beyond stealing money from his peers and pocketing it offshore."

"What do you mean?"

"I'm not sure anymore. I mean, the contract between Silverman and ITA is a legitimate money-transferring mechanism. What was crooked was the fact that it was never filed with the SEC, which meant the money flows were kept secret from shareholders."

"So that's the crime," said Damon, taking her cue and leaning away from her.

"Well, it's *a* crime," said Sharon, convinced something was still amiss. "It's just that the instructions for this transfer could have also been part of a different scheme."

"I'm not following," he scratched his head.

Sharon was sure that a piece of this puzzle was still missing. She couldn't open up to Damon about the trail, not yet. But she could throw heat on the mastermind of the enforcer scam, who had no doubt colluded with Ivan and Katrina. "Damon, the vice president is involved. I'm not sure how to prove it, but he was running this group through the SEC—the Enforcer Unit. They took bribes from companies, big bribes, to throw dirt on their competitors."

"Like WorldWell Bank?" Damon didn't question her statement.

"Exactly like WorldWell Bank," Sharon said. He hadn't been entirely off base with his story, just with the details.

"So, my story? None of it was real? It was Silverman, I mean Katrina, planting information to me, while paying the Enforcer Unit to prosecute WorldWell Bank."

"It's something like that, maybe." She tucked her hair behind her ear. "Katrina was covering all bases, conspiring with Ivan and the media." She had seen Katrina's signature on the contract, but Kevin had never mentioned her at all. Something was missing. Some obvious connection. She couldn't let it go.

The flight attendant for American Airlines announced the final boarding call. "I need to mull this over, okay?" she told Damon, and stood up. They didn't touch. They didn't embrace goodbye. He reluctantly joined the other passengers walking out the glass door, heading to the tarmac for boarding. He turned to wave, but Sharon had already disappeared inside the terminal building.

CHAPTER 52

Sharon's friend and former lover, Pedro Amilla, was of Mayan descent, like many Belizeans. He lived outside of Dangriga, in a small town of two thousand people called Johnston, but spent most of his time working up and down the coastline.

Pedro made his living taking tourists diving; this was how Sharon had met him. He owned a boat in which he captained the wealthy and powerful in the midst of their monetary activities. Sharon knew he hated them. But his services were in high demand, mostly because of his reputation for trustworthiness. It was said that he would never compromise his clients' secrets. It was dangerous to give anything away, anyway. Too many locals wound up dead in the sea following botched laundering operations.

The payment for quiet service was good. It supported his family, consisting of two sets of grandparents, aging parents, and four younger brothers. He was steadfastly single, not having the time for a personal life, something Sharon could relate to. They had spent one week together, mostly on his boat making love and under the sea, diving. She had retreated to Belize to escape her divorce, her near-death encounter, and the ever-inescapable guilt.

This time, he stood waiting outside Belize City's tiny terminal building, leaning on his battered white jeep. He beamed when he saw her. She hadn't said much about what she was doing there, but the two had become email friends after their romantic encounter. Their enemies were the same; she didn't need to explain much.

"Pedro, it's so good to see you." said Sharon. As they embraced, a booming voice came from behind them.

"Hey, kiddo." Mickey stood panting and sweating, wearing a baggy pair of tan pants, a Hawaiian floral shirt, and a straw hat.

"What is that ridiculous thing on your head?" asked Sharon, not surprised that Mickey made the trip.

"Just trying to fit in with the locals." He nodded hello to Pedro, wiping some sweat from his brow.

"Then take the hat off, man. I'm telling you," Pedro smiled.

Mickey kept the hat on. "Nah, I'm good the way I am."

"Suit yourself," said Pedro. "Okay, let's roll!"

Sharon wanted to board the *Ides of March* once everyone else left the scene. To check around. Pedro knew where all the boats docked. He also knew the local security guards that the U.S. Coast Guard hired to do their job at night while they headed off for the bars. Access to the boat was easy. Finding evidence beneath the surface—that could be tricky. Pedro entered the jeep and opened the manual locks. Sharon got in the front. She was about to turn her head around to make fun of Mickey's hat again.

An ear-shattering pop pierced the air like several truck tires bursting at once. A second blast followed almost immediately, coming from the same direction, the end of the parking lot. Her body was suddenly alert, and her eyes scanned the lot at full attention. Then she heard what sounded like an animal groan.

"Mickey!" she screamed as she watched her mentor slide to the ground. Blood was spurting from his right thigh. Then she noticed a separate leaky pool forming, over the bird-of-paradise flower in the middle of his hula shirt. "NO!"

CHAPTER 53

Sharon leapt in front of the car where Mickey had fallen. "Oh my God!" she gasped. She knelt in front of him. He was half-propped up against the thick rubber tire of the jeep, clutching his side.

"I'm okay, kiddo," he wheezed, between short, sharp breaths, "got a lot—of padding..."

"You're going to be fine," she whispered. *You've got to be.* The buttons flew off his Hawaiian shirt as she ripped it open. Pressing both palms on the stomach wound to stop the blood flow, she yelled, "Get me a towel!" Pedro ran around the car, offering his T-shirt.

"Get some help!" Sharon yelled. While Sharon dabbed Mickey's midsection, Pedro dashed to the back of the jeep. He returned with a first-aid kit.

"Let me," he said, pressing thick gauze into Mickey's thigh to stop the blood spurts. "We gotta get him to a hospital!" Pedro punched something into his pager. People were running over from the parking lot and terminal building.

"Kiddo," panted Mickey, reaching for Sharon's elbow.

"Shh...don't try to talk," said Sharon, dabbing harder. "Stay still."

He turned with difficulty onto his side, reaching for something in the back pocket of his pants. "Take this." He handed her a 9mm gun. "Just in case...fully loaded...safety catch on..."

She thanked him with her eyes, securing the pistol in her jeans pocket with one hand, the other still pressing into his body. She looked down at the bleeding man, this man who had been like a father to her. She knew that if she had to, she'd shoot to kill. "You'll be fine," she repeated.

"There...!" he lifted his head, gesturing to the grassy patch between the runway and the ocean.

She turned to where his head had pointed. Darting like a scared rabbit through the fields was a tiny blonde woman. Sharon scrambled to her feet. Jumbled thoughts. *Stay with Mickey. Follow the woman who had shot her friend.* She was torn between heart and mind.

"Go," said Pedro, gently. "Be careful. I'll meet you at the hospital."

"Go!" said Mickey, before he passed out.

"I'll be back," she said and raced off after the sniper, pushing through the gathering crowd. The blonde had a huge head-start, but Sharon was fit. And determined. As she bolted forward, she patted her pocket to make sure the gun was still there. The woman was heading toward the docks past the airport.

Sharon willed her legs to carry her forward. She saw the woman hop sharply, as if she had hit a rock with her foot. It slowed her down enough for Sharon to close the gap. The two women ran only twenty yards apart, hurdling over rocks and island brush and tropical bushes.

The woman looked over her shoulder. Sharon noted the freckles spotting her face. She had never seen her before. The woman was young, Sharon thought, late twenties or early thirties, incredibly agile. During that second, the woman raised her gun without breaking stride.

Sharon dove to the ground, crashing onto her bad side. "Ow!" she yelped. "Shit!" The sound that followed left her momentarily stunned. The bullet sped through the long wild grass beside her, missing her by inches. She panted and pulled out her own gun, unlocking the catch.

Steadying the gun, she aimed directly at the blonde's legs. The woman cackled. *She's insane*, thought Sharon. Her eyes widened as the woman cocked her trigger again. A second shot just missed her. Sharon cocked her own trigger. She felt a familiar anger. The rage she felt at the brute's first visit. *It's you or him*, she had thought then. *It's you or her*, she thought now. Another shot pulverized the ground by her knee.

She jumped aside. This was about survival. Not about rules. *You can back off and figure it out*, Sharon thought, *or you can run out of time*. "Wait!" she called, rising from the ground, stumbling as she straightened her legs to lunge forward. She figured the woman had one shot of a six-round cartridge left.

"Fuck you!" the woman screamed as she darted on.

At that moment, Sharon realized, *this is personal*. This woman was far too emotional for this to just be some job. She didn't have time to figure out how or why. Her legs propelled her as the woman picked up speed. *If I can get her to shoot once more*, thought Sharon, *I can take her down*. Get some answers. *As long as I don't get hit with that last shot*. Her palms were moist, and the butt of the gun grew slippery. She noticed the woman wore white gloves. She was a professional. Wasn't leaving anything, like sweat, to chance.

Sharon was panting like she'd finished a marathon as she pursued the woman to the docks. The blonde raced up one of the uneven wooden piers. Sharon willed herself to go faster. This was it. The ocean would stop the chase. *Just keep away from that last shot*.

The woman stopped at the end of the pier. She turned to aim at Sharon who had just reached the beginning. "Bye, bitch!" she shrieked, before executing a perfect dive into the glistening sea. Sharon sprinted toward her. This woman was nuts. *Where did she think she was going?*

Sharon inspected the lapping waters, crouching down to avoid any other surprise shots. The tide was coming in, gathering waves. The woman would have to come up for air shortly. Sharon scanned the ocean as she pointed the gun, cupping her right hand with her left for steadiness. She could see nothing.

Where the hell is she? Sharon thought after almost two minutes had gone by. Even the best spear shooters rarely held their breath for more than three minutes at a time. Sharon gazed inland. There didn't appear to be anyone else in the boat yard. The early-rising fishermen had gone home for the day. The sun was setting, striping the ocean with rays of burnt orange and hot pink.

Sharon lay flat, her stomach pressed against the wood planks, searching between them for signs of the shooter. Waves licked the pier's wooden stilts. The water was shallow and crystal clear. She saw nothing but barracuda, some jellyfish, and a thin trumpet fish swimming too close to shore.

Where is she? Sharon could hear her heart thumping as she scanned farther out into the sea. Then, in the distance, past the swell of the waves, she noticed faint bubbles. Sharon recognized them instantly—bubbles from scuba gear.

Sharon turned back toward the land and spotted a red and white flag flying over a shack in the dock yard, just off the pier. The international diving sign hanging over a PADI dive shop. She looked back toward the water. The woman still hadn't resurfaced. She decided she could either wait for that to happen, or go underwater herself. She sprinted toward the shack. "Hey anyone there?!" she called on approach. There was no answer. She tried to loosen the padlocks on the shop's doors, but the rusty locks were shut tight. *Dammit.*

Sharon noticed the shop's dive boat in front of the shack, anchored in the shallow waters between the shore and the dock. She knew there had to be some stray equipment on it. She dashed over to find it.

Creeping quickly aboard the boat, she saw that a few tanks remained on board, probably ready for next morning's dive. She searched for a BC vest below the boat's bow, where dive-masters sometimes stored spares in case of malfunctions. She extracted two and examined them. One was huge; it could have fit Mickey. Grimacing, she told herself not to think about Mickey just now. She held up the second one. Extra small. She put it on, removed her sneakers, and searched frantically for a regulator.

Where would it be? Then she remembered Pedro stored his extras under the captain's chair. As she reached for the latch underneath the white plastic chair, a shot rang out. Sharon jumped. Her pulse raced. The bullet hit the mast of the boat next to her. *This woman's still close. I can get to her.* Fear was replaced by a sense of purpose. *Last shot*, she thought as she untied a tank and hooked up the regulator between it and her BC. With the weight of the tank heavy against her back, she strained through her thighs to stand up. She stuffed a couple of three-pound weights in her BC pocket for ballast.

Scouring the vessel for fins, her spirit dampened. None were around. She knew swimming with no fins would greatly hamper underwater speed. Her feet would feel lighter than the rest of her body. She grabbed a sandy mask lying on the boat's floor and placed it over her face, wrapping the strap around the back of her head, and stuck the regulator in her mouth.

It's show time. Sharon rolled backward into the water, in the direction of the shot. The woman had to be close. She headed down, distancing from shore and equalizing quickly, as the depth increased: ten feet, twenty, thirty below. She hadn't checked the air gauge on her regulator, hoping the tanks were full and ready. A major diving mistake. She examined it now. *Shit.* 300 PSI. A tenth of a tank full.

Sharon's lungs were efficient; 300 PSI would last her about seven minutes. Unless she went too deep. The deeper you went, the faster you went through the tank. She had to get to this woman in a hurry. *Her air was running out.*

CHAPTER 54

Sharon spun in a quick circle, hoping for a glimpse of the woman. *She's got to be near*, Sharon thought, straining for visibility. She shivered from the chill in the water. She scanned the underwater reef, alive with corals, sea fans, and innumerable creatures coming in to feed. About a hundred yards off the reef, Sharon noticed a sharp dark drop; the barrier ledge seemed to become an underwater mountain. It looked like it could be a thousand feet deep.

Sharon felt a sudden tug at her BC. Swinging around, Sharon came face to face with the blonde shooter. Or more accurately, goggle to goggle. Their eyes locked. The woman's eyes glared cold into Sharon's; even behind the cover of the goggles, they were menacing.

Reaching into her pocket, struggling against the weight of the water, Sharon felt for her gun. Not to kill the woman, but to threaten her to the surface. *Damn it*. Her pockets were empty. *Shit*! It must have fallen on deck when she was rushing into the scuba gear.

Too much thinking. The woman smashed her palm into Sharon's goggles, pushing them upward. A burst of water bubbled around Sharon's eyes. The salt of the sea stung, momentarily blinding her. As she struggled to replace the goggles on her face, Sharon lost sight of the woman, who kept grabbing at her hands. Without the mask, Sharon was fighting blind.

Sharon crooked her hand into a boomerang position, another Aikido move, to release it with a snap, reached round the back of her head for the mask and refastened it on her face. With the other hand, she gripped the woman's wrist and bent it away from her. The blonde yanked her wrist away, adjusted her regulator to her mouth, and swam around to Sharon's back.

She felt another tug. This time, it wasn't on her BC, it was on her regulator. The woman was trying to take her air supply away. Sharon hunched her shoulder and shimmied down to free her regulator. She made a grab for the woman's fins. The woman kicked at her head, as Sharon worked herself up the woman's thrashing legs, until she could wrap her own around the woman's body. The woman reached down to pull again at Sharon's regulator as Sharon held onto her with her legs.

The blonde thrust herself toward the surface and wriggled out of Sharon's leg lock. She kicked Sharon in the face as she hoisted through the deep water. Sharon could feel her goggles flying away, completely this time, no hanging strap around her hand to keep them in place. Her breathing rate increased as she realized she would have to beat this woman without the use of her eyes.

Sharon felt a strong kick at her neck, snapping her head sharply backwards. She had to bite down hard on the regulator's mouthpiece to maintain connection to the air flow. With all the survival strength she could muster, she brought her head back forward. She knew she was sucking too much air because of the adrenalin flowing through her body. As her head snapped forward, Sharon gripped a chunk of the woman's blonde hair and yanked back on it. *Take that, you freak.*

The blonde's head strained back as she raised her hands up to loosen Sharon's hold. She folded her legs up to her chest and pumped both heels up. Hard. Smack into the bottom of Sharon's nose. On land, she would have broken it with that maneuver. The water's buoyancy provided more resistance.

Sharon sucked in a lungful of air to fight the staggering pain. She felt blood leaking from her nostrils. Underwater, she couldn't inhale the blood to clear her nose; every breath now had to come through her mouth. Her lips tightened on the regulator's mouthpiece. Her teeth clamped on its plastic grips inside her mouth. She saw stars. Her shoulders heaved. She felt faint. Everything started going black.

It was all she could do to focus on breathing through her mouth, despite the pain rushing up her sinuses. She felt her grip loosen on the woman's hair. Inhaled another lungful of air. She couldn't concentrate on slowing her heart rate. Couldn't help burning through her tank.

The blonde swam in back of her. Sharon could feel the woman's hands circling her throat, tightening down. Her orientation was shot. *Come on, Sharon, stop thinking and just react! One quick move. Do it!*

She bent her heels up behind her, toward her butt, and arched her back away from the tank as much as she could. She needed the angle in order to reach the most sensitive part of her attacker, between her legs. With all her strength, she shot both feet into the core of the woman's body. *Take that!*

Sharon felt the woman's hands release her throat. Then she felt another tug on her air valve. *Focus, Thomas*, she told herself, knowing what was coming next.

The woman managed a grip on Sharon's tank with one hand. With the other hand, she cranked Sharon's air valve all the way off. Sharon sucked in hard through her mouth, gasping for air. The flap of her regulator made a sickening thump against the tank. Like a large gulp. The sound of the end. As Sharon tried to contort her body to reach the valve, desperate to turn on her air again, her attacker whacked her in the nose once more with the heel of her fin. Sharon couldn't concentrate on the massive pain; her only thought was to find a way to breathe or surface. While still struggling for her valve, Sharon felt the woman's thighs clamp around her torso, like a boa constrictor. *She's gonna hold me down!*

Ten seconds. Twenty. Every movement Sharon initiated was thwarted by this killer. She felt herself slipping away. She knew about drowning. Had studied it, anyway. First your lungs collapsed from lack of air, then they filled with water. *Thirty.* She could voluntarily hold her breath around thirty to forty seconds, but it was a task much easier done given the luxury of breathing when it was over. This was a sense of claustrophobia she had never experienced. She kept thrashing to loosen the woman's leg grip around her body, but this woman was strong as hell. *Forty.*

So, this is what's it's like to have time to think about your death, thought Sharon, while spiraling her body to find a weakness in the woman's hold. The killer's legs squeezed tighter around her. Sharon was left with no other option. She ceased all movement, out of seconds, as she relaxed her body. *Keep your attackers guessing.*

It's her or me. In one motion, she twisted her body around and punched into the blonde's mask. The mask whirled off into the depths below. *Now, we're both diving blind,* she thought, *I just need some fucking AIR!* The woman's legs released as her head jerked back. Sharon got hold of one of the woman's feet, reaching for one of her regulators tubes. *Sorry, sweetie, NEED AIR NOW!*

The woman fought for control of the regulator, but Sharon managed to yank it away, and brought the mouthpiece to her own mouth. She sucked in a huge lungful of air, and started to regain clarity with the oxygen. *But not enough.*

The woman pulled the regulator out of Sharon's mouth and shoved it back in hers and kicked Sharon in the nose once more. As Sharon reeled, the woman kicked again. The pain was excruciating. Sharon, out of oxygen again, felt her body pulled backward. This time, the blonde didn't need to hold her down. Sharon was beginning to sink.

It's her or me. Sharon raised her arms to tunnel for the surface. She calculated that she had about twenty seconds before blacking out. She catapulted herself up, scooping water out of her way, pumping her arms to get to her attacker, who was swimming ten feet above her, back to the surface.

While rising, she saw a little black rubber object floating away—her regulator. She reached out and grabbed it. There was 100 PSI left on the valve. The woman propelled up faster, dumping weights out of her vest to ease her lift. Sharon harnessed herself for a final effort. Giving every bit she had left to pump upward, she grabbed the killer's ankles once more. They were about twenty feet from the surface; now, they both sank back down.

The blonde smacked Sharon's regulator from her mouth with her fin. *No way I'm gonna stop breathing because of you,* thought Sharon, as her fingers extended toward the woman's back-up hose. She managed to suck in a lungful of air. *If we have to share, so be it.* The woman spun around suddenly to get away from Sharon, and reached for something attached to her inner thigh. She extracted a dive knife from its latch and plunged into Sharon's vest, with the viciousness of a barracuda intent on blood.

The blade missed her body by a hair. Now it was all about instinct. Sharon whipped her body in a half-circle, bringing her hand to the knife sunk into her vest, got a grip on its handle, extracted it, and jerked back in the other direction, plunging the knife into her attacker. One motion. One second.

This time, the knife punctured skin, the skin covering the woman's heart. All her movements ceased as the woman's blood slowly drifted into the sea in a muddy brown-red. Her body sank into the sea depths. If they had been farther out, Sharon realized, a school of sharks would be swarming already. She didn't want to stick around and see how long it took for them to figure it out. And she needed air. Sharon surged upward, sputtering frantically as she broke the surface of the water.

CHAPTER 55

I t had never felt so good to breathe. Pedro raced toward her on the dock. A tank strapped around his bare muscular waist, no BC vest. Part merman, he had the experience to go in air apparatus and tank alone, no extra gear. "Sharon!" he shouted, holding a face mask. "Are you okay?"

Sharon swam to him, panting with each stroke. She clambered herself up on the dock, heaving, "That was a diving exercise I won't be trying again," she gasped. She examined the spot where she had resurfaced. "Pedro, she's in there, somewhere," she said, pointing to the ocean.

"Stay here," he told her, throwing his mask on and jumping into the water. Sharon stood shivering on the dock. Pacing. Moments later, Pedro resurfaced, carrying a limp woman. Her eyes were shut, her head back, and a dark clot of blood saturating her vest. He laid her carefully on the dock.

"Who are you?" Sharon asked, kneeling beside her, cradling her head.

The woman stared directly into Sharon's eyes, with a lifetime of hatred. "You...killed...him," she sputtered.

"What? Who?"

"It was you," answered the woman, between gasps, "He was all...I...had."

"I don't understand," said Sharon, bending her ears over the woman's mouth to hear her better.

"That night...the FedEx truck...you killed him...Lester... internal bleeding," she panted.

The brute. The pieces were coming together. "I'm so sorry," said Sharon instinctively, even though this woman, and apparently a man named Lester, had tried to kill her, and Kevin, and Mickey.

"My fault," murmured the woman, losing consciousness, "I never should have involved him."

"Please, who are you?" There were still so many unanswered questions.

"You…should be done…you took everything from me," she said almost inaudibly.

"I'm so sorry," Sharon repeated. "Maybe I can help you."

The woman let out a quiet huff, something like a low laugh. "R trail."

"R trail? What do you mean? Please. What do you know about the trail?"

"Rrr. Saa." The woman fell silent, her blue eyes frozen.

Pedro examined her pulse and slowly closed her eyelids. "She's dead," he said. Sharon nodded, shuddering, getting a closer look, digging into the woman's back pocket from which she extracted a soaking wet passport. She opened it up and inspected the inside. It had been issued to Elaine Northright, born in 1979. "This must be the woman shooter who was at Damon's house, the same night the brute came for the trail." *Only a week and a day ago.* "I wonder what she was doing here now?" Sharon asked out loud. *Besides trying to kill me.*

"Huh?" said Pedro, wiping the leaking blood from the dead woman.

"Nothing," said Sharon, looking off into the horizon at the sunset, rubbing her upper arms. "It's just that, she was late."

"I'll say," he said, shaking his head.

"I mean, I don't get it. The bad guys were already caught." She pinched her nose, rubbing away the blood caked in her nostrils.

From Pedro's pile of clothes and shoes next to them, his pager emitted a shrill beep. He ignored it while he continued cleaning up Elaine. This was not the first time he had seen a diver die. She might be a criminal, but she still seemed too young for this fate. The pager beeped again. "Excuse me," he said, both to Sharon and to the corpse.

"More bad news, Sharon," he said, showing her the screen:

IDES OF MARCH. BOMBED.

Sharon wasn't surprised. It all made sense. Elaine worked for Ivan. In case of any problems, she was supposed to destroy the evidence. "I guess she wasn't late after all. She was just in time. Sent as a decoy. To keep us here and away from Ivan's yacht." She glanced at the body; she was unable to feel sadness for the death of this woman who tried to kill her, and yet felt a modicum of empathy for her ultimate, and worthless, sacrifice at the hands of Ivan Stark. "Oh my God, I can't believe I haven't asked yet—how's Mickey?"

"He'll be okay. The bullet he took in the stomach grazed his side, didn't penetrate any organs. The one in his leg will be removed. He's at Belize General awaiting the surgery."

"Alone?" Her eyes bulged.

"He's okay. My brother was the ambulance driver. Here," he fished in his pocket, "he wanted you to have these." He handed her a set of keys.

She rolled them around her hand.

"He said you should stay and write your story at his place. Said you'd know the combination to his alarm. Something about your first trade."

She recalled that first FX trade, under Mickey's leadership. The profit was $285,492. He had made a poster of it at the time. Plastered it across the trading room. "I can't go back without seeing him first," she said, choking back a tear.

"He told me to tell you that if you didn't fly straight back to New York to scoop this piece, he'd never talk to you again," said Pedro, giving her a hug and a lingering kiss on the cheek. "Next time, you should stay a bit longer, we'll go diving."

Sharon frowned. "Or maybe just go explore a rainforest."

"You're on," he said as an ambulance pulled up to the foot of the dock. "As soon as we take care of her, I'll drive you back to the airport."

"By way of the hospital?" she asked. Mickey would understand that she had to see him, after she had dragged him into this mess.

CHAPTER 56

The last thing Sharon wanted to do back in New York was enter the Silverman building again. That rumors about Katrina and Ivan were flying around the Street wasn't the problem. It was that it looked impossibly and increasingly likely that Sam Peterson was clean.

No matter how much she played it in her head, she came to the same conclusion based on the evidence. Ivan and Katrina had colluded. They would probably do jail time. The Enforcer Unit was a criminal scheme directed by the vice president. But, like every other possible fall of the powerful, it would be swept under the Washington carpet. Relegated by the media—and thus the Justice Department—to the category of *"yesterday's news."*

As Kevin told her, the fact that the enforcers really did process some fraud cases, or at least cases with evidence of fraud, meant they came off as a legitimate group of elite white-collar crime fighters. Not extortionists. Not killers.

For right now, there was one remaining element of protocol that Sharon had to take care of: Quit Silverman. For the last time. Sam, however, beat her to the punch. His assistant had called to set up a Thursday morning meeting with the CEO.

Sharon was staying at Mickey's Gramercy apartment while he recovered at St. Vincent's. He didn't want to stay in Belize more than one damn night, he had said. The fire in her apartment hadn't destroyed her clothes, just her main living room and study, so she had plenty of suits to choose from for the event. She decided on a pretty egg-shell colored linen one, which she complemented with cream pumps, no stockings. Riding the 6 train downtown, she realized she had selected Katrina's signature color. She suppressed a laugh as she sipped her third morning coffee. The subconscious worked in mysterious ways. Another one for her therapist.

Promptly at ten a.m., Sharon appeared at the door of Sam's fiftieth-floor office. Seated behind his desk, he greeted her like a favorite daughter. "Sharon, please come in, have a seat. It's so very good to see you."

Sharon searched his eyes for signs of sarcasm. "Thanks," she answered, opting for his black leather couch, not one of the two chairs in front of his desk. Let him come to her.

Sam cleared his throat. "We've had an interesting history, you and I," he said.

She crossed her legs and leaned back. *I'll say.*

"I called you here today because I wanted to discuss an opportunity with you."

"Opportunity?" she asked. Something was up.

"You impressed me, Sharon," he said, bead eyes capturing hers. "Despite your reservations about my company in the past, you helped put the lid on a very serious crime."

She heard the sounds of leather shifting as she leaned forward. Her stomach contracted as she considered the fact that she had helped Sam. "I didn't do anything for you," she said.

"Maybe not consciously," he said, "but our interests were aligned, yours and mine. We both wanted to clean up some rather nasty corruption. And, I just wanted to," he came over and sat beside her on the couch, "to thank you."

She leaned away from him, sniffing, wanting to stand and run. His breath smelled of expensive peppermints. His cologne of power. His clear blue veins added an eerie outline to his skeletal hands.

"I also wanted to offer you a job here," he said. "A promotion, as it were."

"What?" She couldn't think of anything she wanted less. He had to know that.

"That's right. Your credibility. Your integrity," he seemed to struggle with the word, "would help repair our reputation, after this...incident. Our CTO aligning with such a corrupt company—unthinkable. I was stunned. I, of course, resigned from ITA's board immediately upon hearing of the bust."

"Of course you did," she said, rising. She straightened a non-existent crease in her skirt. She didn't think the bust was public information.

He grabbed her wrist, bony fingers encircling it. "I would pay you, Sharon. Very well. Seven figures. Maybe eight."

Sharon retracted her hand from his grasp. She gazed out the window onto the street below. Men and women like ants, scurrying about, no awareness of the world around them. She inspected the huge flat screen. Silverman's stock price arrow was green. It had changed to green after Sam's press release about the need for strict corporate responsibility, following the "incident." His eyes, imbedded in the wrinkles of his WASP lineage, were the same color.

She looked around Sam's office. Considered the money. The security it could buy. Maybe a dive shop in Ecuador. Then she turned around and walked toward his door. Before she exited, she turned to face him. "Sam, there are some things that are not for sale. I wouldn't want to work here again if it were the last job on Earth."

"Sometimes, Sharon," he replied, "you don't do things because you want to. You do them because you can." He didn't rise from the couch.

She dug into her purse. "Here," she said, taking one slow step toward his desk. She placed her Silverman ID card on it. "I won't be needing this anymore. Goodbye, Sam."

* * *

A few minutes later, Sharon burst through the front doors of Silverman. The August air was thick with humidity, and the curb reeked of old garbage, and Sharon was thrilled. She felt free. As she turned north, she knew that now she could focus on what was really important.

Sharon needed time alone to figure out what was gnawing at her. She walked back from Wall Street to Gramercy. She needed this thinking time. Having rolled the pieces around in her mind a hundred times, she realized there was some link she was overlooking. The fact that the vice president—so smug about his fight against corporate crime—was so intricately involved in perpetrating it. This wasn't the end. By Fourteenth Street, she was completely stuck. She had to call Trevor, her technology saint, who was still feverishly working on figuring out the links in the Enforcer Unit network.

"Sam Peterson, CEO of Silverman—what's his connection to Julian Elliot?" she asked. There was no need for small talk between them.

"Julian is his nephew. He's going to plead self-defense. He'll get off light." Trevor was enjoying his investigation role.

"Do you have that email connecting Sam and the vice president to the money transfer?"

"Yeah, but it's a printout; it'll be inconclusive—could have been created at any time."

"Trev, we need to resurrect that enforcer network. We need to—"

"Whoa. Is that all?" Trevor said sarcastically.

"All? That's everything! How can you be so nonchalant about this?" The vice president had deflected all involvement onto Ivan and Katrina. *He is in the clear*, Sharon thought angrily.

"Well then you'll be happy to know I have the entire network on my burner."

"You have what? When did you...?"

"While you were tangling with the twerp, I was downloading. I figured you could handle yourself."

"Trev, I love you!" She wanted to wrap her arms around him.

"Promises, promises."

"Excellent. Keep it safe, not at your place."

"Share, with all the goons after you, I wasn't going to, like, take any chances. It's safe. I assure you."

"Where?"

"Nuh-uh, not on the phone. Think donuts. Dunkin Donuts. I'll talk to you later."

CHAPTER 57

Sharon made sure Trevor's copy of the Enforcer Unit's network was handed over to the United States Justice Department. They launched a full investigation, promising it would be quick. A week later, they announced that none of their probes into the vice president's computer systems indicated he had ever sent an email about a wire transfer to Sam Peterson, exonerating him from any possible criminal link to the old Enforcer Unit.

The White House decided that the best way of dealing with the enforcer incident, now that the media had sniffed a story and was poking around for leaks, was to admit, rather than deny, its existence. The day after his exoneration, the vice president held an elaborately orchestrated press conference.

In a self-righteous tone that made Sharon's blood boil, he said: "I am deeply sorry that the Enforcer Unit had to be closed due to lack of appropriate funding. I also am saddened that the Justice Department's time was wasted on an unnecessary investigation into its credibility. I am happy to report that we are winning the battle against corporate crime everyday."

Though rumors about the investigation dampened his popularity, and though a few progressive groups demanded the impeachment of the president and resignation of the vice president, the administration remained. The vice president's old-money pal, Sam Peterson, was also not implicated in any wrongdoing. The Silverman-ITA contract didn't contain Sam's name, after all. It had been signed by his former CTO, Katrina Sullivan, and former ITA CEO, Ivan Stark. Both of whom awaited sentencing.

With the help of his influential friends, Julian claimed self-defense and plea-bargained to the minimum eighteen-month sentence for third-degree manslaughter. The Capitol killer case got relegated to the bottom of Sergeant Rodriquez and Officer O'Harris' pile, by White House decree.

* * *

Just after Labor Day, Damon sat behind his *Riche$* desk reading through the drafts of Sharon's story on ITA's scandalous crash when his phone rang.

"Hey, Damon," Sharon said cheerily, "how's it going? I've got something I think you'll be interested in. Can I stop by your office?"

"Of course." He hadn't seen her since Belize. She had been holed up at Mickey's apartment, working on her story, and avoiding him, he suspected. He missed her.

"Great, I'm in the lobby. Be up in two minutes."

As she walked into his office, Damon pointed to his desk. "This is an awesome story!"

"I wish I could have used the email trace between Peterson and the VP. Useless Justice Department!"

"Yeah, but you know Stetson would never let a story run with so much info denied by Washington."

"The independent media strikes again. Right. Whatever. Anyway, take a look at this." She handed him an 8-K report.

"What am I looking at?" He stared at the piece of paper.

"The money that was supposed to hit Ivan's fake company in Belize—it never surfaced."

"Really? What does that mean?"

"He and Katrina were bagged on conspiracy to commit fraud—on account of the Silverman-ITA contract they signed, right?" She leaned toward him, her palms flat on his desk.

"Right. So?"

"So where's the money?" Her face beamed.

"I thought the Feds decided the mission was never accomplished, right?"

"Wrong." She cracked a wide smile.

"Wrong?" He frowned in return.

"I mean, right about the Feds, wrong about the mission. The money did leave the accounts of those fifty companies. I checked all their current financials to make sure."

"Then where did it wind up?"

"In Belize."

"Belize?" He scratched his head. That's where transfers were unconfirmed.

"Take a look at this." She extracted a transfer receipt and handed it to him.

His eyes widened as he inspected the piece of paper. "Where did you get this?"

"A friend of mine down there," she stated matter-of-factly.

"Who the hell?" he asked, with a tinge of jealousy.

"Pedro—the captain who manned the boat I used for all my diving trips down there."

"And he happens to work part-time at..." Damon squinted at the blurred ink, "...PSS, Partners, Plc."

"No," she said, propping her hands on her hips. She was proud.

"No? Then what's his deal? Who are PSS?" He wasn't enjoying this as much as she was.

"Damon, come on," Sharon goaded. "This is *so* not hard. PSS. Peterson, Sullivan...."

"Stark."

"There you go," she snapped her fingers. "Now," she teased, "guess who Pedro *has* worked for."

"Ivan Stark. The *Ides of March*." He was getting it.

"No," she shook her head.

"Then who? Who else has a boat down there?"

Sharon couldn't contain herself anymore. *That's what Elaine tried to say before she died. 'Saa' —Sam.* "Sam Peterson—And guess who happened to be in Belize the day of the *Ides* raid?"

"Sam Peterson," Damon announced, finally catching up.

"Uh-huh. See, I think Katrina believed she was out-maneuvering Ivan, when in fact Ivan was one-upping her, and working with Sam. But Sam double-crossed them both."

"How so?"

"He planted that contract to implicate both of them, no matter what happened to the money."

"But he's a billionaire, why would he want the extra money at this kind of risk?"

"It's not the money, Damon. Sam's a power fiend. Ivan and Katrina were conspiring to supplant Sam's investment banking world with their technology. I think they wanted to cut out the banking middlemen. If the networks that ITA constructed were airtight, they'd gain huge credibility. The test was these fifty companies—the best network companies in the world. If they couldn't track where their own money went, then no one could."

"Then Ivan is deeper in this than we thought." The thought of that man tightened Damon's gut.

"Well, Ivan was doing other things as well, like cooking his own books in case this didn't work."

"That's where my wife came in, right?" He felt a chill.

"I'm sorry, but yes. She was helping him doctor every acquisition. You can tell from all the massive bump-ups in the value of each acquired company before and after ITA bought them. She would have gone down for that, Damon." Sharon watched his face fall.

"That didn't mean she deserved to die," he said with pride and pain. He did still love her.

"Well, someone needed her dead."

"Ivan. To keep her quiet."

"Maybe."

Damon changed the subject, hoping to ease the rage building in him. "And the Enforcer Unit, the vice president—how does that all fit in?"

"It was easy to set up the unit and have the vice president oversee it; it made all of Washington pleased that corporate crime had a new watchdog. Meanwhile, the vice president had his own ideas of how to control how companies did business. So he brought his buddy Peterson in on it, made it look as legit as possible, hired real lawyers, eager young men wanting to make a difference."

"Enter Kevin, your source," said Damon.

"And Simon. And Julian. Julian must have been the vice president's plant. To make sure the transfers happened. To make sure you were involved for media attention—in addition to whatever Katrina was dishing out about WorldWell to keep you off track—and I guess, to help out Ivan. I was supposed to be involved to cast a shadow on ITA and away from Peterson's real plot."

"So he walked away clean."

"Until now, until Pedro got me this document. I've contacted the Feds to bust into the PSS accounts. My guess is that within an hour, they should find a billion dollars, less expenses."

"For?"

"Yachts, hush money, assassination money. Elaine."

"Elaine?"

"The blonde nut job that threatened you. And tried to kill me. I had my buddy in the D.C. police department do some research. It turns out Elaine met Sam a few years ago at an art forgery bust. She used to be a cop. They kept in touch. Did business together."

"So she took out the first enforcers?"

"Yeah—the ones that asked questions. They were shot in the eye and the hand to destroy the prints and the retina—the two IDs that were used as unique access to the Enforcer Unit. So that the floaters couldn't be traced back to the unit. But Elaine won't be standing trial."

Her cavalier tone surprised him. "What do you mean? Why?"

"She's dead, Damon. We–I–it was her or me. We had an underwater scuttle. I needed air, I—" She was choking up. He put a hand on her shoulder, where it felt too comfortable. Sharon composed herself by shaking it off, flicking the memory aside, too. "Anyway, so that's the deal on the enforcers."

"Nice work, Thomas," he grinned. "You did all that this morning?"

"The calls this morning, the rest while I was putting together that cover." She tapped his desk.

"And what are you going to do for the rest of the day?" he said, trying to joke with her.

"Help you sort out Marsha's murder," she said, thinking her therapist would be proud of her.

"What's that?" he stuttered.

"We need to figure out who killed Marsha," she repeated, sensing his apprehension.

"We?"

"Yes. I'll help you. You need to know. To move on." This was new territory for Sharon. She was trying another route. She knew that avoidance would no longer work for her. She knew that you weren't supposed to do it that way. You were supposed to face your demons and work with them, or through them, or something like that. Otherwise, they could just kill you.

CHAPTER 58

Twenty minutes later, Sharon and Damon entered the lobby of the Pierre Hotel on Sixty-first Street and Fifth Avenue. "So tacky, isn't it?" said Sharon, as they climbed the Persian-rug-covered stairs that led to the front reception desk.

Damon noted that nothing had changed since that horrible night. *In places like this,* he thought, *nothing ever does.*

"Thanks so much for letting us check out the room," Sharon gushed to the hotel's manager.

"You're in luck, it being between guests at the moment," he responded defensively.

"We won't be long," said Damon. If it were up to him, he thought, he wouldn't be there at all.

"The elevators are past the main stairway, through the cocktail lounge," said the manager, "but you already know that, Mr. Matthews?"

Damon swallowed. "Unfortunately, yes."

"Come on," said Sharon, grabbing his arm and shooting the manager a dirty look. At the sixth floor, she and Damon exited the elevator and stepped across an intricate Oriental carpet. Soon, they stood in front of room 605.

"I haven't been here for over a year," said Damon quietly.

Sharon clasped his hand. "Are you okay?"

"I'm okay. Let's do this." He inhaled deeply.

She inserted the heavy gold key into the gold lock. As

she was turning it, she remarked, "Guess they don't believe in electronic entry cards at the Pierre."

"Old style," replied Damon.

"Old money."

"That's why I could never understand what she was doing here. Why the Pierre?"

"It does seem...snotty. Very Sam, actually." She was surprised that was the first connection that popped into her head.

"Are you saying that...?" asked Damon, picking up on it immediately.

"No, I'm not saying anything. It was just an observation."

Damon walked over to the four-poster bed, covered with a thick floral fabric of vibrant cranberries and mauves and limes. He removed the thick spread to expose pale blue silk sheets and goose-feather pillows. Only the best for the Pierre. Trailing his hand over the sheets, he said softy, "I never examined this part of the room. I was only by the curtains, where she was... strangled. God, this is hard." He swallowed hard.

Sharon whispered, "Yes. Look, if you don't want to do this now, we can come back."

He straightened his back and walked over to the gold and silver twisted curtains. "I'm okay," he said as his eyes welled up.

Sharon followed him, counting the steps between the bed and window. She looked up at the curtain rod, about eleven feet above them, and followed the bronze hooks that clasped the upper folds of the curtains. Then she examined the tassels that divided the curtains in two separate cascades of material. "This is odd," she remarked, touching one of the hooks that pinned back a tassel.

"What's odd?"

"This hook," she gestured to the one she was holding, "it's bronze, and aged, like the hooks at the top of the window."

"So?"

"Well, if she was strangled with one of these," she pointed to a tassel, "she'd have to be standing near enough to these tassels for it to reach around her. There's not much material here," she tugged the end of one, "not much give."

"But the police report was very specific about the cause of death—asphyxiation," Damon said, and then softly, "from the tassels."

"Yeah, but unless she wasn't moving at all, the only way to strangle someone with these tassels is to pull them from their hooks."

"Well, maybe the killer pulled them then."

"Maybe, but they're old. They're probably irreplaceable."

"This whole place is old."

"I know, but," Sharon tugged at the tassel. The hook popped out of the wall and fell on the carpet.

"What are you doing?"

"Look at that hole," she said, sticking her index finger into it. "It's huge—you couldn't screw an old hook back into there. They would need to replace it with a new one."

"Well, maybe they have a whole stash of old bronze hooks."

"Maybe. Or maybe..."

"What, Sharon? What are you saying?"

"Maybe she wasn't strangled by this tassel at all. Because she was already dead."

"Then why?"

"Strangling someone, it's a very...personal way to–to... kill, isn't it?"

"I'm not following."

"You have to be close to the person. Whoever killed her knew her well."

"That's why it has to be Ivan. That bastard. Oh, God!" he gulped through his tears.

"I just don't think it was Ivan."

"Why? He had the motive to keep his scheme quiet, especially since he failed at it the first time around."

"It doesn't make sense. Even if Marsha was threatening to expose him, he wouldn't take that risk. The fact that he set up multiple business strategies to win big—even had each acquisition doctored to show an exact business growth pattern—he wasn't that kind of a risk taker. Unless he was set up," she mused.

"Who else wanted her dead? Kat?" Immediately Damon was embarrassed he used her nickname.

"Silverman was their IPO banker. Lots of money and reputation would be lost if it got out that all of ITA's numbers were false."

"Particularly Katrina's, right? You think Katrina could be involved?"

"Maybe, but I think she was confident she could ride out any negative press. She had you for that, didn't she?" Sharon couldn't resist the dig.

"Yes, she did," he acknowledged, avoiding her gaze.

"Anyway, Sam had more to lose, because he's the big picture guy. But he doesn't seem like someone who'd get his hands dirty by actually committing murder."

"And she wouldn't have been waiting for him, dressed like she was." The thought of his wife in that lingerie, meant for someone else, still made Damon furious.

"Which is why, no matter who did it, she had to be dead by the time she got here. My guess is she died from something she ingested—and the strangling was for dramatic effect."

"But there's nothing in the records. The coroner said she was completely healthy, internally," he cringed.

"That doesn't matter."

"Why?" Damon never understood Sharon's distrust of standard police procedures.

"Because the NYPD, the medical examiners, the coroners can all be bought off. When I used to work at Silverman, Sam would boast about how he owned this city. Katrina used to say everyone has a price. Sam lived to pay people off to do what he wanted. That's why he hated me. I didn't play ball. He could have put me away. He can put anyone away. Including Ivan." *And maybe the vice president*, she thought, but didn't share. *That would be huge.*

Her cell phone rang. "Hello?" she said. "Yes. Excellent! Thank you, Sergeant!" Her left thumb flexed up, to get Damon's attention.

"Who was that?" asked Damon.

"Sergeant Rodriquez from D.C. Seems that PSS received a rather sizeable deposit last month."

"For one billion dollars?"

"You got it. Come on!" She grabbed his arm.

"Where are we going?" he said hesitantly. She hadn't touched him like that since their night together. Or rather, the morning after, right before he skipped out on her. He promised himself that if he ever had the chance again he'd act very differently.

"Downtown. I'm not about to miss the big raid on Sam's office. While we're at it, let's take some of these hooks and get this investigation reopened."

Damon stood still, resisting Sharon's pull, gazing at the spot where Marsha's body was found. "It's still a mystery, isn't it?"

"Maybe," said Sharon, "but something tells me we'll get to the bottom of this. Let's go."

CHAPTER 59

They took a cab downtown in order to maintain communication contact with the outside world. As the cab sailed down the FDR, Sharon could sense that everything was breaking apart. Sharon's cell rang as they reached the Water Street exit. It was Sergeant Rodriquez, telling her the raid had been called off.

"What? What do you mean?" she asked shrilly. This was going to be it for Sam.

"After they got notice of the billion dollar transfer to PSS, they immediately received notice that it had been a mistake," he explained.

"That can't be," she swallowed. "How can it be there one second and gone the next?"

"I don't know. I never understood technology anyway," said Rodriquez. "I'm sorry."

"Thanks for letting me know," said Sharon, letting out a deep sigh.

"What's the matter?" asked Damon, placing a hand on her arm then removing it.

"There's nothing there. No trail of any transfer. Nothing." Her lips trembled. Gone like the Enforcer Unit. This time with no traceable copy.

"Hey, it's okay," said Damon, putting a hand over hers, keeping it there. "Your ITA scoop is gonna hit tomorrow. You'll be a star."

"Maybe," she said dully. Fame wasn't what she wanted. "But I'll know it's not really over."

"Cheer up," said Damon, squeezing her hand. His search for Marsha's killer wasn't over either. "I'm sure there'll be other crimes to solve. Let's get a couple of mochas in the meantime. On me," he said, hoping to cheer her up. *Avoidance seemed to be the easiest route. Again.*

CHAPTER 60

The following Saturday night, Sharon was looking forward to catching up on her sleep and having a late Sunday brunch of a cheese omelet, home fries, a fresh cappuccino and a strong Mimosa, like a normal New Yorker. Maybe Damon was right. Put this crime to bed. Move on to the next story.

She slipped into her robe and popped an Ambien. She had selected one of the smaller rooms in Mickey's apartment to sleep in until she found a new place of her own. It was farthest from the front entrance and had the most adorable antique writing table in it, with a delicate gold holder for an eighteenth-century quill pen. The kind that real writers used with real ink, before the invention of pens, typewriters, and laptops. Sitting at the desk made her feel like a Renaissance poet more than a reporter. The room had nothing to do with Mickey, she knew. It was like a secret compartment from a former life of his.

She hopped under the white Egyptian cotton sheets and rested her head on a stack of fluffed pillows. She had actually bought a book for the occasion, Hunter S. Thompson's *Fear and Loathing in Las Vegas*.

Let the drug culture of the 1960s replace the offshore money culture of the 2000s for an evening, she thought as she got comfortable. But after four pages, her exhaustion, aided by the Ambien, overtook her. She placed the book on the Victorian nightstand next to her cell phone and switched off the light. Sinking back into the goose feathers, she drifted off to sleep.

Moments later, she woke with a start to the music of her cell phone. "Hello?" she flipped it open and whispered, eyes blinking. Orienting to the dark bedroom.

"It's me. Trevor." He sounded rushed.

"What time is it?" she yawned.

"Share, are you okay? It's, like, not even nine yet," he said, fingers clicking on his keyboard.

"I'm fine. I just decided to do something unusual—sleep. What's up?" She sat up in bed.

"You know how you can't let go, if you've left something... unfigured?"

"Unfigured?"

"You know, not figured out. Anyway, I was going through the enforcer network for the tenth time—we should definitely talk about it, by the way, there's like a ton of shit here. It could keep you in stories forever."

"That's what you're waking me up to tell me?"

"Yes—well, no. There's something else. So I'm going through the network files, memory usage, timing, when it hits me what was bugging me. The wire transfer."

"The one in Belize?" She had had the same thought, but nowhere to go with it.

"Yeah, well, here's the thing. No money was wired."

"Right," said Sharon, confused, "we know that. The transfer failed."

"No, I mean the transfer didn't fail because no money was ever wired."

"What, Trev? I'm not following."

"Smoke and mirrors, Share. It was all faked." He was panting, like an excited child.

"What do you mean, faked?" She was fully awake now, soaking in his vibe.

"The thing is, when you transfer any kind of information, like money, it doesn't take a lot of memory on the network. That's why things flow so quick when you do an electronic bank transfer."

"And?"

"And this transfer that failed? It never even started. What you all saw on the screen was a picture of a transfer. Well, a failed transfer."

"A picture? Okay, Trev, help me out here, I'm drugged and tired and not a techie." She stood up and wrapped her robe around her. She tucked her hair behind her ear and pressed it tighter to her cell.

"The amount of memory used over Ivan's private network at the time of your yacht bust was like 1500 times that for a normal wire transfer. Someone wanted you to see what you saw. A remote network was transmitting a picture of the screen to Ivan's screen."

"Wait!" said Sharon, blood pumping overtime. "I think I get it. I knew something was missing. This is huge! I'm coming over. We need to...hold it a second." Her call waiting beeped in. The number was unavailable. She thought maybe it was from the hospital. "Hey, Mickey?" she said as she switched over.

"Sharon."

A chill ran up her spine, spread over her shoulders. She had almost forgotten.

"What is it you want now?" she asked the low, mechanical voice.

"You gave up too soon, didn't you?"

"What are you talking about?" she asked, stalling, her heart pounding.

"You didn't look beneath the surface like I said. You really disappointed me." The voice turned cold, and human. Just as she recognized its owner, she heard footsteps creeping down the hallway. Toward her room. She switched back to Trevor. The connection was gone. Her pulse quickened.

She reached beneath the bed. She could hear the footsteps getting closer. She was fumbling to find Mickey's revolver when the door sprung open.

CHAPTER 61

"This what you're looking for?" asked Sam Peterson, pointing the gun at her with black-gloved hands.

"What are you doing here?" She inched away from him, toward the window above the antique writing table. She knew the answer.

"I gave you a chance, Sharon," he said, stepping toward her, his thick black shoes compressing the light blue carpet. "You disappointed me. Twice."

"I don't understand," she said as she steadied her breath, keeping eye contact. *Don't show him your fear.*

"Do you really think you figured it out—the *trail?*" He laughed, closing in on her.

"Sure," she said, still moving away from him. "The money extractions from all those tech companies that never happened, throwing Ivan and Katrina under the bus, you were behind all of it—you're brilliant, what's not to get?" Her only hope was to keep him talking, until she could find an out.

He threw his head back and laughed more loudly. "Little late for the compliments, Sharon." He shook his head; he was enjoying this. "You missed the most important point."

"What was that?" she asked, actually intrigued, despite the gun pointed at her.

"There was no trail."

"No trail?" she gasped, trying to still her heaving chest.

"Come on—you really thought you were solving some big mystery? A document appears and then disappears at the SEC with everything you need to uncover a mammoth money-laundering scheme?" He was towering over her now. Inches away.

"But, the Enforcer Unit, that wasn't—real?"

"Oh no, that was real—to the enforcers."

"I don't get it."

"You see, Sharon, like I told you in my office, sometimes you do things because you can."

"You mean you created this whole scheme for–for fun?" The thought seemed implausible. Then, another thought struck her with the intense force of total clarity. Elaine's muffled and dying last words. 'Rrr trail.' *Wrong trail. A decoy crime.*

He laughed again. "On the surface. Not beneath it." He stuck the tip of the gun against her throat. She gulped. There was no out.

"But, wait, I, please—you're going to kill me anyway, tell me what you did." *Appeal to his ego.*

"I took a billion dollars from clients who'll never notice it's missing, and then I deflected it."

"How?"

"Easily, just like what you thought you saw. Only the money isn't in Belize, that damn second-rate country."

"Where is it then? And what is it for?" Silverman had branches everywhere. Why would he set up a separate bank? Then it dawned on her. *Because he could.*

"It's safe. In a Saudi Arabian bank."

Her eyes widened. *That was out of left field.*

"See, there are too many snooping reporters and do-gooders around here, like you, and like Kevin Waters. The only way to get anything done is to deflect attention away from it. This country has spent too much time bending backward for people who question government activities, watching the president's budget, keeping the administration from doing what's best for

America. So, instead of bothering with taking taxpayer money and dealing with all the whining, we simply extract corporate money to give to our long-term allies, buy arms, and keep relationships. The old fashioned way—with cash."

"The trail, Ivan, and Katrina. The crime that covered the crime." She finally got it. *They had all been pawns.*

"The crime is that we have to cover up the good we're doing. Defend ourselves to the moronic public," he sneered. "If a few people get killed in the process, to keep people away from our mission, so be it."

It was all so crystal clear now. "So, the enforcers, Roger, Marsha—you killed all of them just to—"

"To keep the plan alive," he interrupted, "though I had some help from a lovely young woman."

"Elaine?" asked Sharon, knowing the answer. Elaine knew more than she let on. Maybe her plan was to double-cross Sam, but she never stood a chance.

"Ah yes, Elaine. Such a talent. Good with guns and bombs."

"Ivan's yacht? But, why blow it up? It didn't mean anything in the end."

"That was more sport, really. I always hated Ivan. It was beautiful to watch."

"So, Elaine planted the bomb somewhere under the boat and then came after me?"

"Apparently," he said, losing interest in the conversation, "though that was her decision, not mine. You did take care of her for me, though. How did it feel to kill someone?"

"You bastard," winced Sharon, "I was protecting myself."

"We all are. It's easy to step over the line, isn't it? Elaine used to be a cop, you know. With the NYPD. Always helps to have police experience on your side. Like in Washington."

"Officer O'Harris?" He had always seemed sketchy to her.

"Yeah, I needed someone on the inside. He wasn't hard to buy. Most people aren't."

"Is that why he arrested Kevin immediately, broke police protocol? Kevin told me there was no body at his house when the cops came."

"Protocol is for cops working for a pension, not real money, the kind I can offer."

"And Elaine? Did you buy her too?" prompted Sharon, trying to divert his attention with questions, to gain time to find an opening for escape.

"You could say that. She enjoyed her work though. She was gifted with a gun. Dead-on aim. A bit crazy, though."

Roger Francis. The enforcers. Sharon's eyebrows raised. "So, she was your designated hit-woman?"

"Yes, she loved shooting people. Used criminals for target practice on the force until she shot some sixteen-year-old kid, creating all sorts of department complications. She turned, became a hired gun for a drug dealer. Used her oaf brother as thug-support."

The brute. Another piece of the puzzle. Lester was Elaine's brother. No wonder she hated me.

"You involved in drug trafficking, too, Sam?" she goaded.

"No, I found her through a friend of a friend."

"Someone in D.C.? The vice president?"

"Maybe." He cocked the trigger. "The vice president and I go way back."

"Wait. Were you having an affair with Marsha? Is that why you killed her?"

Sam chortled, "Please, she was just a way to Ivan and the press to me. Collateral damage. Like you." He squeezed his index finger to his thumb on the trigger.

Sharon's eyes darted over his shoulder, her body tensed.
A single shot fired.

.

CHAPTER 62

S am's hand exploded into a bloody mess. The gun he was holding flew from the grip. His body slumped to the floor. As he looked up at her, his green eyes bulged, and then they cringed.

"I promised you I wouldn't fuck up this time, kiddo," said a welcomed familiar voice.

Sharon opened her eyes; she was both shocked and not at all surprised. "Mickey!" she shouted, running toward her mentor, who stood in the doorway, his 9mm smoking.

"I told you she needed our help," said Trevor, in the hallway behind him.

"Trevor!" She rushed to hug him as Mickey limped toward Sam.

"I don't believe I invited you into my apartment, you little fuck!" said Mickey measuredly, standing above the heap of Sam. Bleeding. Panting. Looking far less in control.

Sam's snake eyes narrowed as he sat crumpled on the rug, holding his bleeding hand. Mickey closed in, pointing the gun at him. "Give me one good reason why I shouldn't blow you away right now!" he said, his sweat dripping on the top of Sam's shiny bald head.

"Please," Sam's voice dripped with contempt, "you don't have the balls."

Sharon wrapped her arms around Trevor's waist, ignoring Sam's words, "Then we can't put him in jail, forever," she answered.

"Didn't ask you, kiddo," said Mickey, not turning away from his prey, his eyes full of years of hate and disgust. He cocked the trigger. "There's nothing that would make me happier," he told Sam.

Sharon buried her face in Trevor's shoulder. She was shaking uncontrollably. She covered her ears with her hands. "Don't, Mickey. He's not worth it," she urged.

Mickey lowered his gun. "But then I'd be just as pathetic as you are." He shivered through his entire body, "Nah, I think I'll just let my buddies at the NYPD take care of this. Boys?"

Two police officers entered the room, cuffing Sam, who didn't seem in the least bit nervous all of a sudden. "Don't think you've won," he told the room in general.

"Wait a sec," said Sharon. She broke away from Trevor and ran over to the bed. Reaching beneath it, she pulled out her recorder. She carefully extracted Sam's confession tape. She said, "You'll need this," and handed it to the cops. She shot a glance at Sam. Now, he looked a bit more nervous.

EPILOGUE

Aweek later, Sharon moved into a new apartment, a block away from her smoke-saturated one, and bought a German shepherd, Kira. For company, and for security. She returned to her regular workout and boxing routine, though she switched trainers.

The NYPD re-opened the Marsha Matthews murder case. *Riche$* editor-in-chief, Ralph Stetson, offered Sharon an editorial position after her cover story on the fall of the ITA empire. She declined. There were too many stories to investigate on the ground. She didn't want to be encumbered by the day-to-day business and internal politics of the magazine. She needed her freedom. Thanking Ralph, she accepted a raise for her pieces instead. There was reporting to do out there.

A series of oil pipelines were suddenly coming up dry in the Middle East. It was all over the news. They had been gushing millions of barrels daily. The two companies responsible for pipeline maintenance and oil extraction were seeing huge spikes in their stock prices, as fears of oil scarcity hit world headlines. It was still summer. Things would only worsen as fall came. She smelled international fraud and political collusion. The two got her adrenalin flowing

* * *

That weekend, Sharon decided to reconvene with her social side, partly in response to Nina's thousand phone calls and partly to Trevor's. "So you just parachute into Silverman, take

357

down the wicked blonde witch and the scary turtle man, and scoot off into the sunset, forgetting your old friends?" Nina, her investment banker friend, accused. "I don't think so."

"I was going to call you back," replied Sharon. "I was just busy with some...personal things."

"Lame. You know, some of us are stuck here. And must drink heavily on the weekends to cope."

"Fine, I get it. I'm lame. Sorry I didn't call you."

"Whatever. You can redeem yourself tonight. A bunch of us are going down to Arlene's Grocery to hear my fabulous trader-trying-to-be-superstar boyfriend's band. Your techno babe, Trevor, is spinning at Irvington's for the late shift afterward."

"I know—he left me a hundred messages about it. And he's not my babe."

"Whatever. So you're in. Drinks first at Mission. We're meeting there at ten. In half an hour."

"I'll be there. I promise."

"You better be. Carver's dying to quit the oil trading biz and become the latest Lenny Kravitz. Rumor has it that one of the reps from Atlantic Records is coming."

"I said, I'll...wait a minute, did you say he's an *oil* trader?"

"Yeah, why? You plan to crack some big new oil scandal or something?"

"Me? No, not at all. See you in half an hour," Sharon clicked her phone off, grabbed a notepad, and flew out the door. In the cab on her way to Arlene's, she made a call. "Hey, Damon, come meet me down at Arlene's, there's someone there who can help us with that oil story."

***

At a deep white sink at the Cornell Medical Center on the Upper East Side, the lead plastic surgeon was finishing his post-op scrub. His patient had undergone six hours of intricate grafting work, the second such procedure in two weeks, in order to repair the puncture wound that the bullet had created.

Sam Peterson sat in his hospital bed, dressed in blue patient garb. His orthopedic surgeon entered the room with a smile. "Well, Sam, quite a wound you had there, but you were lucky, missed major nerves. With a few month of physical therapy, you should be good as new."

"Thank you, doctor," said Sam. He raised his arm to examine the bandages that wrapped his right hand. He closed his eyes, smiled, and reclined on his pillow.

At Manhattan's Supreme Court building, a group of navy blue-suited lawyers finished their business with the head judge, working substantial overtime on this important federal matter. They smiled and shook hands with each other before they went their separate ways into the night. Sam would be back in his CEO seat by Monday morning. The mayor owed him one. So did the vice president.

***

The next morning, Sharon awoke suddenly to a sharp headache and a ringing cell phone. She noted the caller ID. It was the man who never slept. "What is it, Damon?"

"Hey, Share, I thought I'd let you know...well, Sam's been exonerated. No charges pressed."

"Of course, he was. Why should we expect the justice system to actually condemn a man funding international terrorism? That's something that only happens to poor immigrants, not WASP CEOs."

"Glad to see your perspective's intact," answered Damon, with a chuckle. "Now, about your next story?"

"I'm on it," said Sharon, "and this isn't a dead-end yet. I know what he's up to and it's gonna lead me to the center of the Middle East. I'm ready."

"Good stuff," said Damon, before testing murkier waters. "And...about another end that might not be dead?"

"You don't stop, do you, boss?" said Sharon. She wasn't sure where she stood on Damon. Trust needed building. "Let's just see, okay?" With that, she dozed off into decidedly peaceful sleep.